It Shall Be of Ja

AND

Love-across-a-Hundred-Lives

CARAF Books

Caribbean and African Literature
Translated from French

It Shall Be of Jasper and Coral

AND

Love-across-a-Hundred-Lives

TWO NOVELS

Werewere Liking

Translated by Marjolijn de Jager

Introduction by Irène Assiba d'Almeida

University Press of Virginia

CHARLOTTESVILLE
AND LONDON

Publication of this translation was assisted by a grant
from the French Ministry of Culture
Originally published in French as *Elle sera de jaspe et de corail*

The University Press of Virginia

Printed in the United States of America
First published in 2000

∞The paper used in this publication meets the minimum
requirements of the American National Standard for
Information Sciences—Permanence of Paper for Printed
Library Materials, ANSI Z39.48-1984.

Library of Congress Cataloging-in-Publication Data

Werewere Liking, 1950–
[Elle sera de jaspe et de corail. English]
It shall be of jasper and coral; and, Love-across-a-hundred-lives: two novels / Werewere Liking ; translated by Marjolijn de Jager ; introduction by Irène Assiba d'Almeida.
p. cm.
ISBN 0-8139-1942-8 (cloth : alk. paper)—
ISBN 0-8139-1943-6 (pbk. : alk. paper)
I. Title: It shall be of jasper and coral; and, Love-across-a-hundred-lives. II. De Jager, Marjolijn. III. Werewere Liking, 1950– Amour-cent-vies. English. IV. Title: Amour-cent-vies. V. Title.
PQ3989.2.L54 E44 2000
843—dc21 99-056677

Contents

These translations are for Werewere Liking, who has the courage to *live* her convictions and thereby has become an inspiration to me in so many ways. —MdJ

Acknowledgments

The translator would like to express her sincere appreciation to the editors of the CARAF series and to Cathie Brettschneider at the University Press of Virginia in particular for their dedication to this project. She is deeply indebted to Carrol Coates for his encouragement, his many invaluable suggestions, and his unswerving care. Her gratitude goes also to Irène Assiba d'Almeida for asserting the need for these translations and for her fine advice throughout. And always, there is David Vita, who stands by her side with his support and never fails to believe in the value of her work.

Introduction

Werewere Liking: A Deeply Original Voice

Werewere Liking is an artist of extraordinary and varied talent. Known primarily as a writer, she has published as a poet and a playwright and writes fiction in a variety of forms: novels, *récits,* initiation tales. But Liking is also a theater and movie actress, a director of her own plays, and a scholar and essayist who has produced works of literary criticism and art history. When Liking began working at age sixteen, it was as a singer. At that time, in the late 1960s, she also began to paint, which she has continued to do: "When I do not feel satisfied in myself that I have said everything through writing, I paint."[1] She has even worked as a jeweler, and she prides herself in finding old beads from across Africa to make exquisite necklaces.[2]

Werewere Liking, a Bassa woman from Cameroon, born on May 1, 1950, has deliberately chosen to blur biographers' charts, especially in regards to her private life and academic training. When asked pointedly what her education has been, Liking answers with a tinge of irony, "This is the ritualistic question! I am a literary person, but above all, I am self-taught and I specialize in the theater."[3] Pressed further, all she volunteers is that she was raised in the traditional African ways, insisting that everything she learned from the West she taught herself. There is clear implication here that, well-versed in the Bassa rituals of Cameroon, Liking was not schooled in or by the French colonial system and does not adhere to its conventions. The autobiographical ambiguity created by Liking must be interpreted as a form of resistance to being pigeonholed and as an attempt to keep her personal and multifarious artistic lives separate.[4]

Although parts of Liking's biography are shrouded in some mystery, it is clear that she was born at a momentous time. If the personal elements remain obscure, her work yet needs to be discussed against the background of the historical and political contexts that shaped her artistic development. Nineteen fifty, the year of Liking's birth, is situated at the exact halfway point of the century—and close to the end of the Second World War, an event that, ironically, marked the beginning of a new age in African politics. France, like the other European colonial empires, was weakened by the effect of that war and shaken by strong anticolonial sentiments. Indeed, in Africa the 1950s were marked by nationalist movements, struggles for freedom and independence, and efforts to seek a new identity and to discover effective nation-building strategies that would open a new chapter of African history. These exciting circumstances brought forth a unique moment of intellectual effervescence and vigorous political debate on the continent. Not coincidentally, this was also a time that witnessed an explosion of literary production, as the emergence of the francophone novel closely followed the surge of poetry inspired by the Negritude movement of the 1930s.

Within Liking's native Cameroon, those intellectual debates continued well into the 1970s, and, as Richard Bjornson describes it, one of the major polemics of the time centered around the division between supporters and opponents of Léopold Sédar Senghor's Negritude: "By the late 1960's, the Cameroonian government had embraced a Negritude-inspired cultural nationalism. For the politically conservative, predominantly Christian proponents of Negritude, such an ideological position offered Cameroonians the opportunity to integrate a spiritual dimension into the national consciousness while synthesizing a new identity for traditional and modern values. Opponents of Negritude viewed it as an obfuscation that distracted from the need to address urgent practical problems in a rational, socially just manner."[5] Liking, therefore, was the inheritor of exceptional political, intellectual, and literary traditions, which she would turn in a new direction in the 1980s. Like a choreographer who designs her own artistic space, Liking built on the traditions she inherited and simultaneously called them into question. She pointed out issues that the first generation of African writers and politicians ignored: issues of gender in particular, but she was also critical of the Negritude movement and of the distorted or truncated accounts of African history that had emerged in the 1950s and 1960s.[6] These preoccupations—especially that of the need for a female perspective in responding to the demands of development and modernity—have constantly resurfaced in the substantial corpus of her work.[7]

A crucial factor for Liking was that she was born at a time when it was finally possible for women to write, to break the silence culturally imposed on them and to achieve in the world of letters what I term a *prise d'écriture,* a "taking of writing," in the sense of a militant appropriation or seizing.[8] It was only in the 1980s that one could begin to speak of a substantial body of female writing in francophone Africa, and Liking, publishing her earliest work in 1977, was among the first francophone African women to come to writing.[9] Like her female contemporaries, Liking has refused to reproduce established discourses. On the contrary, she subverts those discourses and writes women into the vacant spaces, filling out the interstices left empty by others, namely, Westerners and male African writers. The act of writing for Liking, therefore, constitutes an extraordinary liberating force that makes it possible to *dire l'interdit*—to speak the forbidden; it becomes a crucial tool to challenge patriarchal restrictions, to create a poetics of self-affirmation, and to offer a vision for what the future may hold for the continent, culturally and politically.

If by the 1980s African women were capitalizing on the new medium that writing was for them, they were also building on the oral traditions—in which they had long had an important creative role—thus finding an added source of inspiration and a way of insuring a cultural continuity linking past to present. It was with this concern that Liking embarked in 1974 on research trips to Mali and the Ivory Coast to learn more about oral traditions, particularly rituals and initiation rites. She conducted her research with Marie-José Hourantier, also known as Manuna Ma-Njock, a French ethnographer sharing Liking's research and intellectual preoccupations. In 1979 the two women, now collaborators and friends, settled in the Ivory Coast, and Liking became a research fellow at ILENA (Institut de Littérature et d'Esthétique Négro-Africaines [Institute of Black African Literature and Aesthetics]). There she was able to apply her research in a student-centered and community-based project, helping younger students learn more about their own traditions in order to break away from Western molds and discover in African lore creative possibilities that would lead to different modes of expression.

In 1983 Liking and Marie-José Hourantier opened the "Villa Ki-Yi." Initially conceived as a space for research in artistic theories and practices primarily related to drama, the Villa Ki-Yi became part of a larger project. In her work, Liking has emerged as a social critic deeply preoccupied with the African condition—present, past, and future—and the Villa has become part of a plan for a cultural revival in which art and ritual would play a pivotal role. Liking and Hourantier conceived of the "théâtre rituel," or ritual theater, as an experimental theater based on the principles of African aesthetics as they exist in ancestral ritual. In her research, Liking found ritualistic similarities in different West African countries and, in particular, a common reliance on a very sophisticated system of symbols. In addition to the potency of articulated speech, she noted such common characteristics as the use of body movement as sign, musical instruments turned virtually into "characters," and the incorporation of songs, dance, and incantatory recitals. Taking these techniques as its foundation, her "théâtre rituel" became a total theater, exploiting gestural and vocal rhythms—all the resources of traditional rituals—and adding such devices as shadow shows, and costumes and props inspired by the giant "puppets" of Mali, alongside human faces and masks.

A demanding artist herself, Liking moves her actors to be total performers, who must undergo strenuous mental and physical preparation and sharpen their minds by learning traditional modes of memorization.[10] Because the "théâtre rituel" uses a complex symbolic apparatus and sophisticated techniques, it has been cast—along with Liking's artistic production in general—as difficult, esoteric, and elitist. Liking, however, offers no apology, for she believes that a degree of elitism cannot be dissociated from the production and the consumption of art. This elitism, she contends, is part and parcel of traditional aesthetics: "It is therefore a facile solution to say that ritual theater is hermetic. Traditional rituals are themselves very esoteric. To do without elitist research would be to kill theater. The public can only be reached progressively. An elite is always needed to lead the way for the masses."[11]

Although ritual theater is preoccupied with aesthetics and symbolism, it also has—as did traditional rituals—a therapeutic function. In other words, it is, as Liking and Hourantier claimed, an operational theater, one that is intended to produce important results by involving audiences in such a way that they are transformed by the ritualistic and aesthetic experience: "Today Ritual Theater attempts to bring people to a higher level of consciousness where one no longer expects anything from above, but where one finds within oneself ways of eliminating negative forces and of solving one's own problems."[12] This remark reflects two important aspects of Liking's thought—the importance of individual transformation for the betterment of self and community and her distinctive conception of spirituality: "We will need a superior force to solve our problems, but it is nowhere else but within ourselves. . . . What we need to do is to wake that force, to put it into action: then the trees will grow at our call and the mountains will move at the sound of our voices."[13]

Throughout her work, Liking reiterates that individual betterment and spirituality can only be achieved through knowledge. "Ki-Yi," the name of the Villa, means "Ultimate

Knowledge" in Bassa, Liking's native tongue, and signifies the philosophical thrust the artist intends to give this venture.[14] Located in Abidjan, the Villa is now a Pan-African community of nearly eighty artists—actors, singers, dancers, sculptors, painters—who support themselves through their art. They share everything among themselves and also with the public, as the Villa is open to all.[15] A tireless worker and organizer, Liking believes in collective work and has transformed her belief into productive action. In 1985 she created the Group Ki-Yi, also known as the Ki-Yi Mbock Théâtre, a troupe primarily engaged in theater but also involved in all the forms of contemporary African artistic endeavors: fine arts, visual arts, literature.

In the early 1990s, the "Villa" was turned into a "Village," run like a traditional village, with a chief elected among the artists for a two-year tenure. The Village offers a living and working space to the group—a space for rehearsals and year-long production of plays, songs, dance, and music.[16] With its Pan-African outlook and its multiple artistic activities, the Ki-Yi Village—along with the Group Ki-Yi, which is its heart and soul—is a unique endeavor in the whole of francophone Africa.[17] With this project, Werewere Liking emerges as both a visionary and a pioneer. Indeed, francophone African capital cities can boast of American, British, Chinese, French, and Russian cultural centers, whereas *African* cultural centers are virtually nonexistent.[18] The Village Ki-Yi, therefore, fills a cultural void, generating new artistic currents that may have far-reaching influence in shaping the artistic future of the continent.

Werewere Liking's first published book was a collection of poems entitled *On ne raisonne pas le venin* (1977; One does not reason with venom). Although she has not published any other books of poetry, that early collection remains a point of departure for her literary career, containing key ideas that are developed in subsequent works. The title announces Liking's credo: Africa can emerge as a strong continent only if it finds the will to overcome the ills that restrict its development. "Venom," of course, represents those ills, and, given its lethal character, it is not something to be reasoned with—it can only be purged. Africa is a central theme in *On ne raisonne pas le venin,* and speaking terrible truths, the poet does not hesitate to criticize her continent, being like one of her characters, "a voice that dares speak about a tornado when the sun shines without fuss."[19] Yet Liking is not only critical. She evokes love, friendship, and loyalty; she often ponders the importance of spirituality; and from this very first work she begins to address gender issues. Several poems consider the African woman, in ways ranging from her plight within patriarchal society to the celebration of her body, as in "Est-ce bête?" (Isn't [a woman] silly!), a poem in which the erotic and the ironic are closely intertwined.

Liking's poetry is elegantly simple, marked by a use of repetition and irony, its tone mixing despair and hope. Athough she contends that poetry breathes through everything she writes, Liking was to abandon traditional verse models, as well as standard forms of narrative prose, in search of a new mode of expression. She became particularly adept at mixing genres, creating a "nouvelle écriture," a unique, innovative idiom, which pervades her work.

In part because of that new idiom, Liking's work took critics by surprise, creating widely mixed reactions both within and outside of Africa. The unfavorable critics dismissed her literary production as frivolously experimental, some suggesting Liking's books were not "serious" literary efforts at all, only "a play with words" that did not always produce meaning. Others faulted the artist for being unnecessarily cryptic and therefore jeopardizing the communicative aspect of artistic creation. Clearly, the complexity of her writing, highly innovative and largely metafictional, delayed the critical reception it should have received, and only with the emergence of new critical approaches to literature has her work been accepted. In the wake of those changes, Liking has been hailed as an avant-garde writer and a postmodernist artist, for postmodern theory found nothing wrong with mixing disparate genres, with breaking the semantics of a phrase, working a text within the parameters of the intertext, making eccentric collages, or giving a literary work an unconventional revisionary impetus. This shift in the literary critical paradigm in recent years has caught up with Liking's work, now praising what was initially viewed as outlandish.[20]

It is in fact not surprising that Liking's work was first perceived as meaningless play on words, for, working with the latent energy of the mechanisms of language, she frequently employs peculiar arrangements of semantic and syntactic elements. Liking delights in juggling words, constructing her own large semantic field, one that she constantly enriches. A veritable wordsmith, Liking invents new words—"*misovire*" being a prime example of her inventiveness—uses words in an unusual manner, breaks their meaning, dislocates signifiers, and makes odd juxtapositions. She is also adept at stringing words together, often choosing a succession of substantives rather than using verbs. In such a linguistic scenario, the reader is forced into a dynamic and dialectic interaction with the text, becoming co-creator of meaning with the writer; assuming this active role of participation, collaboration, and even production is the end Liking's technique pushes the reader toward.

In *It Shall Be of Jasper and Coral* for instance, Liking juxtaposes unlikely words to create expressions such as "conspiracy epidemics" (80), which mock the imaginary plots often invented by certain African governments to get rid of their political opponents. Another term among many is *thèses alimentaires* or "potboiler theses" (42), which mocks empty intellectuals who saddle the country with theses lacking in substance (three-quarters devoted to bibliography and the rest being mere paraphrase, as the *misovire* points out). These theses are nothing but "a meal ticket," hence the idea of a "*thèse alimentaire,*" which literally means "a food thesis" and figuratively "a money-making thesis." Her character Babou mentally creates a "*prolétariat-populaire-à-la-langue-de-Moussa*" (popular-Moussa-speaking-proletariat; 10) and both Babou and his companion character Grozi take refuge in "*un ailleurs-*

autrui" (an "elsewhere-otherness"; 4) because they both achieved an "*auto-rejet mal assimilé*" (an ill-absorbed self-rejection; 10). Also, the well-known "*Boulot-Métro-Dodo,*" a French expression to express the monotony of modern life in Paris, becomes "*Foot-Foutou-Froufrou,*" a prime occupation in Lunaï. "Foot" standing for football (soccer), "foutou" (an African dish) for food, and "froufrou" (rustle, evocative of the noise women's dresses make) are aptly translated here as "Football-Food-Finery." With an ironic voice the *misovire* explains why she transformed the expression: "there is no subway in Lunaï and . . . nobody ever goes to work" (16).

In *Love-across-a-Hundred-Lives* semantic innovations also abound, and the linguistic sophistication is coupled with imaginative agility. The innovative words seem to leap from the writer's imagination and to entreat the reader's imagination to share those strong pictorial images.[21] One of the best examples of this technique is the invention of the term *la Machine-Goutte,* which can be translated as "the Dripping Machine," or better still "the Drop-by-Drop-Machine" (121), without fully rendering the brilliance of the French original. The "*Machine-Goutte*" represents repressive contemporary political forces that tyrannically control the population through the stomach (hunger and dehydration), by controlling "the distribution of vital Drops" (142). Here, the semantic innovation constitutes a powerful metaphor that carries a strong ideological meaning.

Another powerful image is that of a hanging rope made of "umbilical cords," to be used by the character Lem, who counts the hours he has left to live in terms of "meat-hours" (122). Later in the novel, Liking describes the French colonial oppressive forces as "the hard Hand of Gaul" eager to "redress its shrinking Gaul" (228) by "vampiring the blood of" Africans (228). It is to expose all these abuses that the narrator writes as she does, to perform "a cesarean on words" (185).

In addition to being inventive, the language is bold, used to break, among other things, linguistic restriction imposed upon women's speech. Here, Liking, like other women writers of her generation (Calixthe Beyala or Véronique Tadjo, for example), uses an uninhibited and provocative language that speaks of sensuality, desire, eroticism—all topics tacitly forbidden to women within conventions laid out by patriarchal society. The transgression of these taboos is deliberate in *Jasper and Coral,* where the all-pervasive sexual metaphor is personified by Grozi, who is, as suggested by his name, defined by his sex. (The name Grozi may well be a combination of "gros" [big] and "zizi," a slang word meaning a "prick.") Grozi's frequent physical masturbation is a reflection of the intellectual masturbation he continuously indulges in: "Grozi has masturbated again. And there he is again with his tail-in-front hanging low and slack a shameful drop dangling shilly-shallying: will fall won't fall . . . " (6).

Liking's transgression of taboos is accomplished not only with new words but also through myth-making. In *Jasper and Coral* she invents a mythical story to explain how women were the first human beings to have possessed Love and Knowledge. In *Love-across-a-Hundred-Lives* Liking goes even further and declares that God is woman. Wanting to create social justice and social balance, she imagines a society that offers an antidote to the practice of polygamy: "Although, when compared to man, woman was wronged, since polygamy but not polyandry was allowed among the Seizers, she had not been completely forgotten: she had the right to a lover of her own choice, she had the right to love" (127). The narrator proceeds to describe all the rules of this socially authorized extramarital love—not to be confused with infidelity—in ways reminiscent of the ancient *"amour courtois"* and of the *"carte du tendre."* These are the ways in which, going beyond mere semantic innovations, Liking imagines the possibility of change in gender-based social norms.

It Shall Be of Jasper and Coral is one of the most complex works by Werewere Liking, one that challenges the readers' engagement in a way that makes it difficult to appreciate the work by superficial reading. It is not a simple matter of comprehension that is at stake here, for Liking intends nothing less than to transform her readers into members of the new race she envisions. The title of the work itself is pregnant with prophecy, for in *It Shall Be of Jasper and Coral* the "it" refers to the new race that must be born if Africans are to escape their present condition. And in fact, while continuing to use the term *race,* Liking deconstructs the traditional conception of the term, one that has been increasingly discredited and that contains the divisive black/white dichotomy, a binary simplification. It is no accident, therefore, that the new race of her narrative will be sapphire-blue and jade-green, or better still, of jasper and coral; that is, made from a multitude of bright colors.[22]

Liking gives her novel a peculiar subtitle: "Journal of a *Misovire,*" which marks the text as gender-centered as well as demonstrating the writer's inventiveness. Indeed, the creation of the word *misovire* is an ideal expression of the transformative concepts and practices that Liking advocates in both her imaginative work and her praxis. The term *misovire,* an amalgam of Greek and Latin meaning "male-hater," serves a manifold purpose. First of all, it is a linguistic invention that reminds us that gender ideology affects all spheres of life, including linguistic formation. In the French language, the word *misanthrope* characterizes someone who does not like human beings in general, and the word *mysogyne,* someone who hates women; but no word has existed to refer to someone who hates males. Hence the importance of forging a word that reflects this "forgotten" reality. And Liking makes her innovation serve another purpose by twisting the original meaning of her neologism to give it her own definition: "A *misovire,*" she says, is "a woman who cannot find an admirable man."[23]

The term *misovire* seems to designate the African feminist woman as Liking sees her; that is, a feminist who, because of social constraints, must go through various balancing acts to reach her goals and create new ways of knowing. In an analogous way Liking invents the very powerful word *misovire* but reduces the force of her neologism by giving it a less absolute meaning. It is a clever device, difficult to grasp if one remains within the paradigms of the Western feminisms that have faulted Liking for not matching the force of her invention with the *misovire*'s discourse.[24] Yet because the word now does exist, even though Liking's definition downplays its significance, one cannot help keeping in mind its etymological meaning. The word, therefore, feigns to be nonthreatening while still powerfully questioning gender relations and making African men rethink gender issues. Liking subverts patriarchal thinking—rejecting the phallus as transcendental signifier, we might say—and all the psychological power it carries, and she champions a time "when woman is a man" (169); that is, a time when gender differentiation will be irrelevant to discovering the fullness of what it means to be human. Although Liking has repeatedly refused to be identified as a feminist, her discursive practices definitely place her in the wide feminist landscape. It is, however, a specific form of feminism, one that Liking invents and inscribes in her own cartographies, drawn according to her specific geographical space and peculiar cultural reality.[25]

The *misovire,* then, is at the center of *Jasper and Coral.* She is a represented narrator who, in both a first- and third-person narration, recounts the story of the inhabitants of Lunaï, a fictitious and squalid village representing Africa. The main action of the novel, however, is the metanarrative showing the process by which the *misovire* writes a journal and creates through that writing the new race she is heralding. Instead of holding daily entries as a conventional diary would, this journal is composed of nine "pages," each dedicated to a specific theme. The first page describes the impossibility of finding in Lunaï worthy people to whom the *misovire* can dedicate her journal; the second deals with art, desire, and creativity; the third is devoted to women; the fourth, to the creation of a new language. Page 5 addresses artistic criticism, while page 6 deals with choice and the importance of paying attention to the senses. The seventh page exalts friendship, and the eighth is dedicated to children—to the necessity of raising them in such a way as to turn them into balanced individuals. The last page is an assessment of the creative work accomplished by the *mis-ovire* and the social implications of this creativity.

Such a brief summary reveals little of the unique structure of the novel, which is paratextually introduced as a *"chant-roman"* (song-novel). And this designation is quite appropriate, because *Jasper and Coral* is a polyphonic work, containing various narrative modes, mixing overt and covert authorial strategies, blending several genres. It is at once novel, diary, song/poetry, and drama. Indeed, most of the drama is expressed through theatrical dialogue, conducted mainly by Grozi and Babou, the two talkative male protagonists, who, like too many intellectuals, confuse speech with action. The poetry or song that creates a narrative rhythm is produced by the narrator herself and by Nuit-Noire, a mythical figure that functions as the historical conscience of the people.[26] There is no plot as such, but a succession of thoughts expressed through dialogues that break down the boundaries between written and oral forms. The blend of these techniques makes it impossible to classify *Jasper and Coral* in any kind of conventional manner.

This innovation in genres is one of the distinctive elements that sets Liking's artistry apart from that of most of her contemporaries, but equally characteristic and original in her text is the ludic outlook of the work. Within the text itself the narrator describes the novel as a *"texte-jeu"* a "text-game." The ludic aspect, this "game-playing," takes an important place in Liking's work, and it becomes, along with the laughter it generates, a device to organize the imaginary, a veritable strategy of narration.[27] Through this kind of writing and particularly through *Jasper and Coral,* Liking recaptures for African literature the cultural norms of laughter. No doubt because of the overwhelming problems that Africa is confronted with, most writers (with the exception of the early writings by Mongo Béti, Bernard Dadié, and Ferdinand Oyono) have approached their creative production with extreme seriousness.[28] Yet even if one understands their stance, one has to regret the absence in fiction of the living tradition of laughter in Africa. Indeed, more often than not, readers are robbed of the incredible *joie de vivre* that is so characteristic of most African societies and that, in everyday life, is translated into deeply felt laughter.

In *Jasper and Coral,* a "text-game," the "game" starts from the very beginning, when the book introduces, within the framework of the intertext, works that were written about Africa by Westerners, which bear titles such as "False Start in Africa," "Africa Betrayed," or "Stranglehold on Africa."[29] The *misovire* rejects the assumptions contained in these writings because they reflect European definitions of Africa, definitions Liking seeks to challenge and eventually obliterate. These assumptions are partial, fragmented, and biased, and, more important, they deliberately ignore the simple fact that "there are other truths. Certainly" (3). That is why the narrator is determined to change the rules of the game: "Yes. For once, let's play at being a prophet, each in his own place for a change" (3). But what is paradoxical here is that after refuting the false ideas contained in the foreign book titles, the narrator uses those same intertextual titular markers to explain, in part, why she is unable to write, why "she goes scudding along from failure to frailty, from a 'false start' to a 'betrayal' without ever managing to get her 'journal' under way" (4).

Liking's approach turns the playful use of titles into a serious game—a game that is both a means of denunciation and a didactic tool. By her allusions to these titles, Liking shows the consequence of the paralyzing inhibition inflicted on Africa by such apocalyptic visions. And the game Liking is "playing" denounces not only foreign forces but also the inhabitants of Lunaï, "a village that is shitty to the core" (8): "Let's play here, in this text. Let's play a game in which we amass every weakness every blockage every veneer every bit of ugliness and every stray impulse" (3). This accumulation is justified because in Lunaï all the villagers, be they women or men, children or adults, poor or rich, are "tsetse flies," with all the symbolism that the figure evokes.

The didactic function of the "game," however, is to admit the truth about African ailments without ever forgetting Africa's resilience and strength: "The most astonishing thing yet is that in all this jumble some flashes of light still linger" (4). The *misovire* insists that the apocalypse will come about only if Africans find comfort in what she calls an "elsewhere-otherness" (4), because, in spite of the West's deep-seated desire to see Africa totally incapacitated, in spite of the death wish that the West cannot help casting upon Africa, and though the *misovire* finds it difficult to write her diary, yet "she still doesn't choke!" (4). A sign of hope, this resilience nevertheless has to be seen in realistic terms because: "In our game there will be no magical solution no dogma" (4).

Liking's game is not only ideological, it is also textual, and the text itself is structured as a game at different levels. First, the narrator announces that she intends to write a nine-page journal (the number nine having a special significance in the Bassa initiation rites), but in the original (French) edition "page 1" of the *misovire*'s journal actually starts on page 23 of the novel and ends on page 55. "Page 2" goes from page 55 to page 74. "Page 3" starts on page 74 to end on page 96. "Page 4" begins on page 96 and goes to page 108, and so on until the end of the novel, where we realize that the "nine pages" have developed into 156 pages. In the printed text, then, Liking effectively weaves (or stitches) together the real and imaginative pages. On page 54, almost at the end of "page 1," the *misovire* is still looking for a person to whom she can dedicate her journal (let's not forget that all the Lunaïans are tsetse flies), and the mere fact that it requires one-third of the book to reach the end of "page 1" demonstrates the creative difficulties she encounters. Once the diary is under way, the other "pages" seem to follow in quick succession; however, when the *misovire* reaches "page 9," supposedly the last page of the journal, she suggests a pause as a moment of reckoning, and here at the end she wonders whether or not she should write the already-written journal.

The manipulation of narrative patterns, also a transgression of conventional rules of narration, places readers *"dans le coup,"* making them double participants who take pleasure in finding the *"fil conducteur"* in order to unravel the narrative cloth. In that sense the *misovire* has total control: she is not only playing a game; she is the game leader, the protagonist who shapes the discursive universe of the novel. In this configuration the plot itself is absent, voice dominates, dialogue becomes a privileged locus where consciousness can be raised by the infinite power of the word, as it happened in traditional rituals.

The playful tone is extended by the numerous interjections infused into the text, and those serve a phatic purpose as well as being a technique of derision. Indeed, when the *misovire* is full of pity when faced by the inadequacies of Lunaï and its inhabitants, or when she is incredulous about, or overwhelmed by, the acts or non-acts posed by the Lunaïans, she exclaims: "Ah the Tsetses . . . " or "The Tsetses! Aïyo!," "The Tsetses!!! oho!" (35–36), or again, "Really now Lunaï . . . " (86). The narrator complicates this game by pretending that she is addressing not the Lunaïans but some strangers whom she invites to see what is happening in Lunaï: "You foreigners who come to Lunaï . . . learn the following terminology so as to avoid any disappointment" (81).

Questions are constantly posed in the text—some rhetorical, others reflective, still others expressing real queries that puzzle the narrator, or Grozi and Babou, her mock male intellectuals. These questions and their now touchy-contradictory answers reflect the individual and collective searches for direction that were made in the years immediately following national independence. The scarcity of punctuation—very rare in African fiction—creates the effect of a stream of consciousness, which is quite striking and emphasizes the importance of meditation and reflection. Of equal interest is the way Liking uses grammatical tenses to manipulate time and space to blur the real and the fictional, melting all boundaries to fulfill the playful purpose of a text that is liable either to confuse readers or to engage them fully into the game, but never to bore them or leave them indifferent.

The text is characterized by an alternate use of the future and the present tenses.[30] The future is used from the very beginning of the text, in the title itself: "It Shall Be of Jasper and Coral." It is a quasi-religious prophecy, incessantly repeated by all the characters who echo the *misovire:*

> There shall be born here
> From our groping our stammering
> . . . .
> There shall be born from our shit our blood
> Humus of magic fecundation and fertilization
> There shall be born a New Race of men. (5)

The tension between apocalypse and rebirth is very clear here, but rebirth prevails as the new race emerges in a transcendent manner, rising above its shortcomings symbolized by the groping and stammering, the blood and shit. The grammatical tense propels us into a realizable future, but then, almost immediately, the *misovire* brings us back into the moment with the present tense, a realized present, to announce that the new race *is* indeed born, "*here*" in the certainty of the textual space:

> I swear it. . . .
> . . . .
> . . . swear by fire that it is the truth:
> Thus it is written. Here. . . . (5)

Thus, the new race is at once a projection into the future and a reality created in the present through the act of writing the journal. In this configuration the narration does not only refer to a possible reality—which the *misovire* refuses to see as a utopia because she is too aware that "It is not Utopia that Lunaï needs but rather concrete and viable facts" (95)—it actually manages to create the time and space where the rebirth takes place.[31] But even this creation is complicated and problematic, because in her ninth and last "page" the *misovire* is still asking herself: "Do I really have to write a logbook? Will I be able to write it? Is it useful? Am I not too presumptuous to expect to be doing something for the Blue Race of jasper and coral?" (109).

In other words, the *misovire*-diary-writer-game-leader is also the creator of the new race born through the power of the spoken and written word. Until this moment, however, the *misovire* is the principal agent, the one who acts, who conceives of the journal, writes it, wants to do something for the new race. But this is changed through yet another playful ruse:

> What I shall do right now . . .
> Is burn this journal project or hide it
> And in hidden terms
> Suggest a wrong direction
> . . . .
> So
> The next Race will search
> Will organize expeditions excavations
> And will never stop the quest. . . . (112–13)

In the first part of this passage, it is still the *misovire* who conducts the action. But in the second part the new race turns from object to subject capable of acting upon a real object—the journal and the quest it initiates. Thus the journal will have served the double purpose of creating a race that will recreate itself through consciousness and responsibility. These indispensable qualities, as important and serious as they are, can also be conveyed in a comical manner.

One of the most hilarious passages of the novel occurs when the *misovire* offers a scathing criticism of artistic criticism in Lunaï. To describe that, she imagines an absurdist dialogue between a journalist and an artist. To each question posed by the journalist, the narrator provides two sets of answers. The "good answers," judged good and even brilliant by the journalist, are in fact ludicrously senseless. On the other hand, the "wrong answers," so labeled by the journalist because they are truthful and well thought through, are, of course, the good ones. To the question "Etes-vous engagé?" (Are you committed?; 81), the "good" answer is to prove one's commitment with a long list of words ending in "ism" (including "séisme" [earthquake], which of course is out of place in the list), the narrator urging the artist also to add all kinds of personal detail to satisfy the voyeuristic taste of the Lunaïans (81–82). The "wrong" response would be for instance to deny that one is "engagé" and to claim instead: "Non mais . . . j'engage" (No but . . . I commit; 82); and of course, the irony is totally consummated when one discovers at the end of "page 5" that the page is dedicated to "the criticism of a culture by cultivated people" (84).

The laughter emanating from Liking's text is in fact a "double laughter"—at once comical and tragic, joyous and sorrowful, the kind of laughter Langston Hughes alluded to, echoing the traditional blues song "Laughing to Keep from Crying."[32] In addition, the laughter in *Jasper and Coral* is one that unsettles and gives an impression of malaise. At the same time, however, it is also a wink of complicity shared by people who laugh because they understand the deeper meaning of that laughter. But her game is never gratuitous, because what is at stake is of vital importance. Responding to the demands of her time and place, Liking makes her game operational, programmatic, always grounded on a moral foundation, the only foundation capable of bringing forth the new race of jasper and coral, of breath and of fire. Liking's art has the power of alchemy, capable of imagining transformational possibilities for the future. A new race will be born, *is* born, that sees the quest as important as the initiation rites capable of transforming the Tsetses into responsible human beings. The goal here is to decenter the old, to find a new balance for the new, for a renewal that the people of Lunaï are condemned to choose if they are to avoid total destruction.

Amadou Hampâté Bâ said that in Africa, "when an old man dies it is a library that is set ablaze."[33] Pierre Nora expressed the same idea when speaking of the acceleration of history, a phenomenon he defined as "an increasingly rapid slippage of the present into a historical past that is gone for good, a general perception that anything and everything may disappear"

(7). Embedded in these two quotations is a certain anxiety about the preservation of history. It is also Nora who made an interesting distinction between memory and history. For him, memory itself has no past—it is spontaneous, in perpetual evolution, open to the dialectics of forgetfulness and remembrance. On the other hand, history is the medium through which technological societies organize the past. It is a construction—problematic and incomplete, and, it must be added, ideological—of that which no longer exists. But what history do these remarks refer to? And to what end should it be preserved?

Werewere Liking adds a mythical dimension to her reconstruction of history, a way of suggesting that myth and history are two instruments of memory, two modes of remembering; that is, two different ways of organizing a past that is inevitably constructed. It seems to me that myth and history differ only by their degree of preoccupation with truth—a criterion that itself has been posited as a myth in the West—based on the determining credence given to the notion of proof. In her fictions, however, Liking cannot be bothered with "proof," and she does not claim to any Truth; she simply offers an imaginary interpretation of a certain "truth," and it is not by chance that her work *Love-across-a-Hundred-Lives* focuses in a large part on the epic of Sundjata, a story partially historical and partially mythical, well known in the realm of African orature, history, and literature.[34] Here Liking uses myth and history for the construction and the comprehension of the present, tying together myth, memory, and collective knowledge, hence her recurrent use of phrases such as "Do you remember?," "Can you recall?," or "Have you forgotten?" In Liking's view, history is not a monument but a practical instrument by which to approach the present. This evolution from past to present through memory is textually marked by the manipulation of temporality, which becomes a way of structuring the story.[35]

Like *Jasper and Coral, Love-across-a-Hundred-Lives* is not a novel that can be hurriedly read or summarized. The work is remarkably rich and complex, with different layers of signification. It is the story of Lem Liam Mianga, or simply Lem, whose name means: "The Habit" or "The Manner of Casting Bridges" (119). Lem is a young man tormented by his navel, which is the seat of all that is vile and base in him. He is a cowardly individual of no consequence, who is introduced at the beginning of the story as suicidal, intending to hang himself with a rope made out of umbilical cords. Yet Lem will undergo a gradual transformation, gaining the consciousness that causes him to become a man in the most complete and the most noble sense of the word; that is, a man "in the fullness of [his] heart's center" (215). However, his metamorphosis can be achieved only through the stimulating presence of Madjo, his grandmother, the one who initiates him, encourages him, loves him, and provides him with the strength necessary for his transformation.

But their relationship is not so simple and direct. Lem and Madjo have known each other for a long time, and they have lived a great love that has endured across one hundred lives. Thus they are not only Lem and Madjo but also Sundjata and Sogolon Kédjou, Roumben and Ngo Kal Djob.[36] In his current life, Lem is a student at the university, where his model and his idol is Professor Ziworé, who is himself associated with the mythical Ngok Ikwèn, "the intrepid hero of the old tales" (143). Liking's characters exist simultaneously in the present and in different times, reincarnating real, mythical, and imaginary people, linked with the historical and political intertext and with the literary motif of the double, multiplied ad infinitum.

Temporality is inscribed in the titles of the different sections of the novel where Liking weaves a new historical tapestry through the dialectical manipulation of past and present. The first part of *Love-across-a-Hundred-Lives* is simply an untitled prologue, which introduces diverse characters and situations, but the second part is entitled "Before . . . In Secret . . .

A Very Long Time Ago . . . ," phrases that recur throughout the novel. Part 3 is entitled "Before . . . In Secret . . . Not So Very Long Ago . . . ," the fourth part, "Yesterday," and the fifth, "My name is . . . Lem Liang Mianga. . . ." The progression in time is quite obvious here, and, in the final chapter, Lem is resolutely inscribed in the present through what can be termed "an act of self-identification" that enables him finally to proclaim his own name. This act of self-identification also signals the end of Lem's journey, as he passes from the state of a frightened child, running away from everything, to that of a man and even a warrior. The novel's last part is an afterword, a kind of metafiction where the boundary between narrator and author seems to dissolve, and which ends with an apostrophe directed to the reader:

> Shhhhh!
> What else do I hear?
> The rooster's crowing? Already? Well, look at that. . . . It is daytime!
>
> OUR DAY
> THIS VERY DAY (247)

This conclusion suggests that for Liking history has meaning only insofar as it is used to construct the present and to construct oneself in the present, in "our day," "this very day." Her approach is consonant with that of the ancestral griots who used to say: "Since God created the world, we have summoned the name of the dead to dry the tears of the living."[37]

The goal being to touch the world of the living, Liking makes the present permanent, even in its imperfections, symbolized by the reign of the *"Machine-Goutte,"* a monstrous political invention Ziworé and his students hope to defeat. The preoccupation with the present and the determination to restructure it calls on the potential of the future, an imagined future which seems to be deadlocked in this fin de siècle. The future must lead to a rebirth, especially if one would leave wide open the "door of surprises" to let in "artists, scholars, mystics, and other strange types who always elicit awkward questions" (138). Closed for too long, this door should have been swung open, because, "any people desirous of progress always wished to be surprised: a new look, a discovery, a re-assessment, an emulative discomfort . . . " (137–38). This discomfort is the starting point from which the present can be reformed; it is the only avenue by which the future envisioned by Roumben can be engendered, like "a child that is created here and now, by questioning yesterday and by acting upon today" (215).

Thus Liking's conception of history is far from being static even though it is expressed through a very traditional frame of mythology; rather, for her, history is in a permanent state of flux and is liable to go through many configurations. Perhaps this explains why, in a technique unique to Liking, which I would like to call "the aesthetics of the lure" and which is also evident in *Jasper and Coral,* the narrator of the afterword acknowledges the historical existence of her characters but then immediately denies that historical link. Indeed, she affirms: "Yes! the names of people and places reminiscent of people who exist or have existed are true and could not be 'purely coincidental.' They exist in African history and mythology." Then she hastens to reverse that assertion by adding: "But . . . don't be rash! There is no historical truth here!" In a similar way, she admits that she was tempted by the idea of reincarnation, but then immediately she undercuts her own pronouncement by affirming: "Here then, we are dealing with a purely literary ruse" (246).

The aesthetics of the lure, the interaction between past, present, and future as well as the reconstruction of the past all carry an explicit inscription of the feminine. The leading intertext is the story/history of Sundjata, newly imagined; and while the versions of the epic written by men often emphasize Sundjata's role as a builder of empires and extol the male characters of the Mandinka empire, the impact of women is untold, and women's history remains unwritten.[38] That is why Liking downplays Sundjata's military achievements and reinforces instead his moral qualities. But, most important, she casts Sogolon Kédjou, the buffalo-woman, the mother of Sundjata, as a central heroine. Indeed, the epic of Sundjata cannot be easily separated from the legend of the buffalo-woman, a legend so long-standing that it has an impressive number of variants. It is therefore important to outline that myth to show how Liking borrows from the story while transforming it.

In most versions the tale is set in the Do kingdom, where the king's daughter has been denied her inheritance by her brothers. Seeking revenge, she changes into a buffalo, which ravages the village, destroys crops, and kills the men. The elders of Do summon the best hunters to rid the kingdom of the buffalo, promising they will have as a reward one of the most beautiful women of Do country. Two hunters consult a diviner, who tells them to befriend an old woman who lives in solitude in the bush. They do so and win the woman over so that she discloses her second identity as a buffalo, telling them how to kill her in her animal form. Her condition for this information, however, is that they choose to marry a very ugly hunchback woman who is, under her disguise, the king's daughter. The older hunter marries the hunchback, but each time he tries to make love to her she begins to change into a buffalo. The hunters decide to give the woman to Maghan Kon Fata, the king of the Mandinka, who was told through prophecy that he would marry a very ugly stranger with a hump who would beget the son to successfully succeed him. But when Maghan Kon Fata marries the hunchback, now called Sogolon Kédjou, the buffalo-woman, he cannot make love to her either, and so finally rapes her, thus conceiving his son Sundjata.[39]

Taking this legend as a point of departure, Liking constructs her own narrative centered around her character of Madjo, who in a previous life was Sogolon Kédjou. In contrast to the classical legend, Sogolon Kédjou's life before becoming the king's wife is told in detail. Because her mother was forced into marriage, Sogolon Kédjou swore that *she* would choose her future husband herself, and so acted contrary to the behavior men usually demanded of women, neglecting her domestic duties and becoming a hunter. Soon she was said to be a witch, and she delighted in the rumor because she knew it would keep unworthy men away from her. In Liking's version, Sogolon Kédjou became a buffalo-woman not to seek revenge over an inheritance but because, as a hunter, she had seen a male buffalo attack a female buffalo in the travails of giving birth. Outraged by the male's brutality, Sogolon ran to the female's rescue, killed the male buffalo, and helped the female bring her offspring into the world.

In gratitude, the animal asked Sogolon what she wanted for her act of kindness, and Sogolon said she wished to take on a buffalo's appearance. The female buffalo gave Sogolon a hump and a terrifying ugliness, and thus created the buffalo-woman. Here then, Sogolon became ugly by choice in order to repel all the "people in rut" (148), as she called them. But Sogolon also received considerable inner strength, so that although she was given as a present to the king, she entered through the "door of surprises," a priceless gift, fit only for a king: "the great king Maghan deserved this amazing virgin" (159). Furthermore, the king did not rape Sogolon, as in the original legend, because she taught him how to see beyond her physical appearance, so they could make love with mutual consent: "He entered her bed, and without a word they gave themselves to each other" (161).

By and large, Liking reproduces the events of the buffalo-woman's legend, and yet she significantly alters their meaning. In her version, women are not reduced to chattel; they are full members of society and their stories are worth being told: even though Sogolon Kédjou is given to the king as a present, she is not objectified. Indeed, she has an agency far superior to that of the king, for it is she who teaches him how not to be repelled by outward ugliness but to learn how to discover hidden beauty. She also teaches him to respect a woman in such a way that the sexual act becomes a loving encounter strong enough to engender a formidable successor to the throne. Sogolon Kédjou could achieve this because of her strength, skillfully used as an instrument to revise the social norms that women find reprehensible. But Liking does not make of Sogolon's achievement an isolated instance. On the contrary, Sogolon Kédjou passes on her strength to Madjo and Ngo Kal Djob, women who will reincarnate her, and through them, to generations of women to come, thus giving them transformative powers. In that manner, Liking's novels enact the ways in which women are able to effect social change.

Sogolon, then, becomes the mother of Sundjata, who in *Love-across-a-Hundred-Lives* is also Lem, a man, but one who owes the success of his life-journey to a woman, since, according to the narrator, "Great men are spirit-ideas that take shape inside the bodies of great women" (189). Madjo is the one who initiates Lem. She is also his *griotte* (and here the use of the feminine form is necessary), since the initiation is carried out through the medium of speech, reviving the memory of glorious times past. She sings him a lullaby, in fact a powerful exhortation to courage, syntactically translated into an imperative form and, culturally, into praise verses. This lullaby is repeated with many variants and constitutes a central leitmotif in the novel:

Child of mankind stop your weeping
Stop your weeping I'll cover you with praisenames (131)

Stop your weeping then
. . . .
Raise your eyes to the heights. . . . (154)

Stop your weeping Child and let History inhabit you. . . . (206)

Madjo's greatest goal, however, is to make Lem come to terms with responsibility.[40] She will make him discover "the meaning of 'lost speech'" (133) and the significance of his name. He will therefore know his identity and the reason he is on earth, here and now: "I cannot have lived an entire life without one single action, without one single thing brought to fruition. . . . I cannot have failed to cast a single bridge between myself and one act, between one act and the next. I have to succeed" (178).

Madjo's voice extends itself in that of Bipol, the leader who imagines a new social and political order, and later in the text, in the voice of Ngo Kal Djob (meaning "the daughter of God's words"; 207), who encourages Roumben to come to revolutionary consciousness.[41] Ngo Kal Djob also encourages Roumben with praise names, delivers exhortations, and protects him from danger, making it impossible for repressive forces to capture him. Under the influence of Ngo Kal Djob's strong will, Roumben is able to go through a metamorphosis and act by himself: "He became body inside her body and clothed himself in her body of flesh and spirit. And it was a man who raised himself up, quickly and with dignity, singing as others speak, speaking as others act, and dancing as others walk, steps that move forward" (217).

Even though Liking seems to mock the whole idea of commitment, or at least she downplays it, there is no doubt that she is an *engagé* writer, and her commitment plays out at several levels to revitalize the multifunctional goal of social transformation that she inherited from the historical context of the 1950s. Thus, Liking's women always bring men to awareness and help them realize their potential, to become warriors of a new paradigm, needing no conventional weapons to achieve their goal.[42] Women are the indispensable agents of change who show that coming to consciousness and the effort it requires is a heroic act achievable by everybody. Indeed, as pointed out earlier, Liking's chief preoccupation is to use myth and history for the reconstruction of the present that requires the efforts of all the children of Africa.

If Sundjata and Roumben are mythical and political heroes, their heroism is reenacted by Lem, a very ordinary man; and the lesson to be drawn from the story is that one must believe that heroism is part and parcel of everyday life—that, indeed, heroism is lived every day by "ordinary" people. As for the woman, patriarchal societies have always refused to acknowledge her acts of heroism precisely because more than any member of society her life is inscribed in the quotidian. But Liking extends the idea of the heroic woman even further:

> God is woman and woman knows it
> And woman keeps it silent
> God knows why. . . . (149)

If woman is God, and if one conceives of God as the ultimate organizing force, then woman has a limitless power that she needs to put at the service of the community (including men) to bring about a rebirth of the continent. Only then, like Lem of the hundred lives, will all the children of Africa be able to say:

> We were reborn every morning as we awoke to start
> again . . .
> to start the world anew!
> We were reborn at every stage to renew the effort once
> again
> A hundred times, a thousand times the very same road
> To go faster and farther with every turn. (232)

Irène Assiba d'Almeida

Notes

1. Liking, "La femme," 6. All translations from this interview are mine.

2. Although Liking started their jewelry business, most necklaces and other jewels are now being made by her sister, Nsèrèl Njock.

3. Liking, "La femme," 7.

4. In their anthology *Littératures nationales d'écriture française* (Paris: Bordas, 1987), Alain Rouch and Gérard Clavreuil state, "After a literary training, later complemented by Theater Art studies in Paris, Werewere Liking starts to paint (1968) and gets involved in journalism (1969–71)" (70; my translation). Even this rather vague statement has never been confirmed by Liking. We find

glimpses of her private life in the interviews she frequently gives to popular magazines, but that private life does not seem relevant to the review of her work. In addition, I would like to respect Liking's own choices in protecting her privacy, keeping in mind that in *It Shall Be of Jasper and Coral,* one of the narrators criticizes the inhabitants of Lunaï for being unduly concerned with "autobiographical art" (82).

5. Bjornson, *The African Quest,* xvi–xvii. This excellent work should be consulted for a thorough analysis of the Cameroonian political climate briefly described in my quotation.

6. For an analysis of the evolution of Liking's position on Negritude as seen through her novels, see Irène Assiba d'Almeida, "The Intertext."

7. Werewere Liking is one of the most prolific female writers in French-speaking West Africa.

8. For an elaboration of this topic, see the introduction to my *Francophone African Women Writers,* 1–11.

9. Indeed, the first collection of poems by a francophone African woman was published by Annette M'Baye d'Erneville of Senegal in 1966; the first novel, by Thérèse Kuoh-Moukouri of Cameroon in 1969; and the first autobiographies, those of Aoua Kéita of Mali and Nafissatou Diallo of Senegal, both appeared in 1975.

10. Liking explains some of the traditional techniques she uses to train her actors in "Le 'vivre vrai' de Werewere Liking" (Werewere Liking: 'Living authentically'), an interview conducted by Christine Pillot, 54–58.

11. Liking, "Le théâtre rituel" (13; my translation).

12. Introduction to *Orphée d'Afrique* (76), the play Manuna Ma-Njock wrote as an adaptation of Liking's novel *Orphée-Dafric.* (All translations from this book are mine.)

13. Liking, *Orphée-Dafric,* 58. For an elaboration of the notion of knowledge as acquired through ritual, see Anne Adams, "To Write a New Language" and Irène Assiba d'Almeida, "Werewere Liking: Initiation" and "Echoes of Orpheus."

14. Liking provides the translation of "Ki-Yi" in the interview by Christine Pillot.

15. In the summer of 1990, I visited the Villa Ki-Yi, where I spent most of the day, shared a meal with the group, and attended the rehearsal of one of Liking's plays, *Singue Mura: Considérant que la femme. . . .* This allowed me to observe Liking's talent as an effective stage director and choreographer. Several months later I saw the play in its final form at the Congrès de la Francophonie in Limoges, France. It was a veritable spectacle, successfully mixing acting with song and dance, offering an impressive display of living masks, daring costumes, and an epiphany of colors.

16. The Group Ki-Yi is now an important organization. It includes the Ki-Yi Mbock Theater, the Ki-Yi Arts Productions, the Eyo Ki-Yi Editions, the Ki-Yi Management (a structure that manages the group's affairs), the Neck-Neck Ki-Yi (which caters for the group and for the dinners included with the shows in the French *"café théâtre"* tradition), the Ki-Yi Gallery, the Ki-Yi Lines (lines of clothing made out of African fabric, whose designs are inspired by

traditional fashion), and the Museum/Theater Ki-Yi. In the late 1990s, Liking was building a new facility to accommodate the growth of the Group Ki-Yi.

17. Perhaps the only other enterprise similar to the Village Ki-Yi and predating it is the artistic Village of Oshogbo, located in Nigeria.

18. Endeavors like that of Liking's may be the only solution to the problem expressed by John Conteh-Morgan in the conclusion to his *Theatre and Drama in Francophone Africa:* "The French government, which has been the single most important promoter of Francophone drama, from its origins to the present day, is adamant that only dramatists using French will receive its support. The Francophone governments, on the other hand, suspicious of a form which has the potential to reach a mass audience and which has recently become increasingly critical of them, are far from eager to promote it—be it in French or worse still in African languages. . . . That the continued development of so vital an art form as the modern theatre should depend on the good will of an external benefactor does not bode well for its long-term sustained growth" (222).

19. Liking, *"A la rencontre de,"* 139. (All translations from this book are mine.)

20. While Liking's work has repeatedly been reviewed in scholarly journals in France and the United States (thanks notably to *Research in African Literatures* and *World Literature Today*), the literary community had to wait for over ten years to see any substantial critical writing on her. In French, the breakthrough was by Séwanou Dabla, who devoted a chapter to the examination of *It Shall Be of Jasper and Coral* in his book *Nouvelles écritures africaines.* In English, the first critic to pay any significant attention to Liking's dramatic production was Richard Bjornson in *The African Quest.*

21. Liking emphasizes the importance of imagination as a source of inspiration, of hope, and even of survival. Through direct apostrophes, she invites her readers to imagine certain scenes she is describing in the hope that her writing might endow people with such imagination (120).

22. It is interesting that the symbolism of stones and their different colors can be found in the New Testament of the Bible, in Revelations 4:3, as well as in Plato's *Phaedo.* In the latter work, just before dying, Socrates gives a vision of an ideal Earth: "The pebbles which we prize in this world, our carnelians and jaspers, and emeralds, and the like, are but fragments of them, but there all the stones are as our precious stones, and even more beautiful still" (trans. F. J. Church [New York: Liberal Arts Press, 1951], 66). If it is not certain that Liking's analogy comes from Plato's work, it is possible that the Bible, which Liking often uses intertextually, may be the source of her inspiration. I would like to thank Carrol Coates for bringing these possible intertextual readings to my attention.

23. Liking, "A la rencontre de," 21.

24. For instance in her criticism of the novel, Madeleine Borgomano contends, "This provocative novel does not turn out to be particularly feminist. The voice of the 'misovire'—whose coined name makes us expect a virulent feminism—often concedes its place to other voices, at least two of which, the most talkative, are male voices" (*Voix et visages,* 77; my translation).

25. Liking addresses the issue of feminism in the interview conducted by Peter Hawkins, "Werewere Liking at the Villa Ki-Yi." Also, for an elaboration on the notion of the *misovire* as feminist, see my introduction to *Francophone African Women Writers,* as well as Juliana Makuchi Nfah-Abbenyi's *Gender in Arican Women's Writing.*

26. For an insightful analysis of the character of Nuit-Noire, see Séwanou Dabla's *Nouvelles écritures africaines,* 188–95.

27. The ludic element is used as a transtextual device in several of Liking's works from *A la rencontre de . . .* (Encounter with . . .), her first fictional work, to *Love-across-a-Hundred-Lives,* her most recent novel to date. Written in collaboration with Manuna Ma-Njock, *A la rencontre de . . .* is a *récit* in which two protagonists, Afrika and Occident, recount their different versions of the same events as each experienced them intellectually, emotionally, and culturally. The *récit,* with its contrasted interpretations of the same experiences, is in fact a twin story, where the game is all the more interesting because the two main characters are cast as doubles. Each succeeds not only in expressing their own version of the story but in serving as a reflection each of the other, as if in a double mirror.

28. Janis A. Mayes analyzes the ludic character of Dadié's work in "Bernard Dadié: Politics, Literature, and the Aesthetics of the *Chronique,*" an introduction of her translation of *La ville où nul ne meurt* (The city where no one dies).

29. The titles refer to works by foreign writers such as the French sociologist René Dumont and others: René Dumont, *L'Afrique Noire est mal partie* (Paris: Seuil, 1962), trans. Phyllis Nauts Ott; *False Start in Africa* (New York: Praeger, 1966; 2d ed., rev., 1969); René Dumont and Marie France Mottin, *L'Afrique étranglée* (Paris: Seuil, 1980, 1982), trans. Vivienne Menkes; *Stranglehold on Africa* (London: Deutsch, 1983); Jean-Claude Pomonti, *L'Afrique trahie* (Paris: Hachette, 1979).

30. I am indebted to Amy Bird, a former graduate student at the University of Arizona. She took my seminar on Liking and wrote an insightful paper on the use of temporality in *Jasper and Coral.* Some of the ideas contained in this portion of the essay are inspired by her analyses.

31. Here, again, it seems that the narrator is playing with the idea of constructing a utopia that she says is no such thing! Yet the idea of a utopia, already made evident in the title, and throughout the text, is reinforced by her choice of the name "Lunaï" for the fictitious village and by the fact that Grozi imagines a new world in "Astral," the names connoting the moon and stars, respectively.

32. Langston Hughes borrows the title of this blues song for his collection of folk stories *Laughing to Keep from Crying* (New York: Henry Holt, 1952).

33. This sentence, uttered by Amadou Hampâté Bâ at a UNESCO conference in Paris in 1966, never appeared in print, but it has become proverbial. Bâ subsequently explained the meaning of his saying in *Aspects de la civilisation africaine* (Paris: Présence Africaine, 1972) and in *Calao,* 58 (Jul.–Aug. 1984). His essay "La tradition vivante" (*Histoire générale de l'Afrique* [Paris: Présence Africaine and UNESCO, 1986]) is informed by the cultural beliefs contained in this phrase.

34. Several literary versions of the epic exist, among them, Djibril Tamsir Niane, *Soundjata ou l'épopée mandingue* (Paris: Présence Africaine, 1960); Roland Bertol, *Sundiata: The Epic of the Lion King, Retold* (New York: Crowell, 1970); Gordon Innes, *Sunjata: Three Mandinka Versions* (London: School of Oriental and African Studies, 1974); Camara Laye, *Le maître de la parole: Kouma Lafôlô Kouma* (Paris: Plon, 1980); Adam Konaré Ba, *Sunjata: Le fondateur de l'empire du Mali* (Dakar: NEA, 1983).

35. One finds the same tendencies in an internal intertext throughout Liking's fictional work. Thus, in *A la rencontre de . . .* there are two different interpretations of a same experience that involve the memory of the two protagonists, Afrika and Occident. In *Orphée-Dafric* mythology is used as a source that makes it possible to construct a transcendental present. In *It Shall Be of Jasper and Coral* myth is primarily used to understand how women lost the "fire of origins." In *Love-across-a-Hundred-Lives* there is a construction of the past that is intended to serve as an inspiration to reform the present.

36. Liking deliberately chooses the name of Roumben to suggest Ruben Um Nyobé, the charismatic leader of the radical anticolonial movement, the UPC (Union des Populations du Cameroon), founded in Cameroon in 1948.

37. Quoted by Adam Konaré Ba (*Sunjata,* 13; my translation), the only other woman who has offered a version of the Sundjata epic. Ba concedes that she interspersed her text with "personal reflections that serve as mediation, as social morality in order to fulfil an essential mission of history, that is, serve the present first" a preoccupation shared by traditional griots as well.

38. Here again, in spite of the misleading title of her book, a female writer such as Adam Konaré Ba not only writes women into the epic, she also announces the subjective nature of history and her intention to recast the Sundjata epic from a female point of view that privileges historically "forgotten" women: "Is it also a fortuitous fact that, under the pen of the woman that I am, Nana Triban (daughter of Sassouma Bérété and Maghan Kon Fatta) and Sogolon Kéju are the real heroines of this text?" (*Sunjata,* 12–13; my translation).

39. This summary is indebted to Stephen Bulman, who makes a synthesis of some fifteen versions of the legend in "The Buffalo-Woman Tale: Political Imperatives and Narrative Constraints in the Sunjata Epic."

40. Jean-Marie Volet analyses the question of responsibility and power in *Love-across-a-Hundred-Lives* in *La parole aux Africaines,* 215–44.

41. Bipol is a nickname given to Paul Biya, the present Cameroonian head of state, at a time when he was a charismatic, inspiring leader, long before he became the president of Cameroon.

42. It is, however, problematic to note that when women have to give incentive to men, it is often done in a sacrificial manner; the image of the sacrifice is conveyed here by the metaphor of the blood, even if this also evokes childbirth: "Take my blood, Son of Nyobè-Nyum / And let it forbid you to abdicate" (216). This injunction is repeated again on pages 217 and 229.

Bibliography

Adams, Anne. "To Write in a New Language: Werewere Liking's Adaptation of Ritual to the Novel." *Callaloo* 16, no. 1 (winter 1993): 153–68.

Ba, Adam Konaré. *Sunjata: Le fondateur de l'empire du Mali.* Dakar, Senegal: Nouvelles Editions Africaines, 1983.

Bjornson, Richard. *The African Quest for Freedom and Identity: Cameroon Writing and the National Experience.* Bloomington: Indiana UP, 1990.

Borgomano, Madeleine. *Voix et visages de femmes dans les livres écrits par des femmes en Afrique francophone.* Abidjan, Ivory Coast: CEDA, 1989.

Bulman, Stephen. "The Buffalo-Woman Tale: Political Imperatives and Narrative Constraints in the Sunjata Epic." In *Discourse and Its Disguises: The Interpretation of African Oral Texts,* edited by Karin Barber and P. F. Moraes Farias, 171–88. Birmingham, England: Centre of West African Studies, University of Birmingham, 1989.

Conteh-Morgan, John. *Theatre and Drama in Francophone Africa: A Critical Introduction.* Cambridge: Cambridge UP, 1994.

Dabla, Séwanou. *Nouvelles écritures africaines: Romanciers de la seconde génération.* Paris: L'Harmattan, 1986.

d'Almeida, Irène Assiba. "Echoes of Orpheus in Werewere Liking's *Orphée-Dafric* and Wole Soyinka's *Season of Anomy.*" *Comparative Literature Studies* 31, no. 1 (1994): 52–71.

———. *Francophone African Women Writers: Destroying the Emptiness of Silence.* Gainesville: UP of Florida, 1994.

———. "The Intertext: Werewere Liking's Tool for Transformation and Renewal." In *Postcolonial Subjects: Francophone Women Writers,* edited by Mary Jean Green et al., 265–84. Minneapolis: U of Minnesota P, 1996.

———. "Werewere Liking: Initiation as a Tool for Social Change." In *Francophone African Women Writers: Destroying the Emptiness of Silence,* 125–44. Gainesville: UP of Florida, 1994.

d'Erneville, Annette M'Baye. *Kaddu.* Dakar, Senegal: Imprimerie A. Diop, 1966.

Diallo, Nafissatou. *De Tilène au Plateau: Une enfance Dakaroise.* Dakar, Senegal: Nouvelles Editions Africaines, 1975. Trans. Dorothy Blair. *A Dakar Childhood.* London: Longman, 1982.

Kéita, Aoua. *Femme d'Afrique: La vie d'Aoua Kéita racontée par elle-même.* Paris: Présence Africaine, 1975.

Kuoh-Moukouri, Thérèse. *Rencontres essentielles.* Paris: Imprimerie Edgar, 1969; Paris: L'Harmattan, 1981, 1985.

Liking, Werewere. *L'amour-cent-vies.* Paris: Publisud, 1989.

———. *Elle sera de jaspe et de corail: (Journal d'une misovire).* Paris: Edition l'Harmattan, 1983.

———. "La femme par qui le scandale arrive." Interview by Sennen Andriamirado, *Jeune Afrique* 1172 (22 June 1983): 68–70.

———. *On ne raisonne pas le venin.* Paris: Editions Saint Germain-des-Prés, 1977.

———. "A la rencontre de . . . Werewere Liking." Interview by Bernard Magnier, *Notre Librairie* 79 (1985): 17–21.

———. "Le théâtre rituel." Interview by Lucien Houédanou, *Afrique Nouvelle* 1803 (25-31 Jan. 1984): 12–13.

———. "'Le vivre vrai' de Werewere Liking." Interview by Christine Pillot, *Notre Librairie,* 102 (Jul–Aug. 1990): 54–60.

———. "Werewere Liking at the Villa Ki-Yi." Interview by Peter Hawkins, *African Affairs* 90 (1991): 207–22.

Liking, Werewere, and Manuna Ma-Njock. *A la rencontre de . . .* Abidjan: NEA, 1980.

———. *Orphée-Dafric* (Liking) and *Orphée d'Afrique* (Ma-Njock). Paris: Editions l'Harmattan, 1981.

Mayes, Janis A. "Bernard Dadié: Politics, Literature, and the Aesthetics of the *Chronique*." Introduction to her translation of *The City Where No One Dies* by Bernard Binlin Dadié. Washington: Three Continents Press, 1985. (Originally published as *La ville où nul ne meurt* [Paris: Présence Africaine, 1968].)

Nfah-Abbenyi, Juliana M. *Gender in African Women's Writing: Identity, Sexuality, and Difference*. Bloomington: Indiana UP, 1997.

Nora, Pierre. "Between Memory and History: *Les Lieux de Mémoire*." *Representations* 26 (1989): 7–24.

Rouch, Alain, and Gérard Clavreuil. *Littératures nationales d'écriture française*. Paris: Bordas, 1987.

Volet, Jean-Marie. *La parole aux Africaines ou l'idée de pouvoir chez les romancières d'expression française de l'Afrique sub-saharienne*. Amsterdam: Rodopi, 1993.

It Shall Be of Jasper and Coral

(Journal of a *Misovire*)

A Song-Novel

Fore Word

"False Start in Africa"
"Stranglehold on Africa"
"Africa in Danger"
"Africa Betrayed. . . . "

The Dumonts. The Duparcs. And other De Baleines. . . .

Titles. Names. Assessments. Prophesies. . . .

Words that express a gangrenous Africa and foretell times when there will be nothing left to eat but migratory locusts, and that only in the good season!!! Words that express that "colonized Africa never did have a future and that independent Africa is going to die" . . . and so on. . . and so forth. . . . All that may well be true. But there are other truths. Certainly. . . .

Let's play here, in this text.

Let's play a game in which we amass every weakness every blockage every veneer every bit of ugliness and every stray impulse. Let's superimpose. Let's pile it up. It won't go very far that's for sure. But it's only a game. There it is: the word no longer has any meaning. Looks, pleasure, friendship are congealed in ambivalence. Original desires have become perverted. Intellectuals are hollow and muddle-headed. Men have no balls and women are real shitfaces. Old people are decayed, children contaminated, and an educational system capable of stabilizing the standards no longer exists or has not yet been found. . . .

Yes. For once, let's play at being a prophet, each in his own place, for a change. . . . There's enough wretchedness and woe on every continent now that any prophet of doom can stay home without risking unemployment. Let's play and let's multiply: one gangrene multiplied by one fault line plus one plague times one apocalypse equals = . . . ? That could have sent all of humanity into a crisis, no? But obviously, it does so only to Africa. . . . Or to Lunaï in our text-game. . . . Of course.

But there are other truths. . . .

A people never falls into complete bankruptcy. To file the petition, it needs to be totally decimated first. . . . And even so, there's always a Lot, a Noah, or a Redskin left to perpetuate the human race. . . . Thank God! And there are still enough humans left in Africa whom they haven't been able to decimate. And they have gone on procreating, those fools. Even though the apocalypse of the Sahel Desert its waters moldering with epidemics with hunger has not yet managed to wipe them off the face of the earth! And the most astonishing thing yet is that in all of this jumble some flashes of light still linger. . . .

In our game there will be no magical solution no dogma. Our heroes will leave us unsatisfied: they won't go far enough (imagine the new race already there!). They're groping, they're fluttering, purring and snoring! And with them an incredible woman, frail in flesh, following them only with her gaze her ear and from afar, stalking the power-word that will formulate and give shape to her dream, a fiery dream inside a body she fears is nothing but "meat." . . . A *misovire* in short! She gets lost in their clichés, tries to hook on to an "elsewhere-otherness" and finds herself to be nothing but a mixture of aspiration-inclination and of ill-accepted nonassumed experience. And she goes scudding along from failure to frailty, from a "false start" to a "betrayal" without ever managing to get her "journal" under way. But she still doesn't choke! . . .

As I was saying, a people never falls into complete bankruptcy.

And, of all the many truths regarding Africa and Humanity, there is one I insist on prophesying:

5

It Shall Be of Jasper and Coral

"There shall be born here
From our groping our stammering
Our pompous vacuity our dust-covered memories
From our hard undigested badly absorbed lessons
There shall be born from our shit our blood
Humus of magic fecundation and fertilization
There shall be born a New Race of men
From human breath and divine fire
And the *misovire* I am now shall encounter a misogynist
And we shall live happily ever after
And we shall be numerous children
I swear it. . . .
You can give up or stand up for humanity
And swear by fire that it is the truth:
Thus is it written. Here. For once. . . .
Don't you see the starlight breaking?
Don't you feel the beating of a pulse?
It shall be of jasper and coral
It shall be of breath and fire."

6

It Shall Be of Jasper and Coral

GROZI has masturbated again.

And there he is again with his tail-in-front hanging low and slack a shameful drop dangling shilly-shallying: will fall won't fall. . . .

"I wanted. . . . I would like. . . . I would have liked. . . . An adventure. . . . No! something else, . . . an encounter that's it! I would have liked an initiatory encounter. . . . "

He hesitates. . . . Then he turns away furiously. What did I do to him now?

"All right, all right! You despise me, I know! You despise all those who are like me, all Lunaï's tsetses. Go ahead! Pretend you're superior, that suits you to perfection. . . . "

And he takes off. Here I am alone again still alone how much longer must that go on?

I would like to hear lighthearted words
The way only words know how to be
And "man received the word from God
All the better to conceal what's inside his heart"
I would like to dance songs
And sing silences
I would like
The unfathomable stances of a glance
The fierce quivering of a skin
And the brilliance of a thousand rays shimmering on seductive teeth. . . .
I would like to be colorblind
And see only red
Color of blood
Color of life
To convince me that I'm still alive
And to expunge the glacial void from my soul
I would like crowds water
Wind fauna
To escape from nightmares . . .
From the loneliness that suffocates with its tentacled colors. . . .

For here I am empty naked
More naked than a blank page
And naked
From wearing out my clothes
From having drenched them in mud then washed them again
Having exposed them to psychological analysis then ironed them again
Lent them to vandals and washed them again. . . .
And empty
From having preached love
When what we really need is willpower. . . .

For I too would like something of an initiatory situation-encounter. I would like to look toward a distant and beautiful horizon, to toil and hoist myself up to reach for an invisible peak to aim high. . . . But every time it ends like this: people masturbate and discharge their glaucous shame and one shameful drop stays dangling there. . . . Then off they go with their tail-in-front hanging low and they accept themselves as inferior with nothing beautiful or strong to offer to teach to give. . . .

It's true I got into the habit of looking upon the people of Lunaï with a certain commiserating glower since I've really been observing them and I expect them to grow another tail at any moment. . . . In back! Disintegrating senile instinctively squalid husked by *soukoukalba*-intuition-heavy-burden-parasites on the backs of their sons on the back of the foreigner of the ancestors of the spirits. It's the old outdated race of Cro-Magnon and I do believe I'm somewhat of a racist. . . .

*
**

Enough! Enough! I don't want to fall asleep any more! It's a curse an illness. . . . I fell asleep!

Every morning I grab some pencils, notebooks I'd like to keep a journal–golden logbook in which I would confide the essence of nothingness or nothingness and the essence. On the cover page I'd write: golden logbook of a dog's life: journal of a *misovire*.

I'd write a dedication on the first page but to whom or what? Everything seems so commonplace in Lunaï. . . . But in reality everything is really rather different here and in fact quite out of the ordinary: Lunaï is a village that's shitty to the core.

Since Black-Night's death, it is impossible to imagine Beauty in Lunaï to dream of Love to glimpse Vast Horizons in short it's impossible to attain Vision here. . . . And in the end you could be interested in almost anything or anyone and find enough inner misery to dedicate yourself to the apostolate. . . .

Take Grozi and Babou. . . .

Let's see. . . . Page one: To Grozi and Babou, the seeds of . . . no! that doesn't work. . . . They're just about anything but seeds they definitely are not.

Grozi and Babou they're a specimen of those accursed couples that haunt Lunaï. As prisoners of time they met here again irresistibly inescapably because of the debts they contracted toward each other and the web their emotions had inextricably woven. . . .

> Six thousand generations let them suffer let them pay.
> This time they really hope to empty their cup of wretchedness:
> Uninhabited and maladjusted
> Intellectualizing and devout
> In a squalid and prurient village
> No better way to hit the bottom of the abyss
> And to resurface nimbly in the light of a peculiar couple! but in the meantime . . .

Babou has a richer fantasy life than he thinks. When Babou wants to escape from poverty-wretchedness he dreams that he's robbing a bank right under the nose of a cop who sees nothing not even his fingerprints. He's thought of everything even gloves! Then off he flies to sunny shores accompanied by gorgeous women with streamlined thighs. There's a metallic blue Cadillac in front of a luxurious chateau an elegant white villa inside a garden green with flowers. . . . Every lovely image the media might suggest floats around lightly in Babou's head. His ancestors fought for equality and conquered the freedom he now has to arrange "pictures for everyone" in any way he chooses. But he's not allowed to think about the unformulated unspoken and never-seen. So he has no imagination but simple people aren't supposed to be creative. Let them consume! That's what suits their personality. It's stuck to their pallid skin their staring eyes.

Babou's dog has lost everything including his instinct for survival to such a point that he even eats poisoned food. He's gained too much of a false sense of security and has become completely dependent on Babou. So Babou risks everything: with his dog he wants to find his atrophied inner perception again together with the pituitary body through the weight of obligatory "aid." Grozi has told him that the pineal gland is the seat of mankind's godliness. It should be reactivated before it disappears completely! Could one bear the burden of the reign of darkness that would otherwise settle in? The secret lies in rhythm Grozi confirmed that as well so Babou risks everything even if he has to pass for a traitor to "the rhythm people" a phony black man in short and that upsets him. . . .

As for Grozi he lives his life as one of the "ordinary people" under a regime where those who hold power are the Ancestors and the Spirits; they allow him to create his support but "astrally"! That is the truth in which he must believe that is his duty: truth lies in the astral. What gives anyone the right to doubt the voice of the Ancestors!

So when Grozi dreams that he's escaping from the mess at last he fantasies: a spirit supplies him with a magic word that opens every door entrusts him with the secret of the life-house that builds itself. . . . He soars up in round-trip night flights! His ancestors receive him like a king fairies fall in love with him at the sound and the beat of his magic word. . . .

Unfortunately, when he wakes up he still has just two eyes and no wings. The rain falls on his head then. . . . Then he's had it is fed up with it all with the astral journeys and houses! He can no longer abide fairies and their shadow progeny who don't even guarantee him live descendants of flesh and blood. He wants what is concrete secure. . . .

So Grozi plays double or nothing: he declares himself a Cartesian commits theses on reason and loses his mother tongue in the process. . . . He negotiates agreements concrete-bombs-management-war-genocide-power-oil dollars. . . . He's re-creating the Grozi world: its lumpish bourgeoisie. Its popular-Moussa-speaking-proletariat. Its weathervane-intellectuals-East-West-longwinded-Experts. Its politics-politicians-puppets. Something secure-concrete even if he has to pass for a traitor to "the people of reason" a phony white man and that upsets him. . . .

Faced with the dead end of history's course Grozi and Babou have embarked on a personality transfer and have managed to achieve an ill-absorbed self-rejection. . . .

BABOU (to Grozi): You're not evolving, you poor jerk. . . .

GROZI (to Babou): You're regressing, you specimen of a dying race. . . .

And Ségar keeps talking to them about *métissage*. And they declare themselves for or against their only intention clearly to assume paternity for a new word. . . . Yet another one! While they're living the switch. . . . Babou dreams of Black-Emotion. . . . Grozi aims for White-Intellect. . . . They see everything in terms of squares, of crosses. . . . They've grown old and they don't know it. They are certainly not the seeds of a New Race. May they at least sire a bloodline that will want to go further. Let them prepare it to go further: they will have done their job. They will have prophesied . . . and, naturally, they will be able to make room for mental rhythm. . . .

11

It Shall Be of Jasper and Coral

⁂

Which poem would strike me more sweetly on that day
Than a glittering thrust à la Edouard Maunick
Trenchant lullaby maddening and captivating
What power would bring me greater security than that of the water that filters in floods flows spurts evaporates
Hardens like a rock
At the mercy of the forces of nature. . . .
What smiles would be more dear to me
Than those of Lem and Lia
Crouched with their heads together
The pinnacle of the triumphal arch on my face
In the morning when they say: "Good morning, mama!"
What anguish would be more useful to me
Than that of reading doubt
On the face of my beloved
When from the depth of my fertility comes pouring out
Every creative imagination that renews the world
Re-creates love re-creates life
Re-creates faith and re-creates power
Every day and any day
Oh rapture!
What tenderness would be more moving
Than that of the faces of those women who have often wept over me
The face with unfathomable designs of Ngo Biyong Bi Kuban
The face with the mysterious triangle your face my mother
The moonshaped faces of Alice and Germaine above a text to be memorized. . . .
All your faces of tenderness dissolving in tears
And touching deeply beyond rivers. . . .
What stringency would be healthier for me

Than yours father yours also Mpek
When you say: "Nothing is worth life, only life is worth life"
And I would become humus on the spot
Virgin Forest to fertilize the entire Sahel
Which gaze would be more revealing to me
Than that of my ghost of a friend who said to me one day:
"Be seated on my life Oh Queen so that I will not stagger"
Which desire for truth would be more obvious to me
Than yours woman friend of my truest truth
You who fight in the shrubs where my excess lies hidden
Oh courage!
So many of you who love me
Oh Passion!
All of you who believe in me
Oh faith! Oh heavenly rapture!
In truth
I am the happiest of all women
Everything has been given to me. . . .
And if on earth I were the only one in agony
At that very moment the whole world would be filled with gladness
In truth
I am the happiest of all women
But you whom no one loves
You who are vilified
Christened with every damned and hellish name
Cloistered
Monitored
Your every instinct curbed
All of you who live in fear
And count your pennies
Count your wars and count your evenings
You who refuse to commit suicide on the threshold of shame
Without any further reaction without any other hope
Survive and keep your body and soul together

13

It Shall Be of Jasper and Coral

And I say this to you
You are my chosen ones
Come here come here
To the end of that suicide
And let us live
But possessed but free
And I disown you
You who cause me rapture
Walk on my sons
I disown you
To hell with my own happiness
Tremble for my sisters
To hell with tenderness
Tremble for love
And so many of you who are happy
I disown you
You of ill repute
You are my chosen ones
Come here. All of you come
To the end of that suicide
We are our own carcasses
Putrefaction of our mothers
Cattle dung manure of bare-boned cows
To the end of that suicide
Strong from our actions
Dead from our words
To the end of that suicide
So that shame will not preside again tomorrow
And I say this to you
You are my chosen ones

*
**

Before the gray nights of Lunaï the voice of Black-Night would speak to me at night. . . .

"The line is not a straight line
The curve is not a curve
If the line doesn't join the curve

Light will not shine at all
That is the secret of mental rhythm
The first trump of the New Race. . . .

It obeys the rules of the sinusoid and will no longer limit some to the astral and the emotional and others to arid-intellectual-masturbation.
It must enable the heart of the trunk to be joined to the heart of the head the body to be joined to the roots.
It will enable the construction of a sturdy bridge between the spoken and the unspoken between the solid and the intangible and it will clear the path toward wider horizons.
And tribe race will no longer mean region skin but community of Vision and of Aspiration.
And the Man of the next Race will appear in a stronger healthy body that lives in greater harmony with richer more solid and more refined Emotions. His thinking will be more rigorous and more creative his will stronger and better directed his consciousness more open. . . . "

*
**

15

It Shall Be of Jasper and Coral

Fine, page 1! To Grozi and Babou, the ancestors of . . .

I'm definitely not lacking in generosity where titles are concerned! Seeds! Ancestors! Everything that is accomplished in itself full of life and promises of life. . . .

Grozi's Ancestors have always stressed the body they cleansed it strengthened it shaped it in the image of the soul that lived in it. Until it was that soul's perfect reflection. Until it had come into full bloom.

To please to the point of admiration is one of the first keys to harmony. To success. And the initiate cannot be "short-winded" or overbearing. His spirit spreads its calm exaltation through every opening and his body breathes this generosity.

To please deeply. To please beyond deformities beyond infirmities. To please in spite of dislikes and jealousies.

The tsetse women of Lunaï who will hear me extol the art of pleasing will take advantage of it in order to destroy their husbands prostitute themselves buy themselves jewelry clothes beauty products. They will find every method to exalt their superficiality under the pretext of wanting to please. . . . But I'm not worried they were that way before, long before I ever said one word, Lunaï is my witness!

Lunaï is a burned-out and weary village. Alas! Bodies seem old scrawny revolting incompatible with dialogue. The people here are truly alone. So they buy or sell their companionship (at a cheap price and rightly so) when their urges become stronger than their indifference. . . . For the driving emotions in Lunaï are reduced to indifference and jealousy. And of course any need for articulation has been buried. How then can they hope to secrete the zest for responsibility and a spirit of initiative? Willpower has been scattered to the four corners of futility and all energies have been wasted. . . .

In the end there is only lack of culture complete ignorance of what is being done elsewhere the efforts of the sons of mankind. . . . Yet the Powers that be in Lunaï bear all the noble parchments of every great institution of higher learning from every corner of the world. . . . They have attended the finest institutes they have learned every Name of those who are working on something interesting for the Race: philosophies sciences arts. . . . But all they know are names! People can come to Lunaï and go from door to door but they'll never sell their merchandise. Nobody wants anything to do with knowledge here! They've imported the trinity of *"Boulot-Métro-Dodo"* from the other side of the lagoons. . . . But since there is no subway in Lunaï and since nobody ever goes to work they've adopted the trinity of "Football-Food-Finery" and then everyone back to his own corner of loneliness if he cannot pay. . . .

And Babou and Grozi keep on babbling. . . .

BABOU (full of conviction): Perhaps we should introduce corporeal expression and breathing exercises into the school system to improve the circulation of energy in the body and increase its magnetism? Attraction would become stronger and the desire to be together would bring in something resembling dialogue from which a new form of emotion might result perhaps. . . . Now that I have become converted to "Black-Emotion" I would like it to be more powerful than ever but also more subtle. . . . We should incite enthusiasm for those activities that stimulate goals other than those of self-interest, in short, light the holy fire once again toward an idea that elates and in the very depths of everything will seek that true Emotion that has lain hidden for centuries because it had become used to losing while being in the right. A black emotion that is truer than Black peoples themselves. . . .

GROZI (in the same vein): You could make fanatics out of them if you were sure of a strong thought, a crystallizing one. . . . Feelings being the driving energy of life, the more powerful they are, the more exalting life will be. The more refined they are, the more life will have a direction . . . toward noble goals. And that is where thinking will come in. It should be deepened and go beyond reason. It should prune and chisel emotion to the point of articulating it, of creating it. For there is only articulation to reveal Human creation, articulation to attain options, choice. I want an intellectual rigor truer than reason, a

Hellenic reason truer than the Hellenes themselves. . . . The rest will be nothing more than a question of willpower.

BABOU: The strength of willpower is the result of making a good choice, of options that have been clearly expressed, you're right! With a direction that is based not only on faith but also on knowledge gained through personal experience it should be possible to avoid scattering and wavering where willpower is concerned. . . .

GROZI: And willpower such as that should automatically guarantee a fair division of energies. . . .

BABOU: Now then, those well-divided energies will ensure evolution itself where consciousness is concerned that is open to a higher vibration, to an innovating force. . . .

Am I then no longer young
Am I no longer young enough
Lighthearted and intoxicated by courage
Flooding over with enthusiasm
As beehives flood over with honey
Am I not brave
Am I no longer brave enough
Capable of seeing and imagining. . . .
What is beautiful is not beautiful enough
And beauty true beauty
Alone is what improves
But am I no longer young enough
Frothing with a fire
That never burns
But always consumes
A fire that swells the heart
And makes it able to love everything and everyone
To love the whole wide world
The young world
I am building here with sand
But I may as well use pink marble!

I may be content with a pittance for my sons
But the banquets are theirs too!
Of course we were told
"Just ask"
But I, I have to clarify
Let us ask a great deal
Let us ask all the time
And we will be humiliated!
Is my youth cowardly and limp
Could my youth have aged
Because it was too quickly satisfied?
What has begun will be rethought
And the beaten paths will be diverted
Youth real youth
Alone will be the one to know
Alone the one to dare
To start again
Old age ends and dies
Old age runs aground

*
**

Grozi has abused himself again!

And here he is again his tail-in-front hanging low and slack a shameful drop dangling there shilly-shallying: will fall won't fall. . . .

Grozi always ends up that way when he is searching for inner unity when he feels ravaging forces teeming in his underbelly his head empty with the void that's so bewitching. . . . So he attempts to let the overflow rise up toward the total emptiness and he no longer knows the difference between the physical emotional or intellectual energies and the purely mental ones: they all weigh equally on his coccyx! He stretches he tautens himself like a crossbow ready to launch them straight into the heart of his head. . . . There. . . . There. . . . The energies are rising. . . . There they are at the level of his navel. . . . There. . . . Easy now. . . . There they are at his solar plexus. . . .

No! They want to go back down again. . . . There . . . a little higher. . . . There. . . . There. . . . There there there disaster! They've fallen back down into a glaucous escapade. . . .

And a shameful drop is dangling there: will fall!

Grozi is completely upset angry bewildered ashamed. . . . But he does it again. Some days his desire rises up to his heart and brushes against his throat. It seems to him he's going to hear what's subtle that he's already smelling it. That is what encourages him. He believes that one day he really will end up by having a full mental orgasm. . . .

Sometimes he is aware of Lunaï's agedness. Inside himself he carries the desire for tomorrow and aware of his own limitations he dreams of another world for his progeny. So he married one of Babou's cousins. He married her particularly in the hope she'll make demands since "she comes from elsewhere. . . . " He needs a woman who knows how to take advantage of the saying: "What a woman wants . . . " From him she would demand that he be the best in everything and for everything. She would shake him every time that indifference or complacency would lay its tepid and sticky fingers on him to root him to the spot forever. She'd want more from him than mere appearances for she would know how to rail against the void and mediocrity even when they lie concealed under tons of gold carats. . . . And his children would inherit some of this exacting nature of her reason and her yearning. . . .

In the meantime he simply goes on: better to be ashamed of failure—it's stimulating—than to feel indifferent about nonexistence about a life that trundles along in a muddle! What if he could not muster a true ecstasy? Well then he swears his children will manage to do so: they'll know the joy of a bridge of light raised up like a sacred cobra linking yesterday to today today to the future in a flickering of the fires of knowledge and consciousness the fires of love that truly creates! So make way. . . .

GROZI (with a cry of passion): They won't be children of the White Woman

They won't be children of the Black Man anymore
They won't be Aryans nor Semites nor Hamites
They will be children of light of consciousness
They will be sapphire-blue jade-green
They will be celestial and ethereal
They will be electric warm and beautiful. . . .
And I love them already
They will be young and they will dare
They will dare to start anew
I love them already
They will be able. . . . They will be able!

BABOU (interrupting him): Stop! Come back to earth! you're becoming a Black man dreaming again!
What's wrong with you to get so carried away without a drum
Come back to earth and talk to me in concrete terms
Tell me about this new society to which our children are supposed to give birth. . . .

"You believed Bathsheba
That the body could sweat
Sweat Blood and water gratuitously
Pleasure private territory of the Spirit. . . ."

GROZI (in a very learned fashion): All right! Let's come back to earth and begin at the top. The leaders must, you understand, they absolutely must be initiates. They must have a minimum of knowledge about the laws of the universe: cycles, equilibrium. . . . They must fit into one phase of the cosmic plan in order to work in harmony with a maximum chance for success. Then they will be capable of unleashing every spark of genius among their citizens and of obtaining a qualitative output resulting from the utilization of every potential, of which barely twenty percent is currently exploited. . . .

BABOU: And what if we began at the bottom?

Grozi (more and more pompously): Well then. . . . You'd have to withdraw all sense of dependency from the masses so that they no longer depend on parents, ancestors, spirits, divinities, the rich, the leaders. You'd have to give them back the freedom to express desire unlimited in time, by space, and to strive for this resolutely without any sense of inferiority. Stop making decisions for them about what they will understand or not: fairy tales for children, photo-illustrated romances for secretaries, sports matches for workmen, all those discriminatory categories that deny a fair sharing of culture between the "spinners of cotton" the "little ones" the "hairy chins" and the "rough heels." . . . Only the desire and the strength of each individual when confronted with the test should decide who will attain knowledge and the direction will automatically take into account those laws that govern the individual: planetary influences, rays, karma, interrelationships.

Oh! children of mine. . . .
(once again caught up in his own enthusiasm)
They won't be the children of the Colonizer
They won't be the children of the Subjugated anymore
They won't have the complacency of the Tyrants' bad conscience
They will no longer have the perverse belligerence of the Slave who loves his chains
They will be free and strong and beautiful
They will be of jasper and coral. . . .

Come come all of you
To the end of that suicide
Strong from our actions
Dead from our words. . . .

Babou: Stop it stop!
Let's talk about right now, before our sons become diamonds and gold, let's talk about the here and now: what is becoming of the economy?

GROZI: Prosperous and secure of course. . . . Sources that delve into a one-hundred-percent utilization of human potential are inexhaustible. These will be discovered through the initiation system and they will be as varied as the individuals themselves and the different genius of each! Besides quality comes at a high price my friend. . . . Can you imagine what our society would look like if everyone would put even the much talked about twenty percent of the potential at the disposal of Humanity? Are you thinking about the new currencies that would replace our old so badly designed bank notes? Do you realize what a promise would be worth?

BABOU: Oh no, I wouldn't dare, I'm too frightened to believe in it! For I assume that such promises would be accepted as hard cash as coin of the realm, if all people would really exploit their twenty percent. . . . But you, do you think that people would be less corrupt, would care less for personal privileges?

Ask a great deal
And you will be humiliated
And youth real youth
Alone will be the one to know
Alone the one to dare all
To start again. . . .

GROZI: But that's so obvious! It's guaranteed by the quality of the Race itself: its children have complete mastery over the physical and mental energies hence better health, the first warranty of any equilibrium and flourishing. Refinement and stability of the emotions automatically reduce selfishness, delinquency, and criminality. A broader awareness and a more judicious direction of purpose allow for foresight, prevention, and the facing of conflicts in a more harmonious way. . . .

BABOU (mockingly): Paradise in short. . . .

GROZI: No, of course not! Don't wreck it right away! How do you expect people to be bored when everything still needs to be done? The evolution toward a superior mental state will just be at its beginning: everything will have to be rethought, rearticulated, reconstructed.

BABOU: That's good! Your wares do please me. As long as it isn't paradise yet. I still have much too much drive to settle there contentedly. . . . But. . . . Let's discuss the details. . . .

*
**

BABOU (to Grozi): What shall we be eating in your new village?

In those days
The voice of Black-Night was still soft and she would invite all young people to her table. . . .
"Come come
Here have some
Fruits of heaven"
There was space and light from the stars
There was water wind huge nimble heavy and warm hands whenever you wanted. . . . A color of perfumes
And you would see the depth of the wind of the lush grasses and of the poisonous mushrooms dressed in music-words and eternal love
"Come come come
See Drink Believe
Honeyed hopes
Come come
There will be no requiem nor cold nor ambiguity
But surely surely
All that germinates and procreates will be there
Those who have been immunized against every venom
Here have some
Make mine yours

Fruits of heaven!!"
And no more were any empty-sudden gestures made
And no one left with half-empty zeal anymore
Skin to the earth
Eyes wide-open
Heart sure-and-filled
Without a quivering break without a sudden start
On the beat of Love
One left determined one day to attain
Ecstasy forever
Fruits of heaven. . . .

GROZI: What do you eat at home these days?

BABOU: Prefabricated food my friend! My wife buys peanuts, tomatoes, and even hot peppers already ground up, full of fly legs and half rotten because it lay out in the polluted open air waiting to be bought. And it's always the same okra reduced to powder for centuries, the same *aloko* drowned in age-old oils. . . .

GROZI: Pure shit, man, that's exactly what I thought: you eat, we all eat shit! It's hardly surprising that we are nailed to the ground, body and soul, eternally trying for impossible "take-offs" when we are ingesting *foutou-sauce-graine* every single day, it's no surprise that the mind atrophies as it sleeps every evening under the weight of the *attieké*-gumbo too hastily prepared and that the lower belly swells up from those tons of fatty "artificially flavored" rice! We are chemically what we eat, aren't we? and we naturally emit the vibrations of our own chemistry. If ours is monotonous-thick, and if above all the spirit doesn't temper it, are we then not doomed?

BABOU: And remember there aren't even any festive meals anymore! We make pigs of ourselves with the same lumpy dishes and, right away, imagination loses any chance to escape from the slag. . . . But tell me then, what will we eat?

GROZI: They will eat a conscious gesture, a carefully held-in breath
They will eat a deeply nurtured intention
A color, an image, carefully perceived.

BABOU: But then there will have to be plenty of food coloring?

GROZI: Moron! And what about natural colors?
Spirits will no longer be bulls lying in wait for carmine-red
Sheep on the watch for bright-green
Nor chicks attacking pink-candies. . . .
They will have the subtlety of the shades of color
They will distinguish the pink-quiver of affection
The mellow-blue of fertility and the cloud-black of the storm
They will feel the warmth of a hand bearing down
The smell of a sifting look
And the weight of a drop of sweat. . . .
They will savor the taste of a protecting heart
The perseverance of a love that lights up to give nourishment
They will eat life with fervor. . . .

BABOU: You're right: the first thing that needs to be changed in Lunaï is bad eating habits. We must absolutely get away from that eternal *foutou-attieké* routine that isn't even enriched with rituals and meanings anymore, those congealed prefabricated meals that nail us to the ground, blunt our tastebuds, and obstruct our vision. We'll have to learn to bite into manioc and bananas again, to chew them quietly and to rediscover the purity of their taste. We must transform our chemistry, that's vital.

GROZI: The kitchen must once again become a sacred place and the one who prepares the food, who officiates, must be aware of his gestures and his intentions. When the chef is no longer the dumbest of them all, hired as a mere "manual laborer," when he is an expert who knows . . . And a priest who knows . . . When the meal is a moment of communion, when the spiritual essence of the food is captured through ritual and not merely through the digestion of far too heavy dishes . . . Well, then our chemistry will go through a metamorphosis and perhaps we will finally give birth to the New Race?

Do you want to be my Master Voice of the Night
You speak of the things I love
When they are thinking of the color of mankind
Gray inside the head black on the lips
Red inside the heart and a cross on the eyes
Do you want to be my Master Star
For whom time and speed are not one and the same
One day you can glitter
Another day explode or be a dead satellite
Without despairing of life in the dark
Do you want to be my Master Light
You know how to be blind while you light up all things
Without killing them. . . .
Do you want to marry me?

*
**

Among the most deadly things of Lunaï the word is the worst of all. . . . It is a carcass emptied of all content and all meaning an encumbering and depressing carcass older than old.

In Lunaï the same words are always spoken and to anyone at all always the same words at any time no matter when. It's quite normal actually: Lunaï is already too wordy! Lunaï is a village they say. . . .

Talk to me then
Voice of Black-Night speak to me of villages. . . .
Speak to me of Timbuktu
Speak to me of Djenne of Zinder. . . .

27

It Shall Be of Jasper and Coral

"The sweltering sun cooks the bricks cooks them again
They were ochre
They are red
Turned toward heaven in a thickened thrust
They pray they fight against the cold
The cold of glacial nights which fights against the sweltering sun
And I ask you tell me. . . .
Why was he reincarnated
The man who planted the last stone that shimmers there
As if to reaffirm we know not which oath
Why was he reincarnated
Did he then couple with a mortal woman
While the moon herself was stretching out her arms to him?
Mysterious Timbuktu remained
And in a mirage the sun still reflects
The image of the lavish lover. . . .
Dressed and adorned in her oath
Djenne waits and waits and waits
Waits for the philosopher's stone
to settle again
On her red walls
And will thrust its momentum in Zinder"

Lunaï a village? Too wordy!

You leave the highway. You take a turning twisting road loops wind around each other between hills valleys and swamps. Trees align their trunks and shatter sheet metal: a thousand and one dead cars are lying around on the road's shoulders. . . .

Then comes the path. Everything is gold and ochre with dust leaves roofs people. . . . And the path snakes around. . . . It really is "the narrow path."

Then suddenly there's the village.

An immense tar-black boulevard bordered with shrubs a forest of cold curved lampposts statues as far as the eyes can see opulent villas luxurious enclosures. . . . You expect a stately welcome: the lampposts become angels who blow their golden trumpets of light in great harmony. And Peter stands right on the edge of the path and the boulevard and says to us: "Welcome to you, guest of honor, welcome to the King's breast, enter into glory." The hallelujahs burst forth and with great ceremony you go up the endless boulevard that leads to the palace underneath enormous billboard-triumphal-arches with the King's effigies. The doors of the palace have been studded with the coat of arms of the King: golden globes in the shape of calves ears. . . . The walls of the palace are impressive there is room for everyone on the father's breast. . . .

But if the visitor is not inspired by the entrance into Lunaï ah well then the electric poles would remain true to themselves: a dull deaf metal with a regularity that becomes hallucinating the more you go up the unending and desperately empty boulevard—empty sidewalks houses—empty empty factories empty hotels—empty empty building complexes empty. . . . Billions invested for only a scraggly few wasted energies for nobody for nothing. . . .

In front of the closed palace doors stands an impassive republican guard armed to the teeth who would let the visitor swoon before the golden calves ears: it was not to calves but to swine that Christ advised not casting pearls and furthermore he never spoke of gold. . . . "We need great men to see things in great terms and to strew greatness across this land," the guard would conclude. . . .

Our intimidated visitor would walk alongside the high walls to the other end of the village where other billboard–arch of triumph–effigies display the message "Lunaï wishes you a good trip. Long live the village long live African hospitality!"

In the evening in Lunaï you'll hear words like amiability hospitality, solidarity fraternity dignity -ity, -ity, -ity, and you think you're asleep standing up: some mishap some calamity must have occurred for men to be able to utter such words without being shaken by them, like robots. . . . Not one gesture not one attitude not one action reflects the meaning of the word.

And Ségar keeps talking about humanism. . . .
What has happened what has become of him?

BABOU: And yet, we still take care of our family here, every man in power enlarges his village, strengthens his clan, beautifies the land. . . . The orphan always finds an uncle an aunt to take the parents' place. And there is always a cousin to "bail him out." . . .

GROZI: Talk of a calamity! We'd appreciate a measure of help better after some personal effort, after we have earned it. But we are in a rush to demolish the militant forces. . . . An uncle helps you and serves himself. . . . He needs you because you close your eyes, your ears, and your mouth. The dumber you are, the gladder you make his heart. The more competent you are, the more you enhance his reputation. The more feeble you are, the higher you will raise his power.

Every able-bodied person becomes the rival who needs to be fought and the horde of invalids clutches onto help, using booby-trapped crutches. . . . And that is the long history of our humanism ever since meaning vacated the word's premises. . . .

Hothead screams in the street every day: a word, it's not a word at all, it's a state of being. And the media go on disseminating: a word, it's not a word, it's an abortion. . . . But people keep walking to the beat of words, to the beat of the names that reverberate in their heads, in their hearts and they bump into a wall, thus causing enormous lesions to their brains. And mechanically they walk, eat, talk, sleep to the beat of the saraband of words:

A word a step
Is not a word is not an action
It is a disavowal an obliteration
A word a step one two one two
Make way the zombie troops
A word a step
Make way headless troops
One two one two
They advance they retreat. They stop one two

They walk all over us, walk all over everything, ever since
meaning vacated the premises of the word. . . .

BABOU: Well then, how will we speak, what will we hold a dialogue with?

GROZI: They'll be speaking with a well-placed look one that
grasps
A hand that knows and holds on
A tone that gives direction
A sound that assembles
They will be shape within speech
Action within meaning
Rhythm within idea
They will speak the original tongue
They will find the lost Word again
They will have a dialogue with open heart and full mind.
They will have a dialogue with the breath of life. . . .

BABOU: With the same repetitious words, the same old worn-out phrases?

GROZI: Nobody will find it absurd anymore that languages and forms evolve together with people. The zombie troops will no longer be there to ask them at the edge of a dream: "For which trend school are you registering?" and they will exclaim: "Oh but . . . That's not traditional! Oh but . . . That's not African! Yes but . . . No but . . . " To prevent them from creating, from living. . . .

BABOU: That's why there is no echo anymore in Lunaï. The word no longer conceals reality for the one who gives it. His truth no longer lies in these words. And here we are forced to seek a new language that might adjust itself to the situation we are in as an old race out of step and putrefied. . . .

It Shall Be of Jasper and Coral

GROZI: A copious language that can address itself to all our senses at the same time, attack us like an octopus from every angle to clean us out, shake us until the crust of indifference, of old age is completely gone. . . .

But my children . . .

They will sing their own life and not that of their forebear
They will dance their own rhythm and not that of their father
They will live the shape of their own dreams and not that of yesterday
They will find freedom once again and the nobility of speech
They will once again be people. . . .

*
**

Do you want to be my Master Life
You often leave but always return
Animating all things bland and lively
Every part of what is truth
A part of what you are yourself
Do you want to teach me how to accept?

Lunaï really is a fateful village.

They say that it is the differences that characterize the twentieth century. Differences that mix in such discordant ways that ecology needed to be invented.

Superpowers next to the third world, cities next to shanty towns, the rich next to the poor, the thrust toward the freedom of the stars right next to the descent into apartheid and the slave trade without any sense of decency and this despite the ecological warning. . . .

It is a global crisis the media keep saying but Lunaï goes a bit too far. So much wretchedness next to so much extravagance is enough of a dissonance to make you puke is discordant enough to make you want to lie down and die. . . .

The poor of Lunaï are poor in body poor in head in heart in spirit in God. For is not the worst of poverty the very incapacity to see several aspects of one thing of one life, of one's own life!!!

Only yesterday before Lunaï had been christened with that too-much-of-a-word name you wouldn't die there from poverty. And besides not all forms of poverty could be piled up on one and the same head. You could be poor in body and rich in heart and rich in spirit. And the dignity of love or of wisdom would encircle the shaggy heads the hips dressed in rags and raise them up like sacred trees. And every man occupied his own place aware of the importance of his role happy with the wealth he had known to draw from it because Monsieur "what-would-I-need" will one day need a grain of hot pepper which the backyard raker will always have.

Today the poor man of Lunaï is poor even in his willingness to work and in that very diligence that makes of the backyard raker a specialist who will never lack for grains of hot pepper. He doesn't even have that transient spark of attentiveness that starving dogs possess. Sure that he would pass by the bone as he would by the treasures of his life without a single hair aquiver in his nose or his ear. . . . It is true that the poor man of Lunaï lacks even the discernment of his five most common senses. Even his dreams his imagination his survival instinct are reduced. . . . Do you see. . . . The Tsetse flies. . . . The Contamination. . . .

And since everything in Lunaï runs on wood the slightest rise in price resounds on every other price: the cost of knowledge of heat of cold of light of health of initiatives of death of prayers of honor of beauty of love. . . .

So four-fifths of the population vegetate in extreme poverty and drift along empty living-dead poor because that has been said, empty because that's been confirmed, dead because that's what they believed, living because they move, they keep their nose to the grindstone and the "praise-song of the day" fosters the zest for living of the Black African when a youth no longer knows how to dance, no longer even dares to dance and becomes a spectator even when faced with the convulsions of someone at death's door who stirs up the pestilence of unfulfilled dead desires welling up from all over in a glug-glug of the intestines during an attack of aerophagia. . . .

And we we allow ourselves to be pulled along with the masses with periodic crises of conscience: we have been devoured by a monster. We are covered with slime inside the transparent entrails that grind us up knead us down. We are being digested in order to be fodder. . . . For whom? We do not know.

And as soon as thoughts like these become conscious ones in our bodies strangely softening saps spurt forth from our digestive system and extinguish us and in a halo the intestines become the guts of Beaubourg: we are going to discover "Paris-Paris" the museum of modern art and all the other miracles. There's a round-trip we have the choice: we have opted for evolution as we pass through the intestine so as to be digested and to feed the regime that fights for us. We should be proud and die from hunger unutilized for Lunaï for Africa. Long live independence. . . .

You shouldn't think, however, that all this happened from one day to the next. That would have been too much and I believe there would have been protests. No it happened insidiously treacherously like a cyst like a malignant tumor: you only become aware of it when there's no way back. . . .

Before, Lunaï's name was "cradle in the heart" or "heart in the cradle" depending on the translation. The village had been established by the survivors of a disaster that goes way way back . . . way back. . . ! Their land of origin had been swallowed up by a gaping hole a mysterious fire glowing red at the bottom of the hole that had made the water boil while the wind created a tornado in the shape of a dragon above the hole. The opening of the hole was growing wider. They had to flee. . . .

The Tellem of the plains the Bantu of the forests and of the high plateaus the Zigui with their long necks all rushed to the coast and invaded the fisherman's regions of the Abo the Ewodi and the Ebrié. They had never seen so much water. The Iladjé themselves no longer dared to swear by the

Mother-of-the-Waters and yet there was nothing left to do but pray. . . .

When every prayer had reached the various gods who were overcome with pity they began to drink the water they who had never before drunk anything but saps and juices!

Then a heart-shaped land was seen to emerge. It was so sweet in the hues of colors and in the textures of its vegetation that the survivors really felt they were being reborn: the land continued to emerge from the womb the gods spat the salty water back out like a placenta. . . .

Centuries were needed to repopulate the land and make it prosperous centuries of peace of war and of peace. Centuries of wealth of beauty of ugliness of poverty and of a wealth of beauty. The people perceived all of this and had the dignity of choice. They shared the fervor the memory of the wise ancestor the rebirth rich in creativity the faith in the passion for arduous reconstruction that would begin with oneself. . . . That was their ideal.

But one day the invader came on horseback and with birds of steel the invader. He told them that the ancestor was nothing not even a mediator—there were Buddha Christ and Muhammad—and he proved it to them: it was written!

He told them also that power freedom and wisdom were to be bought and he proved it to them: he bought their sons and the tombs of the ancestors.

Before they were always fighting over some treasure they wanted to acquire there were so many of them that they could conquer by the power of their head or their heart being poor in money. The invader proved to them that they were wrong: he vanquished them and bought their soul. The ancestor and the image of rebirth disappeared one day and were replaced by the image on the shroud and by the tombs with precious stones. . . . Far more efficient as right away they granted prayers said with the rosary: you'd only have to confess your hatred for such and such a brother who was barring your way and he would be found dead with a bullet in his belly.

The rosary prayers were obligatory the supplications on

one's knees obligatory and charity as well. And there were more and more beggars who were harvesting substantial sums of money with which they bought up everything that was for sale. And everything was for sale. They bought heaven love or they sold themselves to God to the Devil. It was all so easy: all you had to do was ask was knock and God would give to us, Allah would make good to us, Christ would save us. . . .

What could be easier than to beseech to pray always with the same words that you count off on rosary beads always on the same knees and the same forehead nailed to the ground buttocks in the air shame in the face of God. . . .

Then God allowed himself to be represented by kings and commanders then by chiefs and relatives and finally by misery and one day people became pitiful parasites to be seduced with trash and to be cleansed with castor oil. But what is most serious of all is that God began to wither became poorer became weaker depending on one's status, rich or poor great or small strong or weak. Some could permit themselves an immanent God who inhabited them was living everywhere and directed them in everything inescapably toward evolution toward light. . . . Others had to content themselves with a petty God who was jealous of their least little free thought.

Every Sunday in church or on television screens you see big lips droning on with a yawn with empty eyes a fixed stare and you have to read between the lines or in the subtitles to know that this is a chorale a hymn to the joy of expressing one's faith!!!

And this has had repercussions all the way into the heads and the hearts into the dreams and the genes all on account of: the Tsetses. . . .

In Lunaï poverty seems to be hereditary.

The poor man of Lunaï is so filthy that he contaminates his own sperm by his disgraceful behavior and pettiness: when his daughters have barely reached puberty they warm up the beds of the palace guests in exchange for a bit of food. . . . Ah the Tsetses. . . .

The poor man of Lunaï is stupid: like a parrot he recites the formulas of his own condemnation thus allowing his leaders to have confidence in him and not the other way around for he will never see beyond his bit of food. . . . The Tsetses! Aïyo!

The poor man of Lunaï has decaying teeth: these have completely reduced his family and their reason for being to search for some food. . . . The Tsetses!!! oho!

The poor man of Lunaï is uneducated: he has read nothing but the words: "Blessed are the poor of spirit" and it is to be feared that he doesn't know the rest of the verse for he can feel no concern for any promise other than that of a pittance. . . . Thinking seeking and knowing how to reflect how could he afford such luxury? And to what end? They think for him they decide for him they act in his place. All he needs to do is to complete his share of the prayer with "the thought of the day."

And of course all of this had an impact on his creativity. Imagination has atrophied and the desire for perfection seems unknown from here on in. Not only do the craftsmen fail to create anything new but the copies are becoming uglier and uglier. . . .

Never will the poor man of Lunaï evolve if he thinks he was created in the image of this God. Never will he bloom with this faith in a petty and limited God barely capable of transforming his bit of food into a huge dish of chunky *foutou* his rags into polyester and his hovel into a "concrete house" for he will never attain more refined dishes nor diamonds and gold nor any chateau.

Babou: Still, you have to admit that with a great ever-present omniscient and all-powerful God imagination grows and creates more freely. . . . But what do you expect, these days a great God costs a lot. . . . It's all good and well for the Mother Church to preach generosity and charity, masses, weddings, baptisms, funerals are still too expensive even at cost. And when the "Mother's" leader goes to the third world he can't very well leave all his wealth on Saint Peter's tomb! What would the world leaders think whose power depends on God's image in the church?

GROZI: That's true. Still, a little respect for those people who, in order to receive you with dignity, would be capable of chartering every bus, train, and plane to "herd" all faithful and unfaithful populations together when the leader of the Mother-Church comes to visit, even if it means causing a global crisis the night before to justify a delay in the salaries of civil servants, and who would spend more than fifty percent of the national budget of all the nations of all the Sahels stricken by the ideology of the Gods of the Rich-Churches. . . .

BABOU: Fortunately there is a deluge of less expensive religions for the poor and the ignorant. . . .

GROZI: Speaking of a curse! Those are the ones that have diminished God even more. Some of them have begun to restrict the efforts by saying that you won't go to Heaven no matter what you do! They talked about the small herd—segregationists that they are—just one hundred and forty-four thousand specially chosen ones who can go on hoping! When you think about all the prophets the apostles the disciples and the other saints who have headed straight in that direction chariots and all, there isn't much room left to bid for. All you can hope for then is a place on earth to be shared with the leopards and the elephants, you'd think the cutting wire for the *foutou* was invented right after Noah! What a lovely dream to have drowned in the water! Just imagine! You would need a fine imagination and creative effort—a creativity freed from time and space—to attain this: one day, a paradise in heaven, the light. . . .

BABOU: While with those pathetic religions, the greatest miracle is to get rid of a migraine or for a baby to live side by side with a panther, as if you'd never been to a circus!

GROZI: But if there were only just this inconsequential thing called hope! You ought to see the list of prohibitions, the sum total of constraints. . . . My aunt refuses to wear pants because it is written that a woman in man's clothing is an abomination in the eyes of God!!! But what exactly is man's clothing? Among some peoples it is a wrap-around cloth, among others it is a skirt, among a third group it is pants, and elsewhere it is the opposite. Now there's something to make a racist of God and ethnocentrics of people!!!

So God shrinks a little every day according to small imaginations small yearnings and pathetic accomplishments! And the world becomes a keyhole through which the poor man droolingly squints with repulsive eyes of ignorance and pettiness without even being able to enjoy it all. . . .

And right beside them the party leaders hand in hand with the leaders of the rich and powerful churches. . . . Wealth to the point of waste refinement to the point of depravity. . . . Oh Lunaï!!!

Goddam! I fell asleep again!!! Where was I? Ah yes. . . . Dedicated to. . . .

My problem is that Grozi and Babou talk too much. . . . If they'd act according to what they say I wouldn't have any qualms about dedicating my golden logbook to them and I'd be in much better shape. . . .

Nailed to a pillory
Hanging in a precarious balance
In which my only wrong was to be the wife of the other
In the depths of the waves limbo lies spying on me
With broken arms I hang here
Since I've been hanging . . .

Never mind! . . . I'm dreaming that their ideas encounter the Echo-that-moves-to-action! And me, I may still be there to see the living example. . . .

Another crescent moon
One more after the 468,000 others that have gone by

Since I've been nailed here
Tomorrow the moon will be full
Another full moon after the 468,000 others that have faded
Since I've been waiting
And I've been hanging and hanging

While I wait for this miraculous awakening I shall content myself with dedicating my journal to their ideas capable of fruition. . . . With initials only to contain the form that will be born from it

So, page 1
A G
A B
Or with initials that are newer whistling ones clacking full of energy
A K
A F
A Z

"It shall be of jasper and coral
It shall be of breath and fire. . . ."

And so be it.

*
**

On page two I want to write an epigraph. A strong word a word-of-strength that will have to undress the reader carefully and profoundly cleanse him before he lays a finger on me on my private self. . . .

Fine! page 2. Epigraph. . . .

What would be the most interesting subject?

It will have to embrace everything in one line concern everybody. . . .

Let's see. . . .

At this moment in Lunaï every Tsetse is interested in art in the idea of art.

In the streets all you hear is rambling and raving about art everybody is talking at the same time unequivocally wanting to impose his most recent invention.

"Art is a commitment"
"Art is a message"
"Art is the power-idea"
"No, not at all! Art is truth. . . ."

All day long. . . .

And woe to the artist if what one thinks the "message" is does not support the speeches of the powers-that-be: ideologies moralities often just fashionable class struggles and thus automatically of a passing nature. . . .

And they publish articles whole volumes. . . .
Maud, write:
"Art is . . . It is a pastime a poverty-concealer a death-dodger nothing else. . . . "
"Art is . . . Mystification manipulation. . . . With a hyphen between mani and pulation, please, Maud. . . . "
"Film is . . . It's the abbreviated thread of a picture story in full color. . . . "
"Painting is . . . It's a garbage dump of old pictures to keep memory going, it's . . . Eh. . . . Painting . . .? Ah but . . . It's not African! Africans aren't familiar with either paint or brushes!"
"Yes, but . . . What about the Tassili?"
"No, that wasn't really painting! . . . "
"Music, now that's African! It's rhythm syncopated a thousand times to wiggle and sway to and not to have to think. Music is the message of today's African!"
"Sculpture . . . Oh yes, that's African!"
"Oh yeah, why . . . ?"
"You know, form. . . . Yes, you know the African form. What, is that like the African form?"

"Well, twisted of course. . . ."

"So it would be enough to twist every art form for it to become African."

"Eh . . ."

"And theater . . . That's not African."

"Of course! No! . . . Yes, it is!"

"In Africa there were only rituals and rites are not theater."

"Yes, they are! No!"

"African theater is dance music song poetry. It's total you see."

"No! Yes! Total theater everywhere. Besides the word theater comes from *theatron* you know the Greeks. . . . "

"But the Greeks came to Africa before . . . "

"No! Yes!"

"Maud, write! . . . all night long. . . . "

"What is Art? What is African Art?"

Grozi (to himself, in a dream): Grandfather was trying to explain this to me, the night before he died. His voice was clear and melodious. What he was saying seemed true to me but I didn't really understand its meaning too well. . . .

Babou (in his own world): My God, ever since I converted to emotion, I think I'm becoming incapable of taking any distance, of theorizing, how can I organize my thesis and avoid all this historical background?

Grozi (continuing his dream): His voice was beautiful. . . .

"Art is an eternal destruction."

"The reconstruction and the re-destruction of form."

He was saying this and his own form, his attitude were noble and beautiful. . . . And I think of all those men "of art" of today their shrunken spines their turned-down features their legs spread wide over woeful misery. . . .

Babou (still in his own world as well): I really don't need to create any complexes. When you read all those theses, three-quarters of which are devoted to the bibliography, to everything that has already been said, and the rest is merely paraphrase, is there anything left to learn?

GROZI: "Art is a death ritual, an initiation into transcendence over death."

Transcendence! My God that sounded good! that really seemed to have class. . . .

BABOU: I really must convince my thesis advisors that instead of doing eight hundred pages of empty babble I should write three hundred pages of pure thought that truly support my thesis. . . . After all that's what a thesis is supposed to be: a new and personal reflection!

GROZI: "Art is an ideo-flame"—damn! He really had a way with words!!!

It's an abstract memory not bound to time that takes shape in the silt of transient ideas. . . . Art feeds on the emotions of the person who lends it this shape and who receives it. . . .

BABOU: Well, darn it! What do I need a new high-falutin' degree for anyway that will not change a thing in the efficiency of my work? I earn my living well enough not to add to the number of "potboiler theses" that are already heaped upon this land. . . .

Another crescent moon
One more after the 468,000 others that have gone by
Since I've been hanging. . . .

GROZI: "And the shapeless memory not bound by time becomes the power-idea in the conscience or through the consciousness-raising of its two creators: the Artist and the Public. . . . And the power-idea becomes the shape of a sound, the shape of a word, of a color, the shape of a rhythm, of a space. . . . "

BABOU: But since I did register, I should go all the way to the end and here I am forced to cram those pontificating formulas in my head again, "art is the power-idea."

GROZI: "And form becomes art again. . . . And Dambala the snake swallows its own tail." Ah! but his voice. . . .

BABOU (exasperated): You idiot! What are you jabbering on about? You don't really want me to start up again about the old quarrels on form and content? That's as old as the hills! And me, I tell you this: I'm looking for a thesis, you understand? A new idea!

GROZI (coming out of his dream in a bit of a stupor): What? What are you talking about?

BABOU: Don't worry. I can see we're not on the same wavelength; in any case I need to give some very serious thought to African art. What is African art, what is not? Is there just one African art?

GROZI (thinking more clearly again): Of course there's an African art, or rather there have been African arts just as elsewhere there has been Byzantine art, Flemish art, and all the rest. But that was in the time when space hadn't really been conquered yet: the universe was . . . split up into thousands of little closed worlds. . . . Do you hear them talking today about French painting, English sculpture when they're alluding to what's being made now?

BABOU: First you'd have to know who is English and who is French these days. . . . They'd be talking about movements and that has nothing to do with race, with nationality. . . .

With broken arms
I'm hanging here ever since I've been hanging
And limbo is spying on me. . . .

GROZI: So you understand that it is difficult to talk about African art today without falling back into the old clichés again. We can go on copying the ancient African arts or we can be inspired by them if we feel the need. Those arts surely deserve that much, don't they? But the African Artist of today cannot, must not repudiate himself nor repudiate his duty to create as a man: a man in a "sidereal era" who experiences "live" the launching of the Apollos and other Soyuz rockets, a soccer game in Venezuela, the shooting of Christians in Lebanon and in Ireland, who suffers and shares the rise of the price of oil and the fallout of the neutron bomb, and who expresses this through his own particular sensitivity.

BABOU: That kind of art obviously can no longer limit itself to the garish colors of women's pagnes as they pound grain in their mortars, to sunsets over fishermen's huts, and to small dugout boats! It can no longer be satisfied with reproductions of statues, masks, and meaningless dances.

GROZI: And rightly so. . . . The poorest fisherman dreams of a fine motor-driven canoe. The lowliest of peasant women envisions purchasing a mixer and dreams of a white villa where miraculous ovens no longer blacken the sides of her pots. . . . Besides, isn't it natural to want to free yourself from thankless tasks in exchange for others that are more exhilarating? Aren't movement and change essential to life? The blender instead of the mortar, the skyscraper and villa instead of the mud hut, and the quest for a personality that is better adapted to this new environment, are they not also the African reality of today? Why then should artists be consigned to small dugouts mud huts and mortars that nobody else wants anymore, why then pontificate: "The Artist bears witness to his time. . . ." And at the same time ask him to be the museum of an "Africanity of days gone by." . . .

Hanging in a precarious balance
In which my only wrong was to be the wife of the other
I hang here since I've been hanging. . . .

BABOU: But what then makes the African artist different from any other? Aren't we risking too much uniformity, too much standardization even where Art is concerned?

GROZI: Me, I believe that only the form the Inner Vision and the techniques of its approach truly create the distinction between one person and the other. Everyone can't approach the divine by the same methods, by the same paths. And it surely won't be computer science and its machinery that will make any changes here, and in any case that wouldn't be anytime soon. . . .

Consequently, art will continue to be diversified, of this I have no doubt. . . .

BABOU: They even say that "geoclimatological" sensitivity by itself is sufficient to disclose a thousand nuances of the sky. . . . That should reassure both the xenophobes and the claustrophobes. . . .

They brought me here where the other one perished
And I'm awaiting my turn
Since I've been hanging here. . . .

*
**

Oh darn! I fell asleep again. . . .

Every time I think about Babou's and Grozi's digressions I get carried away or I fall asleep. . . .

Here's page two: epigraph. . . .

Am I crazy to think that an epigraph about art would be of any interest to the people of Lunaï?

Outside of the rantings and ravings that give them the impression they're intellectuals and the feeling that they're alive art doesn't really interest them. Anyway, what would they do with it? Art "sells" so badly in Lunaï. . . . Of course I'm talking about the art of individual creation of the contemporary art from this place.

Yesteryear's African art has compelled world recognition and still brings money—and good money—to the copyists and the merchants of those copies. As for contemporary art, it already seems fixed with a kind of glue that some have called the "dross of clichés" invented by Africanists. . . .

It leads one to believe that the famous "abstract memory not bound to time" doesn't much feel like taking shape in the transitory thoughts of the people of Lunaï so poor are they poor in feelings poor in desire. . . . Nothing torments them, they never so much as budge.

And I believe this lack of desire to be a serious problem in Lunaï. For here nobody is ever mad anymore no matter what it concerns: mad neither with love nor with hate. They don't even like money: they're caught up in the system and they'd kill for it but without any passion!!! They don't even despise wretchedness anymore but they'd sell themselves to get out of it without any longing without any further goal. The Tsetses have vanquished the will to Fight!

And I await my turn
And they are waiting too
If they don't feel it as a disgrace
Then why should I?
With broken arms I hang here since I have been hanging
If they don't feel it as a humiliation any longer
Then why should I?

And there can be no true life without desire
And there can be no Art without desire. . . .

Fine page two: Epigraph. . . .
a desire for life
a desire for art
the art of desire. . . .

Alas Night is torturing me in my dreams at night. . . .

"The day will come Bathsheba
Bewilderment will be your master and loneliness your only companion

You thought Bathsheba that you could live on spirit alone
On fruits from heaven
That the body created for sacrifice could sweat
Sweat blood and water! . . . gratuitously. With impunity
Wordly pleasures the spirit's game-preserve
And you were taught Bathsheba
You had to love your neighbors as yourself
Seek first the kingdom of Heaven and its justice
And the rest shall be given you. . . .
So you transmuted yourself into love
And you scattered love to the four winds you dispersed yourself
And you were also taught
That it would suffice to ask in order to have your wishes granted
And you Bathsheba you believed them!
And you have worked to please others
You have nourished them with your pagan zeal
And you have remained deaf to your own desire. . . . "

With broken arms I hang here
Limbo spies on me I hang here
Another crescent moon
One of the 468,000 others that remain waiting for desire
Oh well! . . . Let them wait!!!

*
**

Of course when the people of Lunaï hear me talking about Desire their genitals will begin to tingle and they'll throw themselves at me with all their antennae up. . . . And Grozi will be one of them. . . .

Don't think that Grozi is obsessed with sex or he wouldn't be the only person that still makes life bearable for me in Lunaï. . . . For Grozi has endless potential and many many virtues. . . . And he has talent. That's why I like him quite a bit. . . .

But Grozi disgusts me because I fear that in his genes he carries the putrefaction of the macho civilization that has ruled for so many centuries now and that sees everything as a phallus!!!

I bet that he visualizes the leap of the soul as an erect phallus!

And like all the other people in Lunaï who hear me talking about desire he will think of this phallic desire characterized by the impossibility of attaining eternity; desire that invariably becomes erect in the form of swords rifles missiles architectural monuments desire that relieves itself easily in wars in blood in pus. . . . Desire that is stiff at night and limp during the day conceived merely to engender a sense of time:

Time in the morning

Time in the afternoon

Time in the evening

Eat run drink jump sleep kill die!!!

Die limp and grow stiff and decompose into limpness. . . .

And men have built their lives upon the philosophy of a desire the impetus of which is identified by the stiffness of beginnings and the limpness of ends and its symbol—strength—is supposed to be the key to life. And they've deployed this like a hurricane. . . .

But the wind does not go through walls; sound does! And centuries have gone by. And the phalluses collapse like rotting mushrooms by dint of violently ramming against idiocy and inertia.

What would have happened if there had been nobler desires really strong desires that do not flaunt their squalor at the least little friction like Grozi's? With a shameful drop dangling there. . . .

But I do rather like Grozi because sometimes he is aware. However often he says, "Women don't know how to create, they're really quite destructive; every destructive man is effeminate and every creative woman is virile," he knows the limits of that creativity he senses the breathlessness of his race.

Also, when Grozi has finished masturbating he experiences

his shame. So then he tries to search for another desire: a desire that no longer batters like an attack. A desire that is outside of time and space and finds the original source of "abstract and timeless memory."

How could phallic desire attain eternity?

For you cannot live in a state of eternal tension: constant tension is at the root of such a large number of psychoses. . . .

Neither can you live eternally on the edge of climax: waiting for a culmination that doesn't occur has produced embitterment in so many people! . . .

And living an eternal orgasm is out of the question: is that not the condition that gives rise to the proliferation of the vampire-tyrants who stuff themselves with the human-being body and spirit ever since "independence." They eat myths and faith they graze all initiatives down to the stem and the roots and they gorge themselves to the dregs on hopes and dreams: they eat people whole I'm telling you.

And it is not this desire I want to be talking about. . . .
I picture a sinusoidal desire
A desire that undulates with successive advances
And finds its eternity in rhythm
Such as the ocean: it will never be erect and it will never be limp. . . .

It is a wave
The wave rises with the certainty that it will reach its apex
The crest of the wave undulates as it falls
With the certainty that it will rise again
That it will always give birth to another wave
That it will survive eternally
Since there is no break between the dip and the crest of the wave.

I love you and I survive through this love
Through this love I create and live again

I live on and always give birth to love again
There is not the tension of waiting
There is no more terror of failure and of disappointment
No latency period no void
But a constancy in union and in transference
From one shore to the other without interruption
Because whether by low tide or by high
I love you and I am the wave that keeps on undulating
Sinusoidal rhythmical beat. . . .
I am speaking of a desire that would enrich you without impoverishing me
A desire that would fill me without emptying you

It is not the "victorious quest of the phallus" that penetrates and empties itself in failure: cut!!

It is not the "conquering thrust of the missile" that triumphantly slices the air and is crushed in death explosions: break!!!

It is the here and now of a brimming shore.

The creative mother aware of herself and of the life she is carrying: a continuously undulating plenitude. . . .

A here and now that is linked to the future of another brimming shore an undulating steadfastness in its turn. . . .

The child who receives life and does not return it but perpetuates it: survival!!!

In a permanent wave of desiring. . . .

I am speaking of a desire that would reintegrate spirit and body completely and would develop it to its own beat without anyone "taking on the absent look of an alienated mystic."

I am a rhythm calling another rhythm that responds in an echo because it is my own rhythm and there is space only for what is Matchless in love. . . .

I am beautiful through your beauty and my mouth will never gape in a slack and ugly letting-go my eyes will never wander emptily.

I am strong with the life force that we are that we create in a constancy of desire. . . .

BABOU (mocking, to Grozi): You who have some practice in this, how would you phrase this, how would you qualify a desire such as this?

GROZI (very serious): Let's see. . . . It would be a . . . an essential desire! A breath of life that would exist only through the presence of both breath and life. The desire for a lasting desire. . . . That lasts as long as it hasn't met up again with its source, the divine. As the law would have it.

⁂

It looks as if I will not have to wait much longer
For the downpour of desire that I lost in the shipwreck
In my mouth there is a taste of brown fur
And in my hand
The picture of a hand a flower
And yet
Nothing was more beautiful than the downpour of desire lost
In the shipwreck. . . .

Where are you
Birdlime sorrow

That several birds did smell as they flew off?

What are you doing
Icy cold of abstinence?

From which the monks fled as they crossed themselves

I have drunk your milk
I have anointed myself with coconut oil
And yet
Nothing was more beautiful than the downpour of desire lost
In the shipwreck. . . .

I fill my lungs with the smell of the karité *trees*
To embellish my vegetables on days of dearth

It Shall Be of Jasper and Coral

I scatter seeds of rice for the poor
I hoard your lost hairs you who are watching the hours pass by
I relinquish myself to the fitful rhythm of the impatient
I learn the voluntary breath of generosity again
In my hands I hold a moon-shaped face that is leaving me
And yet
Nothing was more beautiful than the swell of desire lost
In the shipwreck

So, page two Epigraph:
The desire for a desire that lasts like the ocean
To become human beings once again
And to be God's children at last
Creators. . . .

*
**

You who love red roses and you who mistrust black roses
Keep your head cool when facing white roses
And don't let the pallid roses put you to sleep
I know a flower, a single one
That I love and that resembles me
It doesn't grow much in marshland
Nor in solid soil
Just on the edge
Thousands of roses grow there inside a single one
Tiny tiny roses with thousands of petals
White ones and lavender-mauve
They shimmer and spread their scent
They bewitch you and flutter
As if to admonish you
You who are going to an encounter
You who are leaving your home and you who are searching
On the other side of me
There is nothing but strangeness
I know this flower the only one
When I pulled off its petals a bit too passionately
Madly ready to die

When I pulled its petals I depleted
Every adverb of my every desire
And was left with nothing but the crystal white and the porcelain pink
Of its petals piling up at my feet
More petals still in my hands
And no hollows in which to put the pollen
Woe unto her who loses her head
She seeks a quiet love
A simple but voluptuous love that doesn't always ask her to be exceptional
You will recognize her from miles away
From her heavy and intoxicating scents
She glistens and she murmurs to you
On the other side of me there is only strangeness

*
**

Page 3: woman
Why not! Woman. . . . That's it. . . .

I cannot add anything else to this point of completion in which a certain creativity a foundation for harmony should at last become manifest.

Besides, how could I, as long as I'm interested in Babou and Grozi since they say the source of their unhappiness lies in the woman they have approached.

And it must be admitted: if Lunaï is in decline it is because the women have become tramps, real Tsetses. Why did God turn Lunaï into the sewers of the world because the women willed it so!

Every Tsetse on earth can be found in Lunaï: forgers bandits vampires and all kinds of bizarre customers! Lunaï is heaven for them. They parade around there their heads held high their shoulders weighed down with medals: decoration in the Order of swindlers armor-plated cross of corruption banners of the guild of zombifiers. . . . Ah! You should see them. . . .

You should see them when something profitable looms on

the horizon when they think no eye is watching you should see them as they chicken out grovel slither froth kowtow lick claw clutch and as terror seeps from every hair on their body. . . .

You should see them as they swindle shuffle scramble speculate down to their marrow. They're contentious and clammy they shed and they slaughter. They reek of pestilence and carrion. . . .

And the women of Lunaï swoop down chomp chew they suck the larvae oh mama! They're entangled up to their necks stuff themselves up to their noses lick the slugs and the ass of the queers oh mama! . . .

There was a time in the "land of the heart-shaped cradle" when the different gods decided to keep knowledge to themselves: men didn't know how to make use of it. . . . Every time it was given to them they would abuse it degrade it throw it off balance and again the gods would have to wear themselves out by gluing the broken pieces together again. They'd had enough! After all a man seemed happy enough when no effort at all was asked of him no attempt to move beyond his instincts no self-censorship at all. . . . It was sufficient to leave him with just his survival instinct so that he could vegetate as would ruminants or wild beasts in the animal world for the rest of eternity. That seemed to be his "sweet sin."

But Hilôlômbi who had created mankind and had placed great hopes in him took a negative view of this half-life lethargy even though he recognized his creation-creature was far from perfect. So he decided to send him a whole group of Masks whose mission it was to civilize him.

The other gods took umbrage at this generosity that would automatically lead to a new deliverance they were sure of it but out of respect for Hilôlômbi who was their elder they gave in once again and the civilizing Masks swooped down upon the "heart-shaped cradle" and their primary purpose was to initiate men into wisdom that is to say into knowledge and its appropriate use. . . .

They would appear here and there to children women to the eldest ones they would appear the Masks. . . .

It Shall Be of Jasper and Coral

The Masks created associations brotherhoods they proclaimed laws rights they defined and assigned duties to everyone they organized they cultivated.

There were Initiates and Great Initiates. Hilôlômbi regained confidence in himself as well as in his creature and one morning he showed him the view into the sixth heaven the heaven of choice.

That same evening mankind chose to become god and Hilôlômbi sighed with relief and went off to get some rest: the road toward Evolution lay clearly marked and wide open mankind could manage nicely all by itself the civilizing Masks had accomplished their mission. All the gods burst out in songs of joy: they had done well to listen to Hilôlômbi the Eldest. From now on they too would be freed from their mission as Masters of conscience and they could try their hand at creating. They all deserved a vacation. . . .

But when they woke up at the dawn of a new cycle they were taken aback at the sight of mankind floundering around awkwardly in the animal world!

They were enraged and terribly disappointed. In Unanimity, they decided to condemn these cretins of men to vegetate in the animal world chewing their cud or hunting prey and too bad if it was for all eternity and so it was done.

But some civilizing Masks had contracted a dangerous virus: compassion for mankind! They were the ones who came to the gods to plead for another chance for men but the Eldest One would hear nothing of it anymore. . . .

One day Um, one of the most fanatic ones to plead man's cause, decided to try something on his own. He stole a bit of knowledge and went off to the "heart-shaped cradle" where he hid in a hole waiting for someone to pass by who would be able to take it from him without burning himself without setting life on fire. . . .

Alas, not one single male felt like doing anything at all nor would he have dreamed of going in search of anything at all in the heart of the earth and especially not in search of knowledge.

There he is, poor Um, tormented by the fire of knowledge

and by his love for mankind, all alone in the heart of the earth of the "heart-shaped cradle" where heartless people don't know how to respond to his love. He is thirsty he is hot his liver is being roasted his heart is burning up and he cannot call for help without giving himself away. . . .

That is when Soo, the second twin sister of Njock, the Eldest of mankind's twins, passed by. She came to fish for love with love a love she could no longer find among people. . . . She had chosen this river which was reputed to shelter spirits. She chose the deepest spot and built a primary dam upstream. She made a secondary dam and then a third downstream and began to empty out the water. In a frenzy she emptied the basin, singing rhythmically, with all the fire of her desire for love with all the strength she possessed from morning till evening she was driving the water out. And the fish and crustaceans congregated in the silt at the bottom of the empty basin. She gathered them up and carelessly put them in her basket then began to dig and widen the holes where crabs snakes and spirits usually hide out! She reached a point where all the holes converged into a single direction that plunged deep into the heart of the earth. At the end of her tether but still relentless she made a fire with her own love and her self-love and began to smoke out the hole. A voice from somewhere else came out of the hole and spoke to her: "*Woman! Who is this person who found happiness and then set it on fire?*"

The Mask embedded itself on the face crushing the nose, pulling the eyes apart and the lips up in a snarl, it shook the teeth to bits and pushed itself through the throat into the heart this heart that thought it funny. . . . The Mask persevered:

"Do you want to resemble me oh tragic mother
Do you want to delve with me
For bursts of laughter that sound like crystal
For the choral songs when fear is at its height
And for the strength of words on evil lips
Do you want to resemble me Oh tragic mother?"

But the woman loved the brute force of fighting bulls the gluttonous weakness of orphans the flowing tenderness of dreamy lullabies and the solidity of faithful husbands. . . .

The Mask insisted:

"Do you want to love me oh tragic mother
Do you want to descend
Into the depths of perniciousness
The filth and splatterings of dried-up hearts
The burns of passion
The sweat of desire
The dankness of fear
The stings of jealousy
And then to rise up with me
Toward the methods of the mind
The greatness of the heart
And the infinity of the soul
Do you want to give birth to me mother
Do you want to marry me?"

And it was then that Soo made the first female blunder: she became afraid! She was afraid of what she had found of the power of her desire she was afraid of herself. . . . The Man she called in for help grabbed hold of Um and of his secrets and jealously kept them for himself thereby completely dispossessing the woman. But Soo was able to keep the feeling of the warmth of this first contact between the fires of gods and of men, as well as the memory of this voice of Love and Knowledge which she was the first one to have heard and which she would never forget.

And from that day onward women have had the power to recognize strength beauty and honesty at a first encounter by the mere inflection of a voice. And men had to pay attention to the nuance in their voices alone in their gestures and in their least little attitudes if they wanted to feel a bit of that "touch of fire" that only women possessed.

The cowards the mediocrities and the dishonest immediately lost any chance of survival: no woman wanted to provide them with offspring. They would die alone and loveless. No crawler or licker would kiss even the littlest toe of any woman. He would have to shine to be worth his weight in gold in courage and dignity in ability and knowledge in order to call forth that ideal of love and knowledge that Soo the Grandmother had felt one day, before he could hope to build a life on earth with a woman. In those days children used to admire and respect their fathers. . . .

Thanks to this demand to this severity initiations were established and these brought mankind once again into the realm of the gods. It was then that Hilôlômbi in his exultation blessed womankind and allowed woman's desires to be fulfilled always. . . . "From here on in your wishes will be mine your will mine" he told her.

How great the surprise of the Eldest One will be when he wakes up at the dawn of a new cycle and sees that his desires, intertwined with those of women, are nothing more than desires for tinsel fancy clothes food, for the pathetic longings of bitches in heat too easily satisfied by the first wet blanket that comes along!

In Lunaï nobody wants anything to do anymore with nobility or its exigencies. What's the point? Queens sleep with drug addicts swindlers murderers and give them progeny to boot!!! Ass lickers display the titles of officers and commanders of a high order with full support of the women. And woe to the man who dares to speak of dignity of merit if he is not able to provide his wife with the luxury of the "Credit-car-castle" trinity even at the price of his own soul. . . .

What then is left for these poor men but to become queer! For they too have retained the yearning for the quest of a contact that would allow them to rise above to tear themselves away from the slime of the animal world to set themselves a standard and reach for it. . . .

Will my sons be Men
I have left them there where my true life lies

Alone
Without a roof without protection without tenderness
Without any discipline
Who will teach them that a man is first of all death
Well before he is life
And that death is better than shame
Who will teach them if not shame itself
Who will tell them that it is easy to build prisons
Simply by attaching one bar to another bar
By enclosing horses within four bars
Without millet without hay
And the space
In front of them a thousand bars they could jump
And four prison bars to crush their spirit
And an ill-omened bird to count
The seconds fleeing from time
Who will teach them if it isn't prison
If it isn't life itself

To whom to what then should you consecrate your life? Why? When? How?

*
**

It was a celebration that day.

The celebration—the adoration—of the Fetish Tree—of Unity you know that tree of truth whose roots had been brought back from the Stone-with-a-Hole by the sons of Kôba and Kwang. . . .

It was on the birthday of a village or a neighborhood that this tree would be planted on a strategic corner. . . . The new community would thus celebrate its birth by making sacrifices at the foot of the Tree beginning at the first rays of sunlight.

A young black and white goat would be bathed in a mixture of leaves roots bark and words. The guardian of tradition would sing the liturgy of slogans laws ideals of the community in the presence of the Masks of Wisdom and Justice of representatives from every section of the Society: the Wedded the Betrothed the Unmarried the Spearheads and the Patriarchs. Sometimes the representatives would propose different amendments which unanimously accepted would be added immediately to the Liturgy of the Guardian. Everyone swore allegiance and the high priest would immolate the sacrificial animal at the foot of the Tree.

The meat will be prepared and eaten by all members of the community from the smallest to the greatest ones. The Bangui and Dolo will flow in streams as will the poetic sayings of the Masks of Wisdom. Evil will run away by leaps and bounds before the clatter of the Masks of the Hunt and of War. People will split their sides with laughter as they absorb and catch the innuendos and sharp criticism of the Masks of Satire. And they will sing to the rhythm of the Masks of the Dance. . . .

By returning to its source the community is renewed and reintegrated. The dead will never be dead and the living will never cease living. . . .

Yes indeed! It really was a celebration. . . .

So that day there was a celebration in Lunaï. The birthday of a new neighborhood. But Lunaï is truly memorable now, even during the celebration the Dead stamp their feet and the Living wallow in idleness!

On that day at the first rays of the sun the Masks complete with all their adornments had gathered around the Fetish Tree of the celebrating district. The high priest stood with great dignity next to the young black and white goat with a white knife in his hand and his white *boubou* in harmonious contrast with the black pagne of the Guardian next to him.

The women and girls, anointed with humus and resin-scented oils, shimmered with the reflections of their golden jewelry and their white pagnes as they moved toward the Fetish Tree like a swarm of bees in a streak of light. . . .

The young men fragrant with peppery scents were dressed in bright red. Life was teeming above and beneath the earth in search of unity. Everything was ready for the rebirth and we were waiting.

We were waiting for the Minister of State who came from the requisite geopolitical district—"who was to honor this little celebration with his august presence and thereby lend it a special brilliance" as the radio announced.

It was a relatively new area and still quite poor. Streetlights and running water in the public square would be desirable, "structures" that would stimulate the beginnings of tourism a very modern industry with easy and sure profits. The government would release financial credit if the Minister of State would put in a good word and surely he would put in a good word if they were to welcome him with splendor and dignity. . . .

The district chief was putting the finishing touches on the setting which was to prompt the precise mental image of the community's wishes in the head of the Minister of State: young women, their faces shining with oil, formed a guard of honor on either side of the main road in exactly those spots where the streetlights were supposed to shine. The other women young or old, mothers-to-be or nursing mothers with all the available youth in the square formed a glistening circle clucking with crystalline song right on the spot where they were hoping for a fountain or an artificial waterfall where tourists would stand in the evening catching a breath of fresh air and talking about the marvels of Lunaï and its different areas. The raffia skirts of the dance Masks stood in neat vegetable-bed rows to suggest the line-up of benches in a city park. A few tourists who had heard the news on the radio were already raising their cameras to their eyes taking pictures of the Masks of Wisdom posing majestically in exchange for a one-hundred-franc coin as they rehearsed their future roles as tourist guides. The most agile tourists had climbed into the treetops next to the Fetish Tree in order to have a better view when filming the sacrifice. . . .

Everything was truly ready and all they were waiting for was the Minister of State.

They were waiting for the Minister now and the sun was rising high in the sky.

The sun was rising high in the sky changing the musk oil on

the young women's faces into thick drops of sticky and rancid sweat. . . . The color of the men's bright red cloths began to run creating bloody stripes that syncopated the rhythms of the drums a little too much.

The sun was rising high in the sky.

The dead and the living were stamping their feet with impatience. The Tree of Truth and of Unity was languishing. The young goat was decalcifying. . . . The streetlight girls were dehydrating. The fountain women grew doleful. Stomachs were cramping and the Masks of Wisdom ended up by accepting five-franc coins for a pose!

The sun was rising high in the sky.

The sun reached its zenith and the Minister of State was reveling in the flesh and blood of the Easter lamb in the Cathedral where he was showing his new medal and assuring himself of the graces of the Mother Church, more powerful after all than all the Masks and Fetish Trees together. . . .

The sun was grinding down on people's heads and still they waited for the Minister of State.

The cries of starving newborn babies clashed with the gurgling of the fountain. Mothers-to-be were about to faint and the old women were suffering from their gout acting up. The men lowered their eyes. The Masks of Wisdom averted their gaze. The other Masks were melting underneath their flashy duds trying to hold in a coughing fit. The Spearheads and the Masks of Satire were shivering with fear. Who would be the first to open his mouth to ask for a break if only on behalf of the newborns and the mothers-to-be? And if the Minister of State were to arrive while the triumphal arch and the guard of honor were in a state of collapse, who would take responsibility for that?

The sun was showing off high in the sky.

And the men were oozing with shame with fear and with heat.

God! In the evening they'll be oozing with the same abominations. . . . They will pour these out into their women who will swallow them with nauseated revulsion disguised as an orgasm and this will turn them into *misovires*. . . .

Nothing was more beautiful
Than the downpour of desire lost in a shipwreck
Nothing as appalling
As being merely the other one's wife

Finally at three o'clock the Minister of State arrived.

The streetlight women bobbed back and forth lifelessly. The "Fountain" let go of spurts of troubled and bloody water-and-sweat with the addition of the syrupy sap that spouted from the hands of the drummers and the bamboo clappers when their blisters cracked open. . . . The fancy rags of the masks were shed like banana peels catching the government's worthy representative who fell flat on the ground his legs in the air right in front of the empty palm-kernel pots which had been scraped out in his honor since the goat had not been killed nor cooked. They plied him with warm champagne—the ice had melted long ago—the most eager Spearheads wiggled their hips as best they could and the Minister of State finally lit on a shaking rump with which he took off for a belated siesta.

The goat was sacrificed at last under the last rays of sun and the Dead died with it. Its boiling blood completely scorched the Fetish Tree of Unity and Truth which began to spit out flames of mourning to the great joy of the tourists and their cameras: a feast of fireworks!

At the first pale light of Cancer only putrefaction was still simmering in a palm-kernel sauce full of the goat's hair that they had not been able to skin very well because of the darkness. . . . Luckily the Minister of State promised "to see if he should speak about the district of Béhous at the next session of Council." There was hope: he had promised he would while he lay eye to eye with the rump of his siesta. . . .

And that was the end of the night's celebration.

That night not one woman refused the shame of moaning

beneath the cock of a male without balls: not one man had had the courage to speak up about the unspeakable behavior of the Minister of State and not one man had found in his woman the mirror that could have reflected an image of him that would be impossible for him to accept an image he would have refused even if it meant trying the impossible searching for the difficult road that leads to the world of the gods.

From here on in the men of Lunaï will be powerless and impervious to shame. They will slither like slugs for a vague promise made in exchange for the rumps of their daughters. God wills it so the women of Lunaï have willed it so.

It was
The time of belief
We believed because we had said we did
And we were unable to lie to our faith
You loved me
You were unable not to love me
You had sworn this in their presence
They were unable to lie to our faith
Those who spoke to us in the name of God
The sun was born from your half-open lips
And the hibiscus petals of the dawn
Your scents of flowers and of love
Were barely expressing the smell of these worlds. . . .
I was born from the sun of your love
And from the scents of your will
I was born from faith in our faith
In the faith that creates light
I was born from the faith in that word from their word of honor
What fate then changed this word of honor
Into a word that shatters its sun
And you have killed the sun
And they have lied
And you have lied to our faith. . . .
It was

The time of suffering
We believed because we had feelings
And in believing we had mastered feeling
We believed in hatred
And we opened the floodgates of heaven
To a suffering we thought was bounteous
Impenetrable
A suffering that would re-create hot suns
And the hot fervor of our faith. . . .
Vainglory!

GROZI: What I'd need is someone to force me to work, someone who'd starve me or beat me, who'd attack me or oppress me until finally there's a point where some jewel comes out of me. . . .

BABOU: Alas! My cousin is content with your labeling yourself an artist and struts around showing off your sketches without trying in any way to push you any further. And you, you're wallowing around in all those superlatives. . . .

GROZI: What do you expect! Me, I'm just happy that she's pleased. I'm always happy to see those around me be happy, even if that no longer allows me to evolve. . . .

BABOU: If only those who make a calling and a profession out of criticism could take their responsibilities seriously, try to resuscitate the sense of beauty that the women of Lunaï have lost!!!

GROZI: That certainly won't happen as long as woman's desire is also the desire of God! We're in deep shit, my friend, up to our neck! . . .

*
**

And the voice
That dreadful voice of Black-Night that torments and haunts me
You remembered Bathsheba you sometimes remembered
You could ask and you would be given
You were sure of it
You were beautiful that's what they told you
You were generous that's what they sang to you
You were intelligent that's what they affirmed for you
You were loved that's what they had sworn to you
And then you were awaiting the predicted day when confusion was to be your master and loneliness your only companion
And you said to yourself: "maybe that day of want that day of setback maybe that day. . . ."
And the years for giving went by Bathsheba you gave
The years for giving went by you gave yourself
Without asking for anything without receiving anything for giving you gave too much you gave too much Bathsheba.
For nobody ever taught you that by giving too much you become deluged
And that from the very start and forever more the deluge is there to annihilate to destroy to obliterate
And you have been obliterated Bathsheba
And you found yourself to be without any strength whatsoever
Without great beauty
Your hands empty totally emptied of everything
Your intelligence dawdling
But something you did remember: "ask"
And what did you ask Bathsheba
What did you ask?
The hot days after the flood will always be unhealthy
Once the heavy waters have turned back all that is left of the children of the union are only the cold ponds of indifference

Of passions only the humid mud of rancor
And of love only the thick dust of oblivion
So?
What did you ask Bathsheba
What did you ask?
What do you desire?
And here I am not knowing what to ask for
Nailed to the pillory
Hanging in a delicate balance my only fault being that I am merely the other one's wife. . . .
At the bottom of the streams limbo lies in wait for me. . . .

So!

What else am I to say about woman at this point of completeness in which a certain creativity a basis for harmony should finally become visible?

Am I to content myself once again with pious wishes?

Would I dare speak of woman's fertility when she wants nothing further to do with it? While she is talking about a hard-to-define emancipation at the very moment that she is losing awareness of her worth and wants nothing but to become "man," worse than the male . . . at the time that she allows herself to be kept as she indulges in hollow words: equality emancipation feminism will I be able to sing of Existence? Rise and say: I am woman.

I am the primordial atom that could never be content with a masculine rib in order to Exist.

I am the Matrix Mother in which Ideas and Forms and Breath of life are in gestation so that all may be because I am.

And everything is.

I am woman of men and of women who come from woman.

I walk ahead and I am.

I walk behind and I precede.

I am everything that moves ahead and advances toward the divine.

I am the woman of the day and the night.

I give Life and receive Death in order to always be reborn.
I am the Void that attracts Plenty.
I am the Impossible that makes everything possible.
I am woman today.
Woman of tomorrow.
Woman of the light of the Great Path. . . .

And if I were to sing this would there be a motherless orphan girl who, thinking she was hearing her dead mother's voice, would straighten her body and head would regain confidence and pride in being woman eternal mother of the great and noble and generous Sea?

The bed on which my mother sat down
Groans with every complaint from hell
So she crouched down on the floor
Like a dog waiting for a bone. . . .
Why do they all say that I shimmer with light
When they leave without saying farewell
Death's rays are wounding life
Life's delights are made up of death
She stretched out on the floor and smiled
A wan little smile. . . .
My mother's feet have trod pure paths
The paths that come back from beyond
The light of my eyes is the light of death
Extinguished more quickly in order more quickly to forget
Her knees are flaking from her prayers
Her eyes remained stubbornly closed
She stretched out on the floor and smiled
A wan little smile. . . .
My mother's ears have heard lovely lamentations
Her divine contours have been lauded in song
And her soul's magnanimity glorified
When they said: she is no fool
Why then did they speak only of wine
When they brought her back with vacant eyes

And ice-cold skin
Only one mouth spoke of friendship
She stretched out to her full length
And her white teeth were never seen again
While the dogs with a double soul came by again
But my mother's mouth sang only
Of the things of life
While the dogs with a double soul came by again

Today she is resuscitated my mother and she lives in full beauty. . . . If I were to sing her praises would that console the orphan girl?

Because I believe that to be so I will devote the third page of my golden logbook to woman so that at this point of completeness the basis for harmony for a sure creativity will become visible again.

*
**

So now page 3:
Eternal Mother
Mother of the sea
Woman of all time
Light of the Great Path
Manifest again here and now
The next humankind of breath and fire
The race—Woman—light of body and heart

*
**

Page 4. . . .

Let's suppose in spite of my disgust with Lunaï that by some miracle I want to cling to . . . To Grozi to a child to a dog or to a streetlight of the big road.

Let's suppose that my madness exceeds the limits of all insanity and that I decide to erect the temple of my soul in Lunaï that it is in Lunaï I want to beget and raise my progeny.

Let's suppose that moved by very powerful forces I am seized by a desire to build something in Lunaï.

I sell all my stocks immediately. I scrape together every last penny I have. I gather up my jewelry. I capitalize on my virtues and my most secret treasures. . . .

In truth

I can't bring myself to imagine what my foundation might be and I don't even think that by converting every virtue of every Tsetse in Lunaï I would be able to obtain the corner-cubic-stone of which I would have liked to speak on the fourth page of my golden logbook.

"Nothing Bathsheba
Nothing is more hideous than loneliness in a crowd
Amidst so many beings voice sounds thoughts
Who approach you step on you deflower you
And no more motions of communion
And no more gestures of friendship
But the weight of the presence of others
A very cold and stifling presence Bathsheba. . . . "

Still I have to think about it because my life in Lunaï is the only life left in my life and I can't very well write my journal with the elsewhere-otherness-life.

Besides I must think about this journal I must because there is nothing better to do: it's so boring in Lunaï. . . . It's indescribable. . . .

In Lunaï people walk around with their eyes and ears closed. Only their noses and mouths open and close spasmodically in death rattles which nobody hears fortunately or unfortunately I don't know anymore.

In any event one has to live and it is normal that people close their eyes and ears if they want to survive in Lunaï. If it were possible to close up your nose and mouth as well without collapsing that would be even better.

If upon awakening one morning anyone were to open his eyes or ears this is what he would see:

The Tsetses have won the Battle.

Looks no longer know how to look

Vacant eyes settle on gold and carrion with the same indifference. At best they confuse the two.
Ears no longer hear the thunder at best they take it for the sound of snails' steps whose traces must be recovered.
Death rattles are not heard
Sighs are no longer heard
Mouths snatch greedily at the wind and babble in the void
Noses hang over a broth of cultures of rogues and ooze a pus of useless chicanery
For what for whom no one knows.
They scream they squawk
For whom for what no one knows anymore
There is no purpose
There is no more ideal
There is no hope
There is no more faith
They saunter they walk
Where to or toward what no one knows anymore
They talk they chat
To say nothing and hear nothing
To understand nothing about anything or anyone
Listen and hear what he would hear:
Base little tales about asses that take craving away
Hollow laughter testy from ignorance
Demagogic monologues
Wretched rattles
And gulps of death
It is true
The unfortunate one who would take a chance one morning to keep his ears and eyes open
Would hear only hollow sounds
Would see only the void
He'd hear the incoherence of life he'd see the uselessness of his own life and would bash his head against every wall of Lunaï's mother-inertia until death followed.

That's why they close their eyes and ears in Lunaï out of an instinctive sense of survival. And Grozi, he even goes so far as to dream of building a future and of becoming with his eyes and ears closed! When I tell you that Grozi is not a bad guy . . .

GROZI (ardently): Like the sunflower
And knowingly
They will close their mouths again without spitting out any venom
And so as not to ingest the darkness
They will clearly see the ugly side of what is beautiful
They will know death they will understand life
They will be driven by living Love they will hurl themselves without hesitation upon a conscious choice and they will be aware of the opening of their legs and their lips
They will be blue with calm and wisdom
They will be yellow with brilliance
They will be green with vision.

BABOU: So tell me, with what magic do you plan to bring this miraculous transformation about?

GROZI: With a new language, of course! . . .

BABOU: Ah hah!!! !!! . . .

*
**

And this idea of a new language is beginning to please me. For a new race a new language all that seems logical to me.

It's true that there is no effective language anymore. In Lunaï they look away when they greet you. When they do look at you they're thinking of something else. When they do think of you it's with other pictures in their head. And as far as smelling goes . . . The only odor left in Lunaï is the odor of pestilence. . . .

How can you hope for a real moment of communion under these conditions? For true individuality exists only because people can communicate from time to time can be aware of their Unity before they subdivide particularize themselves. . . .

That is why a language that would speak to all senses at the same time objective and subjective senses would certainly be of great usefulness for communication and communion in Lunaï. . . .

GROZI (ardently): In the theater they should stop tempering words by adding purely illustrative gestures that belabor an obvious point. Other vibrations should come into play and move us to the core. The sound of vowels should strike our pituitary and put us back in touch with other worlds. Colors should attack our skin. Smells should make our mouths water. Images should captivate us. Music and rhythm should bewitch us. And silences should allow us to meditate and to widen our horizons. May we receive the ecstasy of the original explosion that created worlds.

BABOU: And above all, they must stop clamoring electoral speeches on stage. There at least may we have the pleasure of seeing beauty or ugliness as they are in themselves and in us.

GROZI: And for heaven's sake let them stop serving us the pitiful everyday fare. A show should be so spectacular that it becomes beautiful.

You can always go further
You can always go deeper
You can always discover innovate create
And you can achieve mastery
Let them merely give us support and let them allow us to make it our own and to be creative in turn, with pleasure.

BABOU: Yes, with pleasure. But can we feel pleasure if we aren't able to watch? We wear masks, my boy. Masks of stereotypes, masks of entrenchment, masks of ignorance and limitation. . . . How can we feel pleasure without seeing?

GROZI: Listen: the arbiter between the gods and men, between the ancestor and us was a vital necessity. And during the initiation ceremonies that were supposed to awaken the conscience, the mask served as a mirror.

We were blind and we see
And we see ourselves
We knew nothing did not know God and we see it all
And we recognize God in ourselves.
And suddenly everything is possible:
We were ugly and we become beautiful
We were weak and we become strong
We were passive consumers and we become active and productive
And we re-create and renew the world.

The mask was helping us with this: it revealed the sacred word to us. It reflected the grating image of our weakness in our ignorance and it stripped us bare in front of the eyes of the initiator. It forced us to react: to know how to accept, accept oneself, to be able to refuse. . . .

BABOU (caustic): In a childish way we might add! And the powers that be were strengthened and we created those who are forever on welfare. . . .

GROZI: Still it was necessary to attain some solidarity: to create a society able to feel united as they share a common global vision. The mask succeeded in this mission: it created whole civilizations. . . .

BABOU: So what are you complaining about? Just keep on living then in your masked society. But don't talk to me about a new language which we won't be able to enjoy behind our impenetrable masks! If the truth be known, and it was all up to me, we'd be getting rid of them! They are nothing more than an inefficient yoke, an additional screen that keeps us from seeing. . . .

GROZI: But that's precisely why we'll find a new role for it, a new reason for being. We're going to learn how to look at the mask:

Because it no longer is a mediator
The Mask
The gods no longer reveal themselves through it
The ancestors no longer descend
The sacred-consecrated word is no longer renewed
And has not been revised, reexamined, readapted to our needs of today
It has lost its effectiveness.

BABOU: So then we don't need the mask anymore! You've said it yourself: the civilizing force has accomplished its mission so why should it become a fixture? Even the mask no longer causes fear in the kingdom of indifference. The Mask can no longer serve as mirror in the kingdom of the blind and I think it is no more than a wolf's mask behind which you can commit the lowliest of deeds, incognito. . . . In my opinion, in Lunaï today the mask is nothing more than an additional crutch, whether it be of wood or steel or canvas, meant for gesture or for the spoken word, nothing more than a device which we must get rid of in a carnival-fire, even if it means finding yourself at the bottom of the abyss again. Down there, you'll be forced to fight your way up again all by yourself, and to recognize yourself: ugly or handsome, weak or strong, just as you are. . . .

GROZI: We'll accomplish the same thing without burning the mask, you'll see:

We'll wear it on stage
We'll magnify its fixed gaze
We'll condemn the missionaries who establish themselves for their personal ends
We'll unseat the "technical assistants" who refuse to be relieved

We'll take apart the mechanism by which the mask is manipulated
We'll break up the attitudes and gestures of those enslaved by the mask
We'll design new masks on stage and heave them into the theater
The oral or gesticulative clichés of the intellectuals, the "businessmen," the "technocrats," the executives, the politicians, the "praying mantises, the termites"
We'll throw them out!
And theater will become an initiation rite that will lead to a frenzy that prepares us for a choice.
And one will have to choose
And everyone will choose or else will be swallowed up in floods of shame
Because everyone will be stripped bare on stage and will be seen by all
We will have to see ourselves! And we shall see ourselves!
Once again
The body will bring forth emotion
Emotion will have access to thought
Thought shall attain the will
And the will shall implant itself in our consciousness. . . .
You'll see

BABOU: So it really is possible! The mask can still be of use. . . . In spite of itself! So then we need a double theater, a split theater where on one side the words are spoken, and the actions are echoed on the other. We must show the African of today to what extent his famous "African word" has no meaning anymore, neither for the one who professes it nor for the one who listens to it. We must make him understand how incoherent the clichés are upon which his life is based, how clumsy the actions that flow from it; perhaps he will feel the need for a new philosophy, a new art of living that will finally draw lessons from the historical experience of colonialization?

GROZI: That's just about it! You've got it! A theater of masks to unmask the masks: civilizers or colonialists, mediators or tyrants, down with the masks!

*
**

Yes that appeals to me
The idea of a new language appeals to me
A language that will adapt itself to our situation as mutants
A comprehensive and aggressive language that will engage all our senses all our faculties at one and the same time to clean them out and resharpen them a language capable of shaking shaking and shaking us until every crust is eliminated every crust of ignorance of indifference of limitations and complexes injected by two centuries of forced inactivity of periods of noncreativity of eras deprived of originality.
Once again we'll discover the belly of things
We shall invent we shall create
The smallest and the greatest
The simplest and the most complex
We shall create the new intestines of the world a center a new navel
Our chisels will carve granite and the alluvium anew into new shapes of genius
Our brushes will move nimbly and sure to find hues well beyond the ultraviolet
Our balaphons will reach more subtle octaves
Our dances will be more conscious and better-felt gestures and symbols
We shall create
We shall reach up to the stars
We shall communicate and we shall share
We shall participate in the galactic action
We shall commune with the clouds
Without any time limitations
Without any fear without any complexes
Yes that appeals to me

It Shall Be of Jasper and Coral

The idea of a new language appeals to me
And I think that I'll hold onto it as the cubic stone to be drawn to be hewn or to be written on the fourth page of my golden logbook and long live the Next-Race

When it is all over it is possible you know
That flowers will grow in the desert again
That promises will be kept again
And that one and one will no longer make a third
You know
Ever since the wind no longer blows over our land
The waters move from downstream upward
Palm wine no longer goes to our head
Our children no longer intone song-fables
You know
Ever since the sun went down behind our savannas
The birds no longer lay their eggs in our forests
The bees no longer visit the irises
And all the while the Holy Trinity rests
When it is all over it is possible you know
That the breeze will rise over our bodies again
That the dew will lie on the taro leaves again
And that hair will grow once more on the heads of the bald
You know
When it is all over . . .
But as we await this moment of dreams
The swell digs deep into our springs and troubles the waters
And just as in years of immense disasters
We see ourselves in nightmares drowned
In pools with our herds
The rumbling turns into enormous rollers
Whose undertow threatens what little hope we have left
But when it is all over
You know
It is possible . . .

"Words are hooks
That catch only starved fish"
So, page 4
For a new language
For the Race of jasper and coral
A Race with a new breath of life of speech of the Word. . . .

*
**

Page 5
He is seated on the cubic stone
At the door of the sanctuary
In his left hand the hand of the heart he holds
The scepter of selection by trial
His right hand sketches a stimulating and admonishing gesture
His eagle's eye hovers and grasps every factor:
Historical and sociological contexts
Individual potentialities
Abilities of development and creativity
There he is enthroned and vigilant
Dispassionate impartial
There he is and channels demonstrates explains
He widens horizons
He enlarges feelings and ideas
Because he makes sure to give them prominence
There he is and beauty ennobles him
There he is and ugliness circumscribes him
There he is
And we shall no longer be ignored
He will speak our words and sing them to every corner of the earth
He will show our forms
He'll reveal our ideas
he'll point to our efforts
There he is
The spiritual Master. . . . Criticism. . . .

*
**

Damn!

This time it's too much. I think I'm dreaming on my feet.

Because I've been listening to Grozi and Babou so much I catch myself dreaming and acting as if everything were possible as if everything were true. I'm confusing states worlds dreams. Look I was busy imagining a critic who would perfect creation. And caught up in Grozi's stride I was seeing creators and critics working for the same cause. . . . I had found where I was. . . .

Lunaï oh Lunaï
Lunaï without mornings and without evenings
Without ups without downs
Congenial Lunaï
Without uncertainties
Without medals without a lunatic opposite
Without uneasiness
Peaceable Lunaï
Brotherly Lunaï
Lunaï without critics. . . .

During the last conspiracy epidemics, those initiated into the "sharp satire of the Begging Masks" were particularly aimed at, touched. Their bloated bodies were found by the dozens, swollen with the pus of not-speaking, blotched with the flagellation of not-questioning.

You know how superstitious they are here. . . .

They thought that it was the query and the distance-taking critical look that were put into question by the powerful . . . , the gods. And to adjure misfortune, they decided to praise, to applaud. Those with preconceptions and the "faces-you-cannot-bear" certainly compelled those whose profession it is to check the surroundings, but the memory of the massacre nevertheless remained solidly affixed, covered deeply below the thrusts of fervor, as all those things that have inspired fear in memory are good at doing. . . .

Since then, it is the same people who hold forth about politics, chatter about sports, jabber about the arts, determined to lynch or bury the "guest of the week" in the silence-of-oblivion, with the same old "proven questions" that require the same old "answers-that-confirm-the-references." . . .

You foreigners who come to Lunaï to show something you want to share with us learn the following terminology so as to avoid any disappointment. And whatever the quality or the form of your "merchandise" may be, for everything is merchandise and marketable in Lunaï, don't pull out the responses I plan to teach you when I hand my golden logbook over to you:

Example:

Journalist's first question: "How did you come to painting (music, politics, sports, commerce, medicine, science, etc.)?"

The right answers: "I think it's my vocation: I have been drawing since I was three (I have been talking politics, I've been taking care of dolls, I've been disemboweling insects to see what was inside them, etc.)."

The wrong answers: "I came to it by plane to save time" or else "I haven't the slightest idea I don't think I came to it, it came all by itself just like that because I was open to it because I enjoyed it. . . . "

Journalist's second question: "Are you committed?"

The right answers: "My God, isn't that obvious! Look! The red here on the seat in my car . . . well, that's my fist in the face of man's exploitation by man. . . . That shot sun lying white across the top of my desk, that is the rifle I hold pointed at colonialization! Those rusted lancets in my first-aid kit are my UN-tetanus-speech at the UN against imperialism, racism, neocolonialism, fanaticism, fascism, earthquakism. . . . " (and do make a concoction of every ism that comes out of your mouth. . . .)

You can sell anything you want and you can even sell yourself if you haven't already. Don't be afraid to talk about your private life they want that: they're voyeurs and they like only autobiographical art in Lunaï. . . .

The wrong answers: "I've already done my military service, you know. . . . "

Or else: "Committed? To what? With whom?"

Or else: "As long as it's art, then yes. But it's very hard and too soon to tell. I'll let you know when I die."

Or else and that is by far the worst: "No but . . . I commit. . . . "

Third question: "What message do you convey?"

The right answers: "Since the cradle I've been dreaming of the staffs of Muslim pilgrims the batons of drum majorettes. . . . You know, I have always been noticed for my penchant for bringing messages and I always used to report my father's escapades to my mother while my grandmother would watch on the sidelines with an amused look in her eye. . . .

So it is quite natural that I should have become a great-pilgrim-messenger of peace-liberty-brotherhood-authenticity-blackness-Africanity-friendship-dignity-summertime!

Of course I also convey the message of equality between all beings races countries and even between man and woman." (If you're a feminist that's still tolerated, it's still in style. . . . You'll gain a point for originality. . . . And the feminist clientele to boot. . . .)

The wrong answers: "What possible message could I bring that hasn't already been offered?"

Or else: "I'm not a leader, and I have nothing to impose. . . . "

Or else: "I am a mirror that only reflects what stands before it; I convey you to yourself."

Those last two answers are especially ill-received. . . .

Fourth question: "Could you explain your work to me?" (this book, this record, this painting, this speech, this carpet, this letter opener, etc.)

The right answers: "You see this line is Africa in reverse. This sound is the cry of rebellion of the Black Man. This capital letter after the comma in line 10 is the sign of my grandfather who was hanged by the colonialists in 1900. This thread is from the first bra my father gave to my mother just after I was born" etc., etc. Above all, don't hesitate to tell every anecdote that has shaped you and could thereby have given rise to the "vision of the world" you so generously extend. . . .

The wrong answers: "How could I since I don't understand it myself?"

Or else: "Has anyone ever offered you an explanation of your rosary?"

Or else: "There's nothing to explain, only to feel, to discover, and I can neither lend you my skin nor my eyes. . . . "

Or else: "Oh no! I'm fed up trying to spoon-feed you!"

Other questions: "Why do you like beer?"

"Which side do you like to sleep on?"

"What hours of the day do you work?"

"What are your sources of inspiration?"

"Are you for or against polygamy?"

"Was your mother a believer or a Christian?"

"What do you think of the 'thought of the day'?"

"You have a degree from . . . But did you ever attend elementary school?"

"What is the last thing you'd like to say?"

The right answer is to tell your life story all the way back to your earliest memories to speak even about your previous lives— especially if you were a king or a fool—to go around in circles if you must but above all never talk about the book, the paintings, or about anything that might have brought you to where you are today. And don't forget to mention how relevant the questions are. . . .

The wrong answer: "Bug off!"

If you answered well everybody will be happy in the end. Your bubbles will be published wherever need be. They will be rebroadcast. They will speak about the urgency of your work, the courageous battle you are waging against demons and other powers. . . . You will be flooded with superlatives. You will be invited everywhere.

But if you answered badly then I can't tell you what awaits

you. Are you curious? Are you courageous? Do you like to gamble? Are you a good loser? If so then give it a try and you'll tell me the results. . . .

Unfortunately, in Lunaï it's our literary and art critic's only game and following in Grozi's footsteps, I began to dream. . . .

Yes indeed, I dreamed and I realize that I'm dreaming more and more often since I've become interested in Grozi and Babou. Careful! One of these days I'll catch myself in the process of philosophizing!

Anyway, since this concerns a page reserved for the Spiritual Master and since I have nothing acceptable left in the realm of spirituality other than dreams even other people's dreams that's better than nothing isn't it?

So for page 5 of my golden logbook I shall hold on to the idea of literary and art criticism to be used in a plan for the cultural renewal of Lunaï.

*
**

There can be no culture without criticism
And there can be no criticism
Without cultured people
So page 5:
For the criticism of a culture by cultivated people.

*
**

Page 6: choice

GROZI (soliloquizing): Don't let them talk to me of choices anymore! Whom are they kidding?
What difference does it make whether you choose one side of a square over another?
Let them stop badgering me I am tired
I refuse to look for a distinction between the smell of one turd and that of another in a latrine
I am not blind in one eye and I refuse to be king in the land of the blind

And you my girl don't try to bring it back up!
Let me live my own square inside the square
Life has stopped dead in its tracks inside a squared matrix
One square per sector
One man per square
Man must have mistresses woman must have lovers
Why how nobody knows and nobody gives a damn
Someone on the fringe must speak in reverse wear clothes inside out
lead a rowdy and dissolute life be addicted to drugs
A fringed square for the fringe people
Let me live in my square in a square amid other squares
And don't let them talk to me of choices anymore
One job is as good as any other
One idea as good as any void
One buttock as good as any foot
And what difference does it make whether a penis is full of water or blood or pus?
Isn't it always the same jumbled mess holding sway
The same impression of apathetic inertia that hardens around us
Aren't we always sloshing through the very same mud
Vegetating in the very same half-life?

BABOU (going even further): Why push for rigor in a land of complacency?
Why rise up against corruption in a world of decay among a race of the already corrupt?
Why seek any further, any deeper when the surface planes look pleasant and easy and offer nothing but sparkling specters
Why take up the battle when the die is cast long before one is born
Why struggle for what's only a sham?

And they were stirring their mud-soaked cowardice they reveled in it they vomited it up it came out in their shit and they didn't give a damn powerless disgusting gorging themselves on an overdose of bitterness the better to abdicate the better to justify their nonparticipation their irresponsibility.

Uncircumcised gang!

And Grozi got himself aroused again!

And there he is again in troubled water. A hesitant glaucous drop is dangling again: will fall won't fall. . . .

He wanted he would so much like an initiatory situation an encounter there in his pants soiled with a hundred years of inactivity and the withholding of real liberation because true exaltation was lacking since no matter what is as good as no matter what! And they're still waiting for the "civilizer" who might want to descend to initiate him right there in his pants but who is late showing up and Grozi just continues to despair.

One of the things that upsets him is precisely this problem of choice. Is there really any will or the potential of choice in this screwed-up land from which exaltation has been banished and where apathy is the crowned queen?

Really now Lunaï. . . .

Now people get married here so that the State will provide them with a larger apartment a free plane ticket a reimbursement for expenses.

People have children to get family allowances. They solicit jobs that have good vacations or guaranteed travel.

The desire for union with a chosen being

The joy of transmitting life through love

The appeal of mastering a trade the effectiveness of competency have all been banished too. They entertain to get ahead. They grimly acquire things they really couldn't care less about. And in the end the only desire is that of the conquest of absolute ownership without any passion without any joy. Simply to possess. And they obtain everything: everything is for sale. . . . They invest the same amount of energy in the conquest of a lady and a chick: they use the same techniques in their approach they pay the same price and they win them over with the same ease and the same indifference since pleasure is cut to the measure of their efforts.

Here they no longer know the enjoyment of that one special look that one special moment that one special relationship. What then would motivate them to make a choice?

For while everything is being done to make ownership easier for all nothing is being done to make people anything but colorless. But we will have rocket ships to take us to Venus to Jupiter. We will go to Saturn for the weekend with just a hop through its ring. We will have everything without becoming anything: we are condemned to supreme nonexistence!

So Grozi masturbates mechanically out of weariness out of habit. A little genie is pestering him draining him and prodding him to think about another art of living about a life that might bring him some joy some opportunity for choice. And he says to him:

"Look. . . .
The spirit blows everywhere and a pearl is born from a drop of snot
And plenty of diamond shards shimmer on the traces of a snail on the belly of an earthworm.
Ah if only the gaze could be stilled. . . .
Could stop for just one moment one whole moment
Long enough to smell its scent and to feel its temperature
To try its taste
And to hear its call or its cry of denial to hear its voice. . . .
Yes still the gaze just long enough to discover and distinguish
Distinguish a buttock from a foot
To measure the level of a delight the weight of a thing the value of a moment the special feature of a being. . . .
And to know the reasons for a choice and the privilege of a preference. . . .
He speaks to him of joy. . . .
Ah joy in every sense and on every level

The taste of a sediment of wine
The flavor of a partly cooked eggplant
The subtlety of meat smoked with herbs

The beauty of a water drop
Of a reflection of gold on black skin
The shimmering flash of silk velour
The curled waves of silken hair on a smooth skin
The evening breeze in your hair
The freshness of a dewdrop on your cheek
The true significance of skin touching skin
Of a caress. . . .
He pesters him irks him the little genie
And grazes his scent of smell:

Ah! once again discover the pungent smells of effort
The intoxicating odors of love at first sight
Friendship's fruity perfume
Yes to sniff the buboes of the plague at a distance of a thousand leagues and to bypass its corrupted traps its bitter-facile lures of dishonest gain to avoid them as you might a rattlesnake a patter jabber chatter snake!!!
He is yanking at his ears to make him listen
And hear once again
The rustling of speechless lips that are confiding a life's secret
The blinking of anguished eyelids that call in silence
The screams of a stone a forest a lump of earth
Of a blank sheet that want to be useful. . . .
The call of a heart to its double
Words of sorrow of joy
And the meaning of a word of honor
He whispers all the things that he could discover in the twinkling of an eye!
A gaze that stills and settles
A gaze that looks and sees. . . .
And suddenly

Grozi loves
And from the depths of all his repression from the depths of all his weary expectations of all his
apathy
Suddenly
Joy gushes forth
A deep-seated joy that does not endure artificiality confusion
Nor half-measures half-portions
It is born from the solar plexus and moves in a thousand rays of luminous soft joy warm with pleasure toward his body's boundaries
And the body explodes
And Grozi realizes that he is no longer that he is not just a body
His body is the world is the universe
And he is inhabited
He is full with himself
A light is shining on his forehead and above his skull
And Grozi sees the Vision
He sees himself bathed in joy and he has seen God joyful in his joy
In his nondesire he is his own desire
He is full of plenitude
He is great and the earth is small
He will create new lands to give shelter to his fullness
Nothing will be too great
Nothing will be too beautiful to crimp his joy of plenitude. . . .
And Black-Night mockingly taunting. . . .
"Why not just bathe yourself in the pools of desire
And I shall teach you the pleasures of the flesh Bathsheba
The waves of hot arousal from the depths of hell
The delusions and mirages of inviolate deserts
The breaking surges of waves and backwash
The infernal squalls of storms and cyclones
The fabled quivering of praying mantises mating

The uncontrollable cries and murmurs of wild beasts at prey
And the mystical silences Bathsheba
All things of which your quiescent body is bereft. . . . "

And he saw all this in the time it takes an eye to focus an ear to listen. The time it takes a nose to sniff a skin to feel the time it takes a tongue to taste a tongue to touch the time it takes to pause. . . .

Then his eyes began to blink again and his hands automatically began to wander across his lower belly: all that is left of the memory of the divine are the miasmas of masturbation there is no choice in this accursed land from which exaltation has been banished and where the gaze no longer knows how to see. . . .

⁂

When we will take the time to really look
Simply the time to see and to perceive
When there will be more of us to have seen joy
And when we will once again take the schoolchild's path inside and despite our doleful Lunaïan bodies
Nobody will ever make us take a head of lettuce for the handle of a hammer again or a drop of oil for a pearl.
A nail is not worth an arm
One face is not as good as any other
One bit of merriment is not the same as a real delight
We will know how to identify any form of alienation whether it comes from abroad from the Ancestors or from ourselves through the power of indulgent habits.
We will know what life we want to lead and in which direction we want to move it.
We will know how to choose our loans and how to rid ourselves of waste
Yes when we will take the time to pause again
The time to look
When we will taste true pleasure again

We will fight to find it again
We will seek the lost paradise
We will rediscover the value of a choice
And the reasons for a battle
We will know why it is that we kill
For what for whom we die.

And Night keeps on going:
"Laugh at your misfortune Bathsheba
And open your eyes wide
For happiness is so small so mangled
Watch out that it doesn't pass you right by
And never accept shared solitude. . . . "

In this accursed land from which exaltation has been banished when I take up the editorship of my golden logbook at the very moment when I am thinking about a new art of living another philosophy of existence when I am about to come to the page of choice, page 6, I will write down the vital importance of the gaze. . . .

A gaze that settles
The time it takes to settle
And once again is able to see and to perceive. . . .

I shall also record the value of joy-filled joy that suffers no artificiality no half-measures no half-portions a joy that justifies the act and explains God continuously renews understanding as well as the power to preserve it. A joy that seeks constancy such as the constancy of desire that may be found everywhere on the condition that one seeks everywhere on the condition that one truly looks. . . .

Look. . . .
Your spirit is breathing everywhere
And a pearl is born from a drop of snot
And many shimmering diamonds glisten on the traces of the snail
You look and you see joy

And you love
And everything becomes possible again everything

Yes I shall record the strange thing that Grozi has discovered
In the time it takes a gaze to focus

*
**

So, page 6:
The gaze of the delay that settles
And sees and perceives. . . .
The Lover of the next thoroughbred generation is choosing consciousness

*
**

Page 7

Mother! Is it wrong to dream of a life in this nonexistence? Is it unwise to name one's wish? Isn't an evil spirit likely to take it away from us?

Do I dare reveal my wish to the night and to the ear of the sorcerers who transform our dreams of transfiguration and gold ingots into maggots?

Do I conceal your name the idea of you your life in short when no idea exists without name no creation before it's been formulated?

Do I let you stagnate forever in the brain-cell-magma-blood or in the writhing-astral-magma in which every nonformulated idea wanders and vegetates?

For fear of mockery?

For they would mock me if I were to designate you as the most enlightening enlightened guide investigator of paths who knows of what he speaks and who speaks to us of evolution. . . . What does it matter!

I shall call you divine guidance. Friend Friendship tangible queen of intuition of the look that watches and perceives. Inflexible obligation that pushes or pulls us the furthest we are able to strive. Sweet companion of the delay that settles observes and appraises itself so that it may feel greater love . . . if inspiration were mine. . . .

And so I desire you and I love the desire more than the orgasm. . . .

And I also love the infinite-eternity-moment the moment of longing for a moment of friendship. . . .

I shall call you Friendship and I shall save you for page 7—the page of divine guidance in my golden logbook when I shall speak of the one truly useful crutch that we all need in Lunaï in order to get off the ground. . . .

To take off not for ourselves about whom we couldn't care less but at least for the other. . . . The other who leans on us counts on us lives for us thanks to us.

I shall speak of the only neutral-Mirror able to reflect our image as we really are inside ourselves and to make us want to purge ourselves pry ourselves out of the rut disinfect ourselves detoxify ourselves deodorize ourselves unburden ourselves decontaminate ourselves if not for ourselves who act impossibly as the ass-wipes of traitors and cowards then at least for the other who inhales us and lives off our smell and dies of us if he cannot be proud of it in order to obey who knows what miracle or what accident of nature inclined to expect more from someone or something else than from oneself.

But you, too, fled from Lunaï in order to help us become more bogged down and since then when we use the word friend here we think of that oaf who slavishly obeys. Of that cursed soul who does our dirty work in exchange for unacceptable reasons of self-interest. Or of that godfather with a bad conscience who allows us to suck him like the tsetses that we are so as to justify himself for breathing his own venom into the flesh of the incestuous homeland as he sucks the lifeblood out of his own sisters at night. . . .

And we have seen you at the village gate thumbing your nose at women who swore each other friendship in your friendship's name and who would get all bent out of shape for some guy's cock when they'd be told as a joke that they could share everything and perhaps they were already sharing everything without even knowing it through the impetuousness of loving hearts that leave to encounter each other during sleep and make agreements for reasons that reason does not know. . . . They'd almost burst with jealousy just thinking about it and for corroboration would go to the marabou who would charitably return their fears conveyed by telepathy supported by names and images and all this in barter merely for a Tabaski sheep and a thousand red cola nuts by way of sacrifice. . . .

It is four o'clock in the morning: two women friends are wringing the necks of chickens at a crossroads as they utter litanies of exorcism. . . .

Oh beak of black-white-sorcerer-chicken!

Give love back to me

And may my woman friend be abandoned and convinced of my power and my superiority: may the bile rise up to her teeth and make them yellow forever more and congeal her smile into a grimace of envy. . . .

At the first signs of daylight: there they are, our lady friends, in each other's arms hugging and noisily kissing each other's cheeks and lips as they throw each other cold fishy looks or a bulldog's look spying the fly on his ear. . . .

We'll buy the same pagne

We'll wear our new jewelry

How much did yours cost

We'll boycott the party of that Mamou who thinks she is the queen of England with her unspeakable hats and who is not all that emancipated as she makes herself subservient to a drunken gigolo. . . .

We'll go meditating transcendentally before dinner you know how good you feel after all the energies come flowing together. . . .

We'll go dancing like "the sugarcane" and we'll make real trouble wearing wigs to stay anonymous. . . .

We have seen you stick out your tongue at those men who toasted their friendship in your name of Friendship but no longer recognized each other on the roads of ambition of gain and ostensible honor. The friend would trip over the proper name of his friend and would smirk when looking at "his photo which tells me nothing worthwhile. In your place I'd mistrust a mug like that even for some lousy job. . . . "

In view of the banality of the stories actions and reactions that your vapid name calls forth how can I speak of Great Providence chariot of great paths and long distances for he who wants to go far and survive the antilife-inertia of Lunaï how can I call you friendship without drowning wholly in the triteness of these words which have no further meaning anymore?

To live for you survive through you and revive a bit more every day and to name you as a disciple to invoke you without being ashamed of my faith. . . .

The Friend watches me watching myself in a mirror that likes to please me with illusions in which I see myself as slender when I have gained weight and as brilliant when I'm stammering. And as night comes to an end he'd say without any smugness: you could lose some weight if you really wanted. You'd look really good if you took a bit of trouble. Because he shouldn't lie to me when I'm lying to myself. . . .

The woman friend is there and goads you and steps on your toes. You study her carefully and see the birth of her intention. She forces you to realize that she'll never act unconsciously nor maliciously through baseness or vile self-interest. Never through forgetfulness or neglect. You are all-encompassing and sovereign. Nobody can impart a word or an action to the Woman Friend for no one knows better than you of what she is or is not capable no one is able to sully her. . . .

It is not a Utopia that Lunaï needs but rather concrete and viable facts. And I am desperately seeking an example a sign that can convince me that Friendship really does exist—that it is the desire for selflessness and what's sublime lurking inside everyone to justify that we've been created in the image of something of someone and that it really is a mother lode that might produce surges of loftiness and excellence. . . .

And Black Night persists in tormenting me:
"Write your name on the list of the skeptics
And I shall entrust you with the keys of carelessness Bathsheba
There is nothing to be done for negative souls
There's no point in sacrificing on the altar of an egotist
And loneliness is a burden best borne alone
What else should I tell you Bathsheba
After the flood only the heatwaves of the flesh pass through
Foaming with dampness and unfit for warming the spirit
The survivors stuff themselves with it like gluttons and become alive again
While alone among all their lonelinesses
You fret
How else could it be for you daughter of the spirit
The day foretold will come Bathsheba. . . . "
Slanderous Night!

But at the first slip the first start as I awake I catch myself thinking: so and so seems to feel Friendship for so and so. Or when I get to the point of asking myself whether my interest in Grozi and Babou is perhaps Friendship I jump right on top of the opportunity and I ponder I promise you you'll see! perhaps I'll manage to find that famous mirror-crutch which I believe we all need in Lunaï so as to look a little farther than our bellies and our genitals and then I'll be able to write page 7 of the triumphal-journey of my golden logbook.

And I'll be able to call you friendship without fear of being ridiculed because I was born with the faith and I am not ashamed to believe in the power of a word and a name.

Ah! a gesture a look even just a sound of true friendship! Even just a simple "faithful imitation." . . .

And that will be page 7. . . .

The mirror of providence
The triumphal journey to the extreme boundary of one-self
And of the other
The friendship
That will hold the reins of the chariot
Of the race-mirror
Of the Woman Friend–Truth

Page 8
Grozi and Babou are really a peculiar twosome. . . .

There are days that you ask yourself what they're doing together what they could possibly still have to say to each other after all these centuries these lives of bumbling about of babbling of tilting and tossing without ever making a choice without ever coming to a tangible conclusion.

But maybe they're doomed to talk and talk still more until they speak the keyword that will at last unleash their bonds with the power-word that explains their life with the pure-prescription that will finally clarify their part in the action. . . .

Their life resembles a rosary of words that stammer stumble stagger but continue to be strung together inescapably stretched interminably scattered in every direction keeping themselves occupied for light-years on end years of time lost with a sense of dreadful eternity:

People will always talk
Will always question themselves without ever finding any answers
Will always add a step to another
A word to another
And the Word-God
And the end of the road will never be reached
Always. . . .

So space stands gaping like an abyss time drags on life tumbles and fear and anguish swallow us up.

We must compensate we must find our balance again bring all our weight our trumps to bear gather up our heredity and inheritances engender progeny anticipate the next generation and retirements lengthen lives extend life remain upright under the penalty of everlasting-nothingness!!!

It was in the era-age when one absolutely wants to prove that one is adult by making babies contributing to the labor force which justifies its own existence and gives the illusion of survival but is also the age when one has nothing but absolutely nothing to teach one's child no suggestions to offer him and barely enough to feed him. Grozi had married a young Black girl from his region who was determined to multiply herself. . . . But all she had given him was one son one wretched only son in this land where infant mortality reaches the eighty percent mark what an idea to bear only one son! She had gone from one abortion to another one miscarriage to another without ever managing to reproduce life again. The doctors had predicted she would die if she stubbornly continued to want the impossible to produce a teeming multitude as it behooves a good woman from these regions otherwise what would people say!

She was determined and, indeed, she died.

Grozi began to dislike this evidence of his inability this tangible proof of his immaturity "this puny bit of an only son who surely wasn't going to take long to die sickly as he was and so it wasn't worth the trouble of getting attached to him of thinking about his education" he sent him off to Grandmother's stable where there was enough *macabo* for everyone and where he could pay for his share by helping in the fields as he awaited his death. . . . After a certain period of time he forgot him altogether.

More time elapsed and Grozi began to mature and tell himself that he would really like to have a child now that he felt he was able to love it raise it teach it those things that expand a person to a point where alienation can no longer reach. . . .

And the more time passed the more Grozi became stronger in his conviction that a man should have only one son. This wasn't for just any man and above all not at just any age. He should have struggled first discovered a minimum of rules to live by and have tested them assimilated them. . . . He should have devised a philosophy of life or at the very least understood why he came into the world in that precise place and not somewhere else before he could think about duplicating himself. That way he could carry half of this over to the child through heredity while the other half would have to be wisely dished out to it until it reached the age where it could experience things for itself. This was the only way in which a true and gradual evolution could be safeguarded. . . .

Yes he wanted a child just one and right away: he felt he was ready. One child but not with just anybody and especially not with one of those black broodmares!!! He wanted a child with a woman a real woman who had matured somewhat as well and who would be ready to pass on who she was to an only son without all those complexes about many litters that had killed his first wife. That was one of the reasons he had chosen Babou's cousin who came from a place where having just one son is considered common and honorable. And damned if she hadn't given him twins once triplets twice and quintuplets one more time because of those pills that turn women into real guinea pigs!

Thirteen brats to whom he could not raise his voice without having their mother carry on about "how he shouldn't traumatize them cause them complexes and emotional blocks cut off their instinctual bond with nature squelch the freedom of their genius"!!! Thirteen brats who would reduce every concept every experience and every educational plan that Grozi had to nothing and in disgust Grozi finally chose to live in the street underneath the baobab where he held forth for days on end with Babou who had wanted "a whole slew of untamed intuitive children" and had married a young black woman who had given him an only son: she had entrusted him as quickly as possible to a Caribbean nanny to refine him and protect him from the flaws of Lunaï and make him into a son worthy of his father an aesthete. . . .

Since then there is always a touch of bitterness in Babou's voice when he speaks of the women and children of Lunaï. . . .

All the same! In Lunaï there are slews of children armored with instinct(s) and slews of children who toe the line with traumas and complexes and children without traumas without emotional blocks children without instinct(s) without anything at all! But when they're at rest they all have that vacant look of those suffering of sleeping sickness so characteristic of all the inhabitants of Lunaï who have contracted it because they don't live within themselves because of their lack of awareness and their ignorance of why they are there, because they've been stung by the Tsetses. . . .

GROZI (exasperated, to Babou): Listen! You're wearing me out with your desire for children! And if you want to know the truth, I don't want any more! You can have mine!

BABOU (beaming): Really? Can I adopt some of yours? Oh how happy that would make me! Because, you know, I ordered a few from Cambodia but it's taking a long time and it costs a lot. . . .

GROZI: You ordered a few? But what are you going to do with them?

BABOU: Well! To have a daughter. To give a sister to our son. And to raise her, you know, to help in any case. . . .

GROZI: That really gives me the creeps: that sense that everything happens mechanically, out of habit, as if you're caught up in a system from which you cannot escape anymore. . . . The habit of living, the habit of making or adopting children, the habit of acting the way your neighbors do, according to labels stuck on by no one knows who since no one knows when, labels with meanings that completely escape us, out of habit. . . . But dear God! What do you want with those kids? What have you got to teach them, to contribute to their well-being?

By simply enclosing horses between four bars
Without millet or hay
And space in front of them
And a thousand other bars they could jump
And four prison bars to sap their energy
Four bars they'll never jump. . . .
And an ill-omened bird to count
The seconds that kill all energy
And the seconds that flee from time. . . .

BABOU: But. . . . My children will be educated in a way that's suitable to their background: they will learn history sciences the arts. . . .

GROZI: Following what model? Evenings of storytelling don't exist anymore: when the model that would foster children's dreams, provoke people's callings, unleash the sparks of brilliance was systematically devised. . . . What your children will be taught is that Ramadier was successful in his diplomatic missions to Africa and other children will learn that he set up stooges in order to better carry on with colonization: what is the truth? Which history is the one to learn? Whom are we to admire? Fathers are no longer respected: they bounce around between right and left painstakingly scraping the bottoms of cooking pots and of wine containers: teachers are no longer admired: they drone on indifferently in their classes using heavy-handed jargon with which they desperately try to cover up their enormous deficiencies. We feel contempt for the godfather who palms a job off on us without valuing us at all. Children no longer play at being teachers or the hero who just managed to get his docile sheep locked up, get his head chopped off, without leaving so much as a tenable philosophy or an acceptable ideal behind. . . . But what is this history what are these arts and sciences you're talking about? What viable truth supports them? What are we to say, to suggest to our children?

BABOU: Listen! . . . If you're born in the middle class, you get a middle-class education and you owe it to yourself to hand that down if only to be worthy of your forefathers. And if you're born in a caste . . .

GROZI: But why should you be born middle-class or casted? What does all that mean: middle-class proletariat or other castes? What is their end? Why should you be born precisely in this position and not in that? Isn't there something in this knowledge that explains and justifies this life?

And four prison bars to sap their energy
And an ill-omened bird to count
The seconds that flee from time. . . .

BABOU: Listen! We in Lunaï are nothing but pawns and the role of a pawn is not to ask questions nor to think up strategies. . . .

GROZI: But merely to reproduce, to make slews of other pawn-babies, is that a pawn's role?

BABOU: I agree with you that it's a contradiction. If the pawn had been created only to mark the position of active thought of the strategist-demiurge who demonstrates his creativity by moving him around, there would be no reason whatsoever for him to reproduce given that reproductivity is already a strategy and creation in itself. A pawn that reproduces itself inevitably has a plan. . . .

GROZI: What kind of pawns are we then in Lunaï, we who reproduce without knowing the why and the wherefore?

*
**

What kind of pawns are we? And so they were actually admitting that they were pawns. The problem was which kind.

Grozi and Babou really are an odd pair. And every time that I think about them I stop wanting to talk. Hasn't everything been said already? Will I ever really write this famous journal? What am I to put on page eight when the foundations of equilibrium have been mowed down from the start?

I would have liked to talk about children. About this necessary renewal that allows for evolution. Then I would have to be discussing their education.

But how can you talk about children when the image of yet another pawn immediately comes to mind a pawn who hasn't even been moved around by his sire and who is nothing but dead weight to himself without any initiative ideal or reason for living.

I'd have all the more trouble discussing children because the urge would grab me to nip mine in the bud if I'd so much as glimpse for even a second the image of vermin of maggots of mollusks on their faces. . . . I'd feel too much like hearing the plopping sound their bellies would make as they disintegrate under my boots but my stomach also turns when I think that I could be tarnished that I could get the mustiness of my own contaminated contagious fertility of my decay my weakness my emptiness back in my own face. . . .

So what else should I write on page 8 of my golden logbook if the gold of the balance of my hands? Not much choice: the pawns no longer reproduce and the demiurge is tired of his old pawns. He is burning them in a bonfire and goes on to other business. The earth is clean and neat and I do not open my mouth. Balance exists and does not have to prove itself at all just as "the song of the kora music for the heart does not have to prove itself."

Or else people are no longer pawns and reproduce. And then in our role as forewarned strategists we must anticipate a harmonious plan of evolution that will automatically come through education. . . .

In this age this era
They will be dead the Africans Americans Russians
Blacks Whites Yellow
The simpleton will be a simpleton everywhere and recognized as such whatever his origins his rank or his skin may be. . . .
The genius will be a genius everywhere he walks his human head held high
In this age this era
Battles will be waged against ignorance and subservience
In the name of Humanity
The region will no longer be a prison a yoke that generates entrenchments limitations and complexes

When Africanity no longer does itself in by trying to prove itself with more neologisms restrictions rifts
When Africanity no longer is a pretext for servitude
An alibi for ignorance weakness poverty the Sahel
When the model is no longer Yankee.
Nor negritude tigritude and other turpitudes. . . .
When fathers and schoolteachers are no longer robot pawns programmed indoctrinated polarized pawns
When a bad conscience is no longer allowed to hide behind complacency
When children no longer play the flunky or the gangster
The transvestite prostitute or drug addict and queer
The model will no longer be the slave who breaks his chains to lay them at his master's feet
The proletarian who becomes the boss of bosses
The master who shares his mistress with his slave to soothe his conscience
The humble person who turns the other cheek
The evildoer who steps on everything and is rolling in money

When mini-stories no longer justify the crime to please heroic narcissism cheaply
When the poor is a man
When the African is a man
And when the blacks and third world populations are men
Without having to shout that out on a podium at the UN
When the apparently weak person is a man
When woman is a man
Without having to brandish a phallus to prove it
As "the song of the kora music for the heart does not have to prove itself. . . . "
When Grozi remembers that his "only son" who is now fifteen years old can still be educated. . . .

In this age-era of a new period when people will have opted for the solution of a true education that responds to the aspirations of a human soul in search of evolution while it resolves the problems of equilibrium which is necessarily called forth by the reproduction of bodies likely to be chosen to take a conscious direction.

I shall keep page eight about justice and equilibrium of my golden logbook for a topic that deals with children and their education and I'll explain why I expect a certain balance without having that stunned look of someone searching for the squaring of the circle in a rectangular triangle. . . .

In the meantime I refuse

I won't make any children in Lunaï for Lunaï anymore as long as I don't know what I'm looking for here while I'm bored like an empty hand what children could possibly be doing here to make their life actually be a life: filled with experience-enriching emotions with sources of inspiration with exaltation with possibilities for creative action. . . .

For my children will be blue and coral-pink of the New Race. They'll know the secret of the fossil-shells deep down inside the heart of the sand the mystery of the tender black roses on the fish-stones the geometry of the stripes on zebra skins the stupid symmetry of the warmongering ideas inside the heads of men. . . . They will demystify

The insipid smiles of indifference

The taint of the taste of gall and discord
The sharp acidity of doubt in the hearts of the weak
The tepid moisture of intimacy
The deceptive depth of the abyss that is no more than the failure of a surface. . . .

Because it is worth the trouble of living it with all its twisting and crooked mysteries its bitter sap of kola nuts and because the most flavorless brew becomes divine after having tasted bitterness.

Because it will have an end that justifies the feverish anxieties of India ink the quivering pleasures of dawn's dew the despair and the ever renewed sources of Love

Life
Their life. . . .
They will encounter you and smile at you
In this age this era
They will smile at you and think they recognize you. . . .
They will smile at you
No they do not know you and you will not know them in Lunaï before the return of the heart-shaped cradle
Yes they will still smile at you
Because you'll come alive again and they'll live with you
In this life
I feel a smile in my heart. . . .

Ever since I've been dreaming of a little black boy with blue eyes I'm rejoicing and I'm waiting waiting and I pray. My eyes will open and I'll know and I'll make children who will be of real jasper and coral of breath and of fire and may it be so! May it be so before I reach page eight of my golden logbook when the moment comes that I must speak about the world's equilibrium about children about their education I who have no more education or children. . . .

"You Bathsheba often said to yourself
That your children would be souls who would love you
With exaltation
You would have revealed to them the love that rises
And rolls and flows and warbles like the sap of the hevea

Those souls to whom you would have given and who would give you
The very best
The essence of themselves and the knowledge of what is essential
And you would say to yourself that there where love is sown
Only joy can be born . . . !!"

And Night strikes up a song blazing with thunderous and star-filled joy. . . . For Black-Night is birthing the egg of the day bedewed with gold
"A day will come Bathsheba
A day will come
When your eyes will shine like the Southern Cross
Your body your heart your spirit
Will shimmer like jewels
Incomparable jewels that will burst
Into a thousand rays of joy
The joys of living one's life
Not like a sacrifice
But like a necklace of cowrie shells!!"

*
**

So
I left them there
Where my true life lies
Where one only lives by love
And dies a thousand deaths of ignorance
And dies a thousand deaths of prison bars
And dies a thousand deaths of shame. . . .
I left them there
Without a roof without protection
Without warmth without tenderness
Alone
So that Initiation may live. . . .

*
**

And so it will be on
Page 8:
For a strategy of equilibrium
Of children of breath and of fire. . . .
Strung together like a necklace of cowrie shells

In the mornings of Lunaï's gray nights
At the first early lights of dawn
And in the ears of Grozi of Babou and of all Lunaï
The voice of my Newborn will resound. . . .

"I am the dreadful specter of fire
The black
The white and
The resplendent
Fire is burning my intestines
Life is burning my veins
Its deviations are devouring my brain.

I am the dreadful specter of fire
Fire wells up from my depths
Spurts forth and foams
Lava vomited out by volcanoes
Eyoyoo! Fire! Fire in the pinnacles of my eyes Eyoo
The fire flares up and sparks Eyoyoyoo!
Like palm-tree torches on the nights of great feasts
I am the dreadful specter of fire
I burn life from every end.

There is fire at the neighbors
It is coming closer
As if pulled by an irresistible magnet
I am the dreadful specter of fire
Carrion lies rotting in distant surroundings
Closer to the fire the carrion burns

Carrion come
Come and purify yourself in the heart of the fire
Carrion!

I am the dreadful specter of fire
I devour and am devoured
For the renewal
For eternal love
And for the ultimate purification. . . . ”

*
**

Page 9
As the good daughter of my ancestors I owe it to myself to stop at the number 9: here I have to know who I am. What I am worth. Of what I am capable.

Do I really have to write a logbook? Will I be able to write it? Is it useful? Am I not too presumptuous to expect to be doing something for the Blue Race of jasper and coral?

Really, since I've been spending time with Grozi and Babou I'm behaving like a male: I never assess myself question myself. Did you ever see a man think himself unworthy of what's fit for a king? The ugliest the most vulgar the most untalented the most inane man doesn't give it a second thought to make advances to the finest of women to the goddess herself and never asks himself what he might contribute to the dialogue. Undoubtedly because men seem to think that their phallus alone is enough to compensate for everything else: inner and outer poverty pettiness of vision and action ugliness and bad manners. . . .

In contrast to the man woman always does her best to please to always offer more and to be at the level of her companion. . . .

But through contact with the machos of Lunaï you lose the modesty that makes you gauge yourself judge yourself and react by searching for what might actually be done if one really wanted to participate in the birth of the next Race. You lose pride in wanting to give something of value that might weigh in the balance of relationships.

And I?
What will my contribution be?
If I write the journal will that count as an effective act?
But still I who claimed to want to dedicate this to the next Race I'm not going to pass this shitty journal on unless I'm quite sure of its value. . . .!
So?
Am I going to write it or not? In any event not now that's for sure for I am still too sodden with shit and with pus.
What I would need. . . .
What we would all need
Is an Initiation
Rigid as a cleaver
An Initiation
It would prune every gimpy foot
Every soft part that sticks to our soul drowning it
An Initiation
Complete like the *Kom-Imboye*
With nerve-fibers heart-pits with water-juice
It would harden the abdominal webbing
And prevent men from being squashed like blobs of spit
Being crushed like rotten papayas
At the least little cloud-squall
At the least little threat
At the first sign of anguish. . . .
What we would all need
Is it solely an initiation
Not just that
But a Shape
Cutting—diamond
Rich—facet—crystal
A Shape
To unfetter Art from empty chatter
Initiation from religiosity
Organisms from corruption

Power from stupidity
Wealth from ugliness
A Shape
That would bring its thousand subtleties back to the white light
Without balkanizing it
Yes
What we would all need
Is a form of initiation capable of alchemy
Our societies would once again become initiatory ones
And our initiations would once again become social ones
The Initiate would once again be
The Great-Man who has influence over the powerful
Overthrows systems
Creates and participates in the renewal
Christ will throw the Pharisees out of the temple
Will conquer Leprosy Paralysis Blindness
And once again
The Man from here will walk tall
His heart strong
His head on his shoulders
His feet on the ground
And his soul in the clouds. . . .
For that Form
I shall pray
For that phrasing
I shall fight
For that Initiation
I shall write. . . .
I shall write a golden logbook of gold
For the next Race
But in the meantime . . .
In the meantime

I anticipate a retreat a hermitage where I shall carry out a series of baths of contrition a magic cure from which I'll emerge without hatred without complacency without complexes so I can speak serenely:

A black man may be treated like a jerk
Without centuries of tyranny permitting him to withdraw behind the argument of racism and to walk with his head held high without questioning himself without judging himself as a man and no longer as a colonized being!
The "white big shot" will look at the Black man's work rationally without patronizing him without a guilty conscience that provokes prejudgments and negates human equality despite the clichés of the UN.
Every man on any continent will search within for his existence without being forced to "play the black man" or to serve as "front man" and without having to feed the thought-shape of the colonizer.
When man no longer acts the pig
When woman no longer is a bitch in heat
When I am no longer a misovire and there are no more misogynists
When there are only Beings in search of a better becoming and a better Existence
Because absolute ownership cannot be everything
And Absolute Being can own everything
So when I can speak of the essential completely cleansed
Of the difficulty of being and of the roads that lead to Being
Because I will have tried the experiment of it
I will have a few little tricks grandmother style
And I will work them into a wonderful story
For these precious little children: the Blue Race. . . .
What I shall do right now . . .

Is burn this journal project or hide it
And in hidden terms
Suggest a wrong direction
That way everyone will think that I've burned knowledge in an attack of madness you know
That madness that is born from the pain of birthing a genius. . . .

It Shall Be of Jasper and Coral

They will think that I've hidden fabulous treasures that must be found again at all cost
In order to make the world take one leap ahead!

So
The next Race will search
Will organize expeditions excavations
And will never stop the quest. . . .
And since they won't find my precious bubbles
It will find itself
It will find itself again
And they will take me seriously
For at last I will have bequeathed a beautiful myth at least! . . .

In the meantime
I am stopping
Like the good daughter of my ancestors
I am stopping on the threshold of the ninth door
I listen to myself and declare myself unworthy!

It will not please you
This evening's poem that sings of the fall
And the descent. . . .
Toward . . . hell you'll say
And I say toward life
Warmth lights births and deaths
Who will tell us the best way
Who will have spoken the truth?
I am reborn out of the ashes
When they think we're finished
Dead and forgotten
Black-Night told me: "Love remains does not know death"
And I say: "Eternity exists for the sake of perfection and we are reborn to accomplish perfection. . . . "
It will not please you

114

It Shall Be of Jasper and Coral

This evening's poem that counts you among the dead
And sings of your death
Love of my life
Eternal love
But it sings of hope
For *if the seed die . . .*

Page 9
Quickly
Retreat to a hermitage
The cure for clichés for complexes
The bath in the sacred word that contemplates itself in silence
Weighs words and places deeds
Here and now on page 9. . . .

Tour Sarah
6 November 1981
3:09 P.M.

Love-across-a-Hundred-Lives

A Novel

To Bertha-Ni, my mother-grandmother
To the Children and the Great Men of Africa
To Ngo Biyong Bi Kuban, my grandmother-daughter, my double
To Njock Ndogbéa-Liking Lem, my grandfather-son-husband
This swatch of our entrails
This endless journey of twists and turns
Only to meet again always
Always Siamese and twins
Mirrors and reflections of Love . . .

W. L.

Some destinies are marked with a special seal. And the beings who live those destinies never know banality. Their cowardice like their courage, their strength like their weakness, their flaws like their virtues always seem exceptional. So it is with the destiny of my brother, Lem Liam Mianga. . . .

Look. . . . His name alone is a set piece all by itself, isn't it? "Habit" or "the Manner of Casting Bridges."

An artist of renown today, married and the father of children, he has been in love with one woman only and, without a doubt, will remain so forever: Madjo, our paternal grandmother! His wife knows it and has adjusted quite well: for this strange being, who had come from some other place, nothing but a feeling just as strange was possible. . . .

One of those feelings that are indescribable, indestructible, but so often misunderstood that they lead directly to the psychoanalyst's couch, if not to the asylum, to prison or to the cemetery for having violated taboos, for immorality, abnormality, or the disruption of the social order.

Then the "experts" explain that "Ugh . . . badly integrated libido, ugh . . . suppressed lust for power, ugh . . . hatred of the father, ugh . . . parents not getting along, ugh . . . postnatal trauma. . . . "

And "the Patient" comes out of treatment with more mental blocks than before and, one day, begins to hit his head against trees, against walls of incomprehension, out of shame, out of fear of the inexplicable. . . .

Luckily, my brother ended up finding an explanation before sinking definitively into the abyss of madness and suicide. One of those very preposterous explanations, but one still worth gold, since it allowed him to survive, to come to life again, and to bring joy to all those who love him. . . .

When you look at the beauty of his sculptures, when you see his children, when you hear his lovely voice start singing the songs of his dreams, you honestly regret there aren't more unhappy people who have the gift of his imagination to invent no matter what kind of story for themselves, so long as it allows the world to see this much beauty and to be open to hope.

And if the outrageous story of love-across-a-hundred-lives could unleash the imagination of a few raging madmen (even among those "who govern us") and permit them to "sublimate those of their drives" that are most bestial, and turn these into shooting stars in the night, glimmers of hope for life, then I would say to myself that, in telling the story, I have shouldered my share of the destiny to which I was born, here by the side of another, so very extraordinary, destiny.

Of course, I am not as talented a storyteller as my brother; and so I will often let him speak for himself, just to have you share more intimately in his feelings, his emotions, his evolution on luminous paths. . . .

Follow me. . . .

Once upon a time . . .
And God created man
And man was double
And man was Siamese like Janus.
He always had a sister on the flip side
She was tails and he was heads.

God created man in such a way that he could always win at every game, at every turn, heads or tails.

But an evil angel, the elder of man, who had been created with wings as his only company, was overcome with jealousy for his younger sibling: he came up with a plan to take revenge on him by putting him in a bad light with the father: he taught him how to cheat, and man began to roll the coins on their edges so as not to fall flat on his double face.

Then God became angry and separated man from his double: "Since you like losing just so you can risk more, you'll play at least five times before finding your tail side up again, and for the rest of your life you'll regret having played the edges."

From that day onward, man goes through feelings of all sorts brought on by his cheating: shame, fear, hope, despondency, belligerence, but exaltation also. And so he runs for entire lifetimes; sometimes exhausted, out of breath, he catches a glimpse of a face from afar, reminding him of his double, and he redoubles his efforts only to realize in the end that he was running after the illusion of a Maya. . . .

But the worst of all the torments is that, while he is running one way throughout his lifetime, he discovers only at his death that his double was right there behind him, at his heels, running after him like crazy. . . . After all, really, what do you think the flip side would be doing all that time?

So stop running, your destiny is right behind you. . . .

*
**

The tree was there, in front of Lem.

The placentas there at his feet, with all the umbilical cords trailing: enough to knot the most beautiful rope with which to hang himself behind a maternity clinic that went out of its way to help birth a thousand of those on public assistance a day, only to lengthen the waiting list for the Drop-by-Drop-Machine. . . .

That is where he wanted to hang himself with umbilical cords
to die of this life held together with rotted ropes. . . .

*
**

For how many hours had his fingers been groping around in that "mess" to knot his rope of dangling umbilicals?

Hours as slimy as these placentas to which no name would ever be attached, or any personal memory worthy of being called back to life, of revealing the truth of the life that had once resided there. . . .

Meat-hours that were breaking up, withdrawing from leathery nerves.

Inside his head, more umbilical cords were intertwining and growing longer. . . .

Meters of sinewy rope were dangling from the tree like an old bridge detached from the sky. Then there were his short gasps of effort like small mouse cries, and grandmother's crystalline laughter like a voice in a canyon, a pebble on a lake, echoes and vibrations. . . .

"What are you doing there, Lem? I know you're in 'the habit of casting bridges.' But I didn't think you'd be casting bridges of meat to the midnight sky. Do you know I've been looking for you since noon?"

Imagine Lem, hanging on to his cord as if to a life buoy, with those mature child-adult grimaces of his, when he ran into an obstacle:

"Madjo, I might as well tell you right here and now: you can't do a thing for me anymore, and you won't convince me again. I've made up my mind, and I'll see it through to the end. My rope is ready, I'm going to hang myself."

Do you hear Grandmother Malice's laughter creeping into the soft and slimy rope as into a baby's hoop, as into a featherlight toy?

"But that rope is much too long and heavy for this shrub. You'll never see it through with that thing. Go to your father's plantation where the trees are tall and more solid. At this hour there's nobody around, you know. . . . "

And look at Lem, disgruntled by that hope one always has to be restrained, which will lead you to fight back even more and show your willpower, so that you can play the headstrong child one more time. . . .

"Actually, Grandmother, this tree is a bit fragile, but it's the only one right next to the maternity clinic, and I really want to die close to a place where babies are born. . . . "

And Grandmother, in a conciliatory manner: "Fine. Let's go

to your uncle's then, all his children were born under the *karité* tree not far from his house; his wife was terrified of maternity clinics. With a little imagination you'll be able to think you're in a life-giving place there. . . . "

Ah! imagine Grandmother-Serpent. A snake coiled around another erect snake: Lem's cord coiled around Grandmother and tying her up like a roast. A joyful roast bursting with laughter, running and skipping in the backyard of the clinic. A contagious laugh-game. A game of catch. . . . Imagine Lem running after Grandmother with outstretched arms. . . . Mad laughter. Was it in the exaltation of that strange moment that he intuitively knew he was facing his double, his one love-across-a-hundred-lives, who had been following him since the dawn of time to allow him to evolve and who would still succeed in showing him the direction of his inescapable destiny as a man, his destiny as a warrior? The fact remains that he accepted eagerly. . . .

"All right, Grandmother. Let's go. It won't be imagination I am lacking today."

And they left, Grandmother in front, Lem behind, his cord-cross trailing. . . . Twenty kilos of meat, perhaps. Thirty meters of cords, perhaps, trailing behind him like a satiated wood-snake, and giving the impression he was following the stations of the cross. For once, the Gods were with him: he was allowed to choose his death, he who had not chosen his life. He, who had always run away from life, rediscovered all his courage in facing death. Grandmother had done nothing to discourage him. He was grateful to her for that. Dragging his cord-cross along brought about an ecstasy in him he had never dreamed existed. . . . He was in the process of casting his first bridge between joy and himself, between an action and himself, and without a mentor. . . .

He was dragging his cross. His bridge, heavy with all the stones, the bits of wood, all the branches and dead leaves, all the grass that clung to his placenta meat. . . . He was dragging his bridge-cross, relieved of the trembling and the instinct to flee. He dragged his cross all the way to his uncle's maternity-

karité tree, and he was telling himself that he had stirred up all the slime of his other lives with it. It would rise up in his nostrils, into his lungs, and he would choke right there under the whirlwinds of memories. . . . Now he had to climb the *karité,* tie his rope-cross of dangling umbilicals. . . . He was shaking and his legs wouldn't hold him anymore. Grandmother pretended not to see any of this, and once again he became furious that he never could manage to hide his helplessness, that he could never conquer. . . . He was weeping with rage and despair.

"Lem, why don't you rest a little; otherwise you'll break your bones by falling out of the *karité* tree instead of hanging yourself as you promised, and then you won't keep your word and you'll fail once again. Catch your breath so you'll have the endurance for the difficult climb up the *karité* with that rope that holds the weight of lifetimes. . . . "

Strange Grandmother, so tactful. . . . She was saving face for him, or at least she was trying everything within her power. But he was so exhausted that he could no longer hold back the cry, an enormous sob escaping from his navel and vibrating through every one of his nerves, his bones, each one of his hairs. It flowed out of him from every pore, as from a dike that has cracked somewhere. . . .

But an odd thing happened; grandmother's voice was cutting across this vociferous flood and asserted itself just as the original sound must have thrust itself upon the darkness. . . .

*
**

In everyone's opinion, Madjo was first of all eyes. Eyes and teeth. Teeth like mother-of-pearl, something truly precious from which vulgarities would never escape. That is undoubtedly why she used to speak so little, why she would laugh more. . . .

Her eyes were sometimes dizzying chasms, lakes that would call for drowning, sometimes magic mirrors that would reflect an image dressed in the fears or wishes of the moment, laser beams that would scan deep into the most intimate of thoughts and feelings, paying no attention to any obstacle. . . .

Tattoos, traces of her initiation into womanhood, snaked up the length of her arms and up her neck, which was exceptionally long, ending in sunflower petals around her mouth; indigo tattoos that threw shadowy reflections on her bronze skin; these tattoos had miraculously resisted the burns that, at Lem's birth, had disfigured her in a very curious way. I will tell you about that in a little while. . . .

Lines, laughter-looks, teeth and lights, colors and voice, Madjo. . . .

Lem was under the impression he had known her for several lifetimes, he would have sworn to it. He had always lived with that certainty without looking into it any further. Was it the burns on her face that prevented Lem from settling his gaze on her and from settling down himself?

But that day, as he saw her there underneath his rope of umbilical cords, an irresistible impatience came over him, an urgent need to place her at last. Who was she really? Who was she for him?

As was true for all of us, he knew her only through her myth: she had been married off to Grandfather when she was nine, just after her initiation as a little girl. They had named her "Ngo Bakénya," "she who was surrounded," "Ngo'Kénya, the Wasp." This name had stayed with her, and it was only by this name that I used to know her. Later on I was to discover her maiden name together with the name of my father. . . .

So she had arrived at my grandfather's house, accompanied by forty servants, with forty necklaces of beads from Venice and Amsterdam around her frail hips, an enormous wealth for that period!

Despite everything, she'd go to the fields very early and return when the other women were just heading out. She used to be compared to the caramel woman of our folktales, who would melt when she was forced to work in the sun, for she used to spend all her time in the shade or in her cooking-hut, simmering delicate dishes, stringing necklaces, and crafting other art objects, so that you would have thought she might die if her hands were to stop creating. . . .

Later on, when she began to have children, she made

layettes for herself that would be talked about by everyone in the region. She brought ten children into the world, Lem's father among them. The latter had married at a very young age and had Lem when Madjo was pregnant with her last child, with me that is, the one telling you this tale. . . . So that her first grandson was older than her last child, which explains perhaps why I have always called her "Grandmother" or Madjo, as Lem did, and why I have always called my father "Grandfather." . . . Besides, for a long time I thought Lem's parents were my parents; perhaps because my mother, very attached to her new role as grandmother, lavished more tenderness and tolerance on Lem than on me, and Lem's mother had to fall back into taking care of me. . . .

But in reality, Lem's father was my older brother, and Lem, though older than I, was my nephew. . . . Having become used to calling him my brother and having much more of a fraternal relationship with him than that which binds an uncle and a nephew, you will allow me to continue calling him my brother. Besides, who knows if we weren't brothers somewhere out there at the dawn of time?

Yet, if the myth were to be believed, Madjo should have adored me, since it was said that I was the offspring of a lover whom she had loved madly, as you know how to love only in your golden age. . . . A lover who had died before I was born, just before Lem had come into the world. . . .

I hope you haven't already passed judgment on Grandmother according to today's standards, nor have thought her to be an unfaithful wife. . . . You see, these countries used to have customs that will soon be considered futuristic, for we may well need to go through the same thing in order to save such institutions as marriage, religion, so "shaky" today. . . .

And this is how, among the Seizers, marriage was not seen as an individual matter of the heart, but as an institution of social duty that would involve the entire community; a matter of reason and, therefore, an adult matter. . . . This would concern two clans who, finding their structures altered, would find each other with new branches in their respective family trees, new alliances that could not merely involve two individuals!

That is why it was families, rather than individuals, who would choose one another. But because the emotional needs necessary for the full blooming of individuals were recognized, outlets as well as safeguards had been envisioned. . . .

Although, when compared to man, woman was wronged, since polygamy but not polyandry was allowed among the Seizers, she had not been completely forgotten: she had the right to a lover of her own choice, she had the right to love. . . . If this lover responded fully to the lady's love, he had to introduce himself to the husband and then fulfill certain tasks, such as hunt small game or bring little gifts, little extras. But the affair was never to take place within the village itself. The lover was obliged to build the "love nest" in the bush and was never to speak to his lady in public. Although everyone knew the secret, the lovers had to continue to act mysteriously: never to admit to it, never to show themselves together, never to give each other presents in public. . . . The woman had the right to bring food to her lover; furthermore, the finest parts of game and fowl were recognized as rightfully belonging to the lover, but the food had to be brought to the "love nest" in the bush. Moreover, the task of bringing the lover his food fell to an intermediary, never to the lady herself, no doubt to avoid having the impression that the everyday character of the conjugal home, with its endless parade of tasks that "kill" Love, was being repeated.

Children born from these love affairs were treated fully as children of the family. Among the Seizers, the concept of fatherhood was more a question of the person responsible for the education and training of the children than that of the sire. Besides, popular wisdom says that even to a dog it is given to have fertile sperm, but it is not given to everyone to establish a home and to create a tribe or a nation. . . .

Thus, the woman could not be considered unfaithful because she had a lover whom she loved. Only when she'd betray this lover with another man, no matter what the reason was, would talk of infidelity begin! Then it was up to the husband to fall into a rage. It was absolutely forbidden for a lover to beat his mistress: he was there to provide her with all the good sides of love, since marriage already required so many sacrifices, so much submission from the woman.

Madjo had spent many years without a lover, so many years that everyone believed she had the good fortune of being married to a man she loved. So she surprised them all when, quite late, she took a lover. . . . But this lover—whose name was never mentioned in my presence—was such an exceptional man that everyone concluded this was a woman who had always been incredibly lucky with men. Surely it was her destiny to encounter extraordinary men. And this lover had loved her so deeply he almost made her into a fetish, a goddess. . . .

So, as I was the natural daughter of so great a love and Madjo's very last child, she should have loved me more than the others; but her preference for Lem, her grandson, was truly very odd to me. Was it because she had suffered so on his account?

In fact, when Lem was born, an electric blackout had thrown the maternity clinic into an almost surreal darkness. . . . Even a simple match was not to be found, while the child had just emerged like an egg with its placenta, still whole, and needed to be freed as quickly as possible. . . . Grandmother ran like a madwoman to the kitchen and quickly put together an oil lamp, which she lit with an ember. . . . It was by the light of this lamp that my older sister, a midwife, helped Lem out of his cocoon! But when at last he cried, it was a cry that froze the entire clinic: a cry like a chant or rather an incantation, a word of magic. . . . Grandmother dropped the lamp and shouted: "Roumben!" and then, fainting, fell onto the flame! The flames licked her face and burned it in the strangest way: it might be said they were dressing her in a mask as if to disguise her, to prevent her from being recognized. . . . Only her tattoos came piercing through the mask as a sort of transparency, a magical sign. . . . Thereafter, her eyes and teeth seemed to have taken on a greater intensity; is that why they became so famous, entering into the myth of Madjo to such a point that they loved talking about it to the children?

We would ask plenty of questions, and I, for one, invariably asked: "But why did she shout out the name Roumben?" And every time they'd stop telling the tale and lower their eyes. . . . I ended up by not asking the question anymore. . . . Later, much, much later, I would understand: the love between parents (lovers or married) always seems stronger to children than the affection they themselves receive from those parents. For Lem it was love, for me it was affection. . . .

Yes, Madjo was a myth we were told in episodes. . . . But from our own experience, what did we know about her? Malice, tenderness, an enigma: sometimes a friend, an accomplice, sometimes a distant, mysterious mother, that is all that I knew. . . .

As for Lem, he had more to say on the subject. . . .

"You know," he said to me one day, "for me Madjo is first of all a fragrance. . . . A heady aroma that always propels me into other bodies, other faces, other feelings, other worlds. . . ."

And he especially remembered one specific day, when he was nine, when he had once again started to play his favorite game with Grandmother: the buffalo hunt. He would be the hunter and she the buffalo. She'd tie a hump on her back and horns on her head, run around on all fours while Lem chased after her. . . . On that particular day, she suddenly turned around and started pursuing Lem, quickly caught him, and nailed him to the grass. That was the first time he noticed the aroma she gave off. He inhaled it deeply into his lungs, and everything began to spin: she really became a buffalo, with a face of astonishing ugliness. And as he remained there, paralyzed with fear and drunk with her fragrance, Grandmother's face continued its metamorphosis and became a young woman's face, extraterrestrial, so unusual was it. And then the metamorphosis also took possession of Lem, and he heard himself say, in a voice from the beyond: "Mother, here is the baobab tree. Cut as many leaves as you desire and rejoice, for you are no longer the mother of a cripple!"

His own voice frightened Lem so much that he shrieked and shut his eyes very tightly. . . . Then Madjo's voice took on its normal maliciousness and said: "You're not going to start that again, are you?" And her enigmatic manner of that moment left him with a taste of forbidden fruit that he would always pursue: every time he'd ask to play the game, and every time his eyes would open onto other worlds as soon as he inhaled the scent. . . . And every time, too, he'd promise himself not to shriek, not to shut his eyes. But it was stronger than he! . . .

"The scent," he confided in me, "I think it's the scent that scares me. It produces indescribable drives in me, which I won't know how to restrain anymore without leaving this plane. And I think it is shame that makes me scream. I see with horror a moment when I'll jump her and lose myself inside her, as I believe I have already done other times, in other places. . . . "

What would have happened then? Wouldn't they have called it incest, immorality, insanity?

And so he would shriek while shutting his eyes tightly, and Grandmother would laugh and sing him a lullaby of tales:

Child of mankind, stop your weeping,
Do not cry, I'll cover you with praisenames. . . .

And everything would go back to normal. It was just a game, wasn't it?

And it was that lullaby, that same lullaby she was singing to him underneath his rope of dangling umbilical cords, in a voice like the original sound, while he was weeping over his weakness, over what he thought of as his helplessness. . . .

Before . . . in Secret . . .
a Very Long Time Ago . . .

And the original sound resounded, throbbing more and more, with ever greater power. Words colorful as pictures were taking on shape and life. Finally, nothing else existed but that voice and all life emanating from it. Lem felt it, heard it, inhaled it, and saw it in all its dimensions. . . .

"Child of mankind stop your weeping
Stop your weeping I'll cover you with praisenames
I am naming you as befits your soul
I am calling your spirit by its essential qualities
By the sound and the tone that recall it
By the sign the color that resemble it
Do not cry stop your weeping
I'll cover you with praisenames
Back-of-silver-cobra
Belly-of-green-mamba
Crocodile egg tortoise egg that hatches without fail
You
Female crab eel crayfish who proliferate
Enrich the world
Do not cry stop your weeping
Everything ugly will perish
It is true
The world never was this ugly
The world is never as ugly as when it proclaims rebirth
And when it prepares for the rebirth of a great man
This will happen soon this will be tomorrow

This will be the hour when your eyes reopen from a long sleep
From the long latency
This will be any time now
This is the way it always is before messiahs
It was thus before Sundjata the Mandinka buffalo lion
And thus before Roumben
The rainbow pillar of the Seizers. . . .
Child of mankind stop your weeping
Do not cry anymore I'll tell you the wonder
The eternal wonder that goes back deep into all memory
So that mankind will survive ugliness
With beauty in its heart
Wonder that goes back deep into the memory of the fetus in quest of a soul
It returns on the tongue of the minstrels of Great Worthiness
Resurges in the lullabies of the followers of Bikoursi
Of the Mévoungou and the Koo
I sing to you of the wonder of time immemorial
I'll explain the coming of the promised child to you. . . .
He never arrives when men are noble
He never comes when women are pure
Not when the young are daring and full of ideals
Nor when the elders are wise and incorruptible
Why should he come at times when commerce blooms
Economies are stable and the powers just
For what reason would he come when the universe is enjoying equilibrium
He only arrives in times of war, in times of plague
Avatar amidst the extemporizers
Anti-evil scourge among evil and its scourges
Under the reign of the rotten-to-the-core and the Pontius-pirates
When everything goes with the flow under the tidal waves of degradations
When the balance breaks under the crashing weight of ignorance

And when purity causes shame. . . .
Thus it was that in the Mandinka kingdom
The Only Virgin Was a Hunchback!
In those days
Men had bowed to dependency and slavery
Were in the habit of
Paying tribute to the king
Speaking the same words using the same gestures
Making love making children
Lukewarm in their tedium
Hands and heads emptied of the essential. . . .
And our virgin was dying of desire to admire
To be exalted over someone who'd break out of his strait-jacket
Who'd reveal new worlds
And our virgin hid her desire underneath a wholesome ugliness
But not so hardy as the desire that made her eyes
Her nose her mouth bulge and catch fire
Made her grow a hump on her back and bristles on her skin
And transformed her into a buffalo. . . .
And the Buffalo's Tail Was Made of Gold
And Gold Belonged to the Blacksmiths. . . . "

*
**

Lem heard this voice, these words, saw these images being born, quarreling over the original sound, and at last he understood the meaning of "lost speech."

"It will never return to the original state, under penalty of denying the love that pushed it one morning to create all things, under penalty of annihilating life. It is lost forever, but it will live eternally in everything it has created and that lives, and that must live. . . . "

Despite everything, a torrent of tears blurred his vision, for he had stirred up too many memories of other lives, and their sludge was going to settle into the abyss of his navel again if he didn't force it out of there! He wanted to die, light and clear, to hang from the tree graciously like a dewdrop of pure gold. . . .

"Speak, voice . . . ," he begged. "Press down on my abdomen, help me to clean out my belly. . . . " And he was weeping, weeping with all his heart, calling the voice of love that echoed in answer to him, Madjo's voice. . . .

"Stop your weeping Child of mankind and I'll cover you with praisenames:
Phantom-tree never shelters parasites
Caterpillar does not let go with a sudden breeze
Hawk's-eye does not confuse chick and pebble
If I am telling lies
May piss make my feet swell up into festering and stinking blisters
For nine moons. . . .
Do not cry stop your weeping
I'll explain the advent of the foretold child to you
When the blood of the highest nobility has been corrupted
Asphyxiated obstructed by the blood of incest
The new blood will ripen at the thousand springs of the blood of castes
The occult forces reserves of energy
Yes. . . . When one is preparing the return of stability
Or of instability which must alternate to ensure evolution
One must seek the ancestral Strong-Soul capable of large-scale action. . . .
For no action on the world's stability can be taken
By the first puny runt that appears. . . .
No peace can be settled by the first right-thinking person who comes along
There are times of peace like pestilential farts that poison the air
Choking like an octopus. . . .
And peace cannot be broken by the first aggressor that comes along
For there are wars that are like harmonics

True promises of light. . . .
And such wars are the work of the Masters of Energy
They control earth and water air and fire
In times like those Child
The Masters of Energy were the castes
And in the shade at those times
The blacksmiths governed over Matter with the fire of bewitching alchemy
The hunters were masters over Space Earth of healing and over Water of clairvoyance
The griots dominated over Time through Speech of pure Air
These were the castes that knew the origin of things
They would do huge and small jobs
They were merchants and craftspeople these castes
But they were aware of the decline of the times in those days
So they were preparing the renewal
While the masses and the nobles were sauntering unhurriedly to
their destiny
Docile sheep unknowingly bringing the work of the Masters to an end
Listen. . . .
I am telling you of the origins of Wonder
Before in secret a very long time ago. . . . "

*
**

But what was oppressing and obstructing Lem? What was holding him sequestered and preventing him from being reborn into consciousness? What was destroying the bridge of light that had connected yesterday to today and that would have joined today to tomorrow? The bridge between Memory and his brain, between his soul and his actions. . . . What was oppressing and obstructing him? He wanted to set himself free. So he had to remember, even if it meant dying for it; he had to imagine, even if it meant living for it, but he had to set himself free, set himself free at any price. . . . Alas! He fled, he would always take to his heels!

Lem would always flee the horror that was lurking there somewhere . . . in his navel; a lump of fear that frightened him! It flung him out of his bed when the light went out. It made him run like an elk into the forest, hurling him against every obstacle, enough to make his skull burst! It made his muscles quiver before a piercing look, and it made the bile rise to his nose with disgust for himself. . . . Really, Lem no longer wanted to endure his enormous navel!

And was it not his navel that began to convulse again and inject him with the drive to flee, that muffled fear of hearing the rest of Madjo's story, as if he sensed the revelation of formidable keys, of responsibilities that he had always feared. . . .

And because she didn't want to see him back down anymore, didn't want to hear him cry out anymore, Madjo made her voice ever more urgent, ever more appealing, and Lem felt himself fastened to the ground as if to an irresistible magnet. . . .

Beloved Child listen to the story of our former lives
Listen and stop your weeping I am looking into your eyes
A very long time ago there lived a king
Maghan Kon Fata
Ah that handsome Maghan, Maghan—Honor,
Ah Wari ya Wari, Maghan—Silver
Maghan was beloved by his people

Maghan didn't bother his people: he asked nothing of them other than to be allowed to have his customs, to have his comfort. Thieves and opponents practiced self-censorship. Sorcerers lived their witches' sabbath peaceably at night. Men had their honor except: their fear was disguised by peace and their servility by public-spiritedness. . . . The rapacity of women held its head high: custom obliged the men to cover them with gold as proof of their love and, pride willed it so, as a demonstration of their honor and their ability. A woman would feel respectable only if she could wear a pagne and sing the ditty of the day: *Mon mari est capable. . . .*

And everything was peacefully festering away under the peaceable reign of Maghan Kon Fata. A rich reign of peace inherited from his fathers. A peace he had not conquered, he had not created. A peace that had immobilized everything: the creativity of the artists, the inventive spirit of the women, the children's taste for innovation, the philosophic readjustment of the elders, the men's desire for conquest. Peace had immobilized everything!

And Child did you know this?
Man is made in such a way that he makes no further progress when he is or believes he is happy
He forgets that he is on earth to grow,
To find his integrity again
To evolve toward the divine
An evolution that is acquired by trial and tribulation
Hardships that will be all the rougher if peace and happiness have been sweeter and more mellow. . . .
It is true
The world is never as ugly as under these reigns of peace
When men resemble castrated pigs
And women cuddly teddybears!
There are times of peace like farts, did I tell you that yet?
The world is never as ugly as during the ends of reigns like these
The ends of times, the ends of races. . . .

In the royal court, Maghan Kon Fata would thus rest under the tree of words, where there were never any discussions held but there was peace. That was because an agreement existed that nothing or no one had come to the kingdom of the Mandinka through the door of surprises; the bolts had rusted: someone had locked it; through negligence, in a mechanical motion, or with premeditation? No one could say, especially since no one seemed to have realized it. . . .

Now, you know that in those days any city worthy of the name had an entrance called "the door of surprises" . . . for any people desirous of progress always wishes to be surprised: a new look, a discovery, a reassessment, an emulative discomfort. . . .

Even though the strongest locks and the sturdiest bolts would always be placed there, this door was never to be under lock and key, at least not as long as the city's policy was meant to be an orientation toward development. It is through this door that artists, scholars, mystics, and other strange types who always elicit awkward questions would enter the city. . . .

And it was often noted that, at the very moment when incredible things were confirmed or supported, a specimen of this sort would pass through and sometimes, quite in spite of himself, raise one of these preposterous questions that might confuse the protagonist or completely pull him out of his embarrassment. And then they would notice that surprise had entered the city! One ended up by confusing these people with surprise itself, and it was not uncommon that this door would be referred to as "the door of scholars" or "the door of artists," "the door of mystics," and whatever else. . . . And so life was lived in a kind of emulative and slightly uncomfortable excitement, most auspicious for creativity and progress. . . .

Of course, History is familiar with tyrants who had locked the door of surprises and who discovered at their own expense that surprise feeds, by preference, on interdiction and repression, as freedom defuses it all the more. . . . The most intelligent ones among them not only hastened to unbolt the locks, but remagnetized the attractive bells placed above these doors to give direction to surprise, making them shine like beacons and ring at the approach of a new idea. . . . And they would then claim it and make it the core of their systems, and so one could hear talk of "light-kings." . . .

Indeed, in the Mandinka kingdom in those days, Maghan Kon Fata's throne was turned toward the door of surprises at all times, but alas, it was a door that no longer inspired expectation but quiescence. . . . It had been half a century, easily, since surprise had entered the Mandinka kingdom! Was King Maghan always right? Did the people and the institutions really have nothing to reassess? Or had the attractive bells of surprise been removed or demagnetized? Might it be definitively confirmed that a flabby peace and permanent comforts turned out to be antidotes to surprise?

The nobles purred like white maggots in a rotting palm tree! The women cackled like geese! The children dozed, their bellies shimmering in the sun! Servants dragged their feet! Courtiers stuffed their faces with kola nuts, hoping for an inspiration, a word sweeter than sugar! Alas! It seemed there was nothing left to expect from the Mandinka kingdom. . . . The king's griot, who understood signs such as these, was beginning to worry:

"I shall relate the battles of your fathers to future generations, oh Maghan Kon Fata. I shall recount your efforts to keep the inheritance of your ancestors intact. But what shall I say of your creativity? You haven't even sired the *heir* as yet. . . . "

Maghan straightened his torso and, with a gesture of irritation, swept these words aside, finding them to be childish provocations. . . .

"Indeed, the soothsayers all say the heir of this kingdom has not yet been born; and yet, I have a son! And quite a strapping one!"

"Kings, as all other men, are the sons of their mothers, King Maghan! A man is worth what his mother is worth, and the heir of this kingdom has not yet found the woman who is to bring him into the world. . . . "

"*Cherchez la femme,*" the nobles playfully sang in chorus.

All eyes turned toward the door of surprises and peaceably turned away again. There was no urgency for the birth of the heir: the king was in marvelous health. Surely he would live another half a century, and peace reigned. . . . Besides, was it not dangerous to rush into siring an heir thus predicted? Would he not be taking the risk of accelerating time?

So the everyday humdrum continued without any surprise coming to the door. . . . No surprise would ever come of its own accord, the little rascal! It's like luck, like evolution: often it must be seduced, pulled in by the hair, coaxed, raped in order to be fertilized. . . . And real men do not believe in chance nor in spontaneous generation.

*
**

At this point in Grandmother's story, Lem began to want to flee again! Had he fallen asleep, or was it that the voice had grown silent? He didn't hear it anymore. He felt a dullness inside that had stuck itself to his skin like glue! And it was lasting. . . . Time was once again playing tricks on him and projecting him into other spaces. A telescoping of images and sounds, a fusion of faces and names, a general chaos inside his head. A long journey full of twists and turns was carrying him from one corner of his memory to the next, from a face to a universe. . . . He had just taken a backward jump of nine months. . . . But let's listen to him tell it himself. . . .

"We had occupied the steps to the chancellor's office, blocking the chancellor's exit, and he ended up by calling the police. . . . Surrounded for more than two hours, the campus was holding its breath: students and police officers were watching each other like cocks before a cockfight, but no signal for shields to be raised had as yet been given. People were going from one group to the next, messages were being delivered, being added to in a whisper as some overheated and unrestrained imaginations saw fit. . . . And suddenly, the whine of a radio station fired everything up. "For god's sake, turn the volume up and be quiet, it's time for the news!" . . .

Ah, that hallucination, the news hour. . . . A gigantic combat between Rumor and "Information." . . . Two monsters riding each other, devouring each other, and mutually re-creating each other. . . . "Oh, come now, be quiet, and let's listen at least!"

"Order: Evacuation of all university residence halls. . . . "

"What do you know, it's the Voice of America! It seems that Gadhafi has assigned a veritable armada to the country to protect us from the counterrevolution!"

"Suspended: all salaries and all fellowships. . . . "

"Hey, guys. . . . They're saying that the Islamic Revolution has promised aid to the comrades of the opposition!"

"Investigation to reassign responsibilities. . . . "

"Africa Number One says that Professor Ziworé is the head of the movement!"

"Measures taken for the return to a sane climate. . . . "

"Hey, they're saying it too! Is Professor Ziworé making this revolution while on a new honeymoon with Didi? My dear boy, how sweet it is now, this revolution, isn't it!"

"Latest decisions of the grand party, which met in emergency session at the palace this morning. . . . "

"Do you think this is going to go on until Saturday? Because the beach outing and the dinner debate might be . . . "

"Come on, stop it, we're trying to listen to the news! What did they say?"

"Evacuate! Evacuate the premises, the school is closed."

Whistles blowing, billy clubs, screams, curses . . . and, indeed, the school was closed! Dazed, we found ourselves "in the street," faculty and students in the street! Hands and bellies empty in the street? For the first time. . . . And I was in ecstasy: our heads were going to be filled . . . at least with fire if nothing else. . . . The word would come to our lips. The Idea would find its shape! This time around we would liberate ourselves, there was no doubt! We would be saved from the Drop-by-Drop-Machine. . . . That octopus Machine that never seemed to have an end. . . .

The former Master had placed it there from the beginning of the new times; it was a fascinating Machine, which spoke in the name of the people, which advocated renewal and a fuel for human enthusiasm and zeal. And the people had intoxicated it with all their wishes, all their hopes, had put uncontrollable trust in it, which thus released them from their responsibility and their power. . . . A dreadful power with which the Machine had become saturated, transforming itself into a many-headed monster that nobody could resist any longer. . . . It was then that they realized that the Machine had a hold on every citizen through some vital spot: through the belly, in the case of people who had let themselves go so far as to owe it everything, through their own laziness, weakness, irresponsibility. . . . Recognition of the belly was thus obliged to prevail at the risk of interrupting the distribution of the vital Drops. . . .

Through the head, in the case of the hair-cream geniuses whose other intellectual brain cells had become ossified: they owed their positions and intellectual titles only to their griot-like activity where the Machine stood, and they stood to lose everything at the slightest sudden movement. . . .

Still others were held through the heart: they had received the grace of faith from God and they carried its fervor and sincerity in their voice just to convince others. . . . One had to take the Machine at its word: it had been there since the beginning and would be there at the end. . . . They were fitted with costumes and crowns. . . .

Thus, if anyone wanted to insist on an action in order to discover the true colors of the Machine's entrails, if anyone attempted the slightest form of inquiry, the mere beginning of an analysis, the Machine would jam, would close the terrifying jaws of its multiple heads, and too bad for anyone who happened to be caught inside it. . . . And even if one managed to escape from the jaws, one was taken care of by the horde of malcontents who could not tolerate the lack of drops, for the Machine's first defensive reaction was, had always been, to turn off its faucets at the first jolt. . . .

A one-thousand-year-old method, with which we were all familiar and which had always worked with the same efficiency: "Walk softly, walk straight ahead to Isba, and no pushing and shoving," and one was certain only day by day, one's maw connected to the daily drop-by-drop-meter that dispensed its drops. . . . It wouldn't guarantee any savings, but "elsewhere you starve to death," so it was better than nothing. . . . Very few people had "extras" put aside, and some teachers would count their change from every tenth of the month on, waiting for the drops at the drop-by-drop-meter. . . .

And here we were, the Machine officially brought to a halt! How long could we hold on without any drops? Certainly it wasn't going to be long before we'd go running for a handout . . . our hands full of support motions, full of "whereas." . . .

While awaiting this moment, anticipated in the usual scenario, we'd be glued to the radio and television stations, for long weeks of silence in which thirty minutes of some burial, marriage, or a visit by some women's group would be inflicted upon us, as if the turmoil existed only in our dreams. Then through the *radio-trottoir,* and meant to mollify, would come a rumor such as: "A list of nonadherents has been opened at the Department of Finances. . . . Name and registration number will be sufficient to be cleared and paid immediately." Then we'd see long lines pass by, heads lowered, and the *radio-trottoir* would mumble again that those folks close their eyes while eating the drop; but then, people say all sorts of things. . . .

Well, at the end of nine days of no drops at all, not a single support motion had as yet been considered on the part of the leaders, while the list of the deserters registered only the small fry!

That was because, for some time now, a kind of creeping flow was shuddering its way to the belly of the Machine itself, and Ziworé, my professor, was mentioned. . . . Tracts, secret meetings, strikes, while the *radio-trottoir* seemed to be changing its sources of information and conveying rumors that contradicted the Machine!

No one before Ziworé had ever looked so closely at the inside of the Machine's belly without being crushed, assimilated! Where did he get this power? Gossipmongers said that he was voluntarily being used this way by the Machine in order to make the youth toe the line better and to inject himself with some new blood when the Machine would take over again, would take him with all his disciples once again. For he was going to be rehabilitated, there was no doubt! The Machine would set the price, he knew that, and would try to raise the bids. . . . Despite everything, we all had faith in him: we were his power, spearheads who wished for the end of the reign of the Machine with such intensity. For us, he was like Ngok Ikwèn, the intrepid hero of the old tales. An old woman had given him a poisoned hot pepper, made even hotter with chili pepper, so he could rid himself of a multiheaded monster who was blocking the road to evolution. . . .

Fortunate is the man who, like Ngok Ikwèn, has sharpened his knife with care and prepared his hot peppers: the conscience of the elite, the fervor of the people! Before undertaking the long descent into the belly of the beast. He slashes the intestines, the heart, the liver, all the "basic organs." . . . The now paralyzed Machine, its monster jaws locked in pain, sent terrifying SOS signals to its condemned soul in a funereal chant that would make cowards tremble, and those hooked on the drops as well! The monster begs for water to extinguish the fire in its belly, the awareness in its gut, and it is so thirsty that it swallows the bucket whole and the beloved spouse along with it!

Dearest spouse daughter of the waters
To Ngo Minyèm Mi Tulép
Please give me a bit of water just a little bit
Pistols submachine guns grenades and armored tanks
Just a bit of water
Since I've been crushing the opponents
Since I've been swallowing the rebels
Bailly Telli Ouandié
Just a little water
I had never before swallowed anything like this
I have just swallowed unexpected brambles
John-John Sankara hard-headed and tough
Just a little bit of water
They're sawing into my entrails and putting pepper in them
They're sucking me dry and deriding me
They're undermining my authority
They're giving me smiles that rip the grimace off my face
Please give me a bit of water just a little bit
A few dollars in billions
Mirages and Phantoms

A few bombs to bomb with
A few tons of vetoes
Operation slam on the brakes
Please give me a bit of water just a little bit
Subversion in their heart
Betrayal for their end
Just a little water
Minyèm Minyèm Minyèm eh. . . .

But Ngok Ikwèn continues his breakthrough until the monster gives up the ghost, even if it means dying with him, even if, God forbid, his knife were no longer sharp enough to open the monster's belly and break the villainous bars! Biko, Mandela, and you, Ngok Ikwèn Manyim!

And so we were becoming overjoyed as we saw ourselves already among the new heroes, those who would have rid the people of this subjugating Machine, we Liberators of the masses. . . .

Alas, quietly the list of names of the deserters began to grow longer and threatened to reach unanimity without the Machine deciding to put its meter back to work! It became necessary to flee the city for the village, where there is enough manioc for everyone. . . .

And the journey went on and on, jostled me about and curdled my blood until I was ready to vomit! And once again I cried out calling for Grandmother.

"Madjo! Is this going to go on much longer? Will this go on forever?"

*
**

I really mean it, my brother is an exceptional being! You've got to admit that when he tells a story it blows you away. . . .

In any event, that was certainly Madjo's opinion, since she answered him so that she could bring him back close to her and take him along into this other tale, where they were together and perhaps happier. . . .

"Yes, too long, Child of mankind.

It always goes on too long for those who want to act and who meticulously prepare their plan in the shadow. It is always like that before the messiahs, it was like that before Sundjata the Buffalo-Lion of the Mandinka, don't you see?

They were counting the moments the moons the seasons
The castes could not take the waiting any longer
They decided to throw the bait into the water
They decided to set the trap
Blacksmiths Hunters Griots Craftsmen
Merchants
The crucial-occult forces of the people
They divided their tasks
The castes. . . .
And they were all there that evening
And they were with a woman
Sogolon Kédjou. . . .
Daughter of pure gold
Daughter of a Master of fire and a Hunter's daughter
Daughter of the land of Do. . . . "

The royal house of the land of Do was in decline in those days. Not only had there not been any alliance with other powerful royal houses, but it had been a very long time since any new blood had invigorated the failing lineage. . . . Therefore, the king of Do decided to seek new blood and chose the daughter of a powerful marabou hunter. . . . Alas, the young girl had already chosen another man, a blacksmith master-of-fire, and was expecting his child. The enraged king had the blacksmith banished and took possession of the young woman, pregnancy and all. . . . And the child was born. A girl. A relief. No problems of succession, of land, which a woman always finds through marriage. . . . Had the child been a boy, the king would have been obliged to get rid of him so that he would not make claims to the throne and bypass his own children, which he was now going to sire with his chosen wife. . . .

The little girl did not resemble the king at all; the insinuations and rumors created just a bit of embarrassment, which would be eliminated as soon as she began to grow up: they would marry her off as quickly as possible and put an end to all this! Is that why she grew to have such an open aversion to marriage, which in her eyes became a rejection of her personality, sexual segregation, and male domination? In any event, she swore that she would never marry anyone at all unless she herself had chosen him. But how? She was beautiful and growing up fast, and women were given away in marriage according to the interest and the alliances of families. In those days her opinion would not be asked.

She told herself that it would be enough to discourage any suitors, to find some way of not pleasing them. . . . So they watched her neglect all those household tasks that validated womanhood and devote herself to the most difficult of masculine tasks, even those that require a previous initiation such as the hunt, first hunting small game before moving up to the largest. . . . Very soon she was rumored to be a sorceress. . . . And she would have wept with joy: the timid and the conformists would thus automatically be eliminated from the list of suitors!

One day, as she was tracking a herd of buffalo, she witnessed a scene that made the masculine tribe permanently nauseating to her: a pregnant female was obviously having great difficulty giving birth; it was very clear she would never manage all by herself. . . . She was rolling on the ground, biting trees in order not to bellow so violently as to lose herself. Throughout all this, the rutting male was running after all the young females in the group, making revolting orgiastic noises! Reveling and wanton romping around the mortified laboring female who was struggling desperately. The male, blinded by his rut and not managing to catch up with a young female, brutally jumped on the female in labor, who was crazed with pain and pointed her horns into the male's belly, literally disemboweling him! In one irresistible leap, putting all caution aside, our huntress pounced upon the male and finished him off, dispersing the rest of the herd. Then her eyes met those of the laboring female, and she sensed the encounter. . . . And she began to speak softly to the animal as if to a friend and helped her through the delivery. . . . And the miracle occurred: the animal spoke to her and asked what she might do for her to give proof of her gratitude. . . .

"Pass some of your appearance on to me so that the ordinary mortal will never be able to consider me beautiful, will never desire me, so that I may be free to marry only the one whom I will have chosen, the one who can see me as I really am inside."

So the female buffalo passed her hump, her blackness, and her terrifying ugliness on to the young woman, together with part of her strength. She in turn gave some of her golden blood to the animal, and so it is that she found herself with a golden tail. The golden tail by which the buffalo who ravaged the country of Do could be described, as she went killing all the males that came across her path, males both animal and human.

The young woman hoisted the male buffalo on her back as if he were a simple gazelle, and went to the king to offer him her first true big game. Everyone fled before her, taking her for a sorceress who had failed in a metamorphosis, for she was now as ugly as a buffalo. And they called her SOGOLON, the buffalo-woman. A great void was created around her, and, having thus eliminated all "people in rut," as she called them, from her life, she was at leisure to seek and discover those who were preoccupied with other things, those who were preparing the rebirth, and they were not among the nobles of the royal court, alas! In those days, the masters of Energy Renewal were among the castes. She aligned herself with them, and they taught her the cause of things and prepared her to fulfill a great destiny. . . .

And so she was there that evening
The woman-buffalo of gold ripe with the desire to serve at last
For she had ripened her desire to lend form to the Ancestor-Spirit
And to prepare her modeling clay. . . .
Stop your moaning Child
And I shall cover you with praisenames
"Sweetness and Slowness child of Running and of Violence"
"Noises of snail's steps one cannot hear you"
"Your tracks are seen." . . .
Stop your weeping I'll tell you the mystery of the male:
He is a myriad of atoms scattered elements
He is dust and grains of sand
So as to be form force
So as to become volume figure rock marble
Woman is needed
Binding him unifier creator
God is woman and woman knows it
And woman keeps it silent
God knows why. . . .
This is why man is afraid of woman
And why he so prizes the first place on earth. . . .
That evening Child there was woman
Ideas are spirit-elements that take shape
Inside the body of woman
And she was ready she for whom they were waiting
SOGOLON KEDJOU
She was there the MOTHER-GOD
And the Occult Ones were going to be able to lay down the Egg of the Spirit.

But in the royal court of the Mandinka, underneath the tree of words, the throne of Maghan still stood, turned toward the door of surprises, surprises nobody expected any longer. . . .

And yet, on the other side of the walls, surprise had begun to tremble for several moons now. . . . It showed itself by the paw prints of civet cats and pagoda cocks in the sand and in the markings of geomancy. It was tormenting dreams of the king, whose mood was beginning to change. . . . And while words and gestures at court were becoming mechanisms, the castes were growing active.

"To the future generations," the griot would tirelessly repeat, "I shall relate the combats of your fathers, oh Maghan Kon Fata, my king, I shall recount your efforts to keep the inheritance of your ancestors intact. But what shall I say of your creativity?"

"*Cherchez la femme,*" the nobles intoned and shifted again into their usual thick laughter. . . .

That thick laughter that would transform crises into cunning latencies, emergencies into proceedings pending, the essential into nothing. . . . But this time the griot insisted:

"What message shall I deliver from you, oh my king?"

"Is a personal message absolutely necessary? Hasn't it all already been said?"

"Not on your life, oh my king! All will never be said, all will never be done as long as the door of surprises is there; discovery and novelty will always be possible, oh Great Maghan!"

"Well, so be it! Listen carefully to me then:

To the future generations
You will recount my message of violence
You will say that I have dreamed of a whip
With which to thrash their buttocks their heads their hands
To get them out of their lethargy
I have dreamed of knives and of billhooks
To recircumsize them and shed them of any soft spots
To straighten them out and put them back into combat!"

"But there is peace, oh king!" the choking nobles exclaimed. "Why do battle and against whom?"

"Against oneself! Against the pretexts bad faith, good conscience

Against all laziness
Against the immobilism-system fear ugliness
I bequeath to the future generations
All knives swords and hooks of my kingdom
To perforate all these obscenities through and through
And to find some of man's dignity again. . . . "

And, since the king caused surprise for the first time, they heard knocking at the door of surprises! A great silence fell. . . .

The griot sent his son to open the door, but the bolts had rusted. Yet, someone stubbornly continued to knock desperately. Who was this lost soul who hadn't been able to find the usual doors?

"Well, surprise of course. . . ." answered the king while he straightened himself as if to welcome a fiancée or someone of great importance.

The nobles, who stood unconsciously frozen at attention, had been literally transformed into a solid block of surprise. . . . The bolts finally gave way, and a hunter stepped across the fragments of the padlocks as he entered, but he almost fell over backwards when he saw all these people, tense and taut as crossbows in wartime; he was about to pronounce the famous formula of invisibility that shields hunters from perfidious attack, when the voice of the griot reassured him:

"Peace be with the stranger who follows or who guides surprise straight to the door of a people worthy of the name. King Maghan Kon Fata accepts you as his guest and asks that you enjoy the Mandinka hospitality to the fullest. . . . "

There was another silence, then the hunter came forward, greeted everyone as ritual requires, the people first, then the king:

"May Kondolon Ni Sané make me a good disciple of my masters, may my tongue never be more nimble than my arm, my abdomen never more skillful than my reason, nor my vanity stronger than my perception of the truth! Oh, Mandinka People, from the land of Do I have been following some game and I have killed it right here at your gates. I have come to give you your share and I thank the king for his willingness to accept this."

"The kingdom of the Mandinka is your home, Simbon Sogosogo Sala Ba, great hunter, you who know and respect knowledge-of-being and knowledge-of-doing."

At a gesture of the king, the visitor was made comfortable. The game was carried in and carved up according to custom; the hunter's share was hung to be smoked with aromatic herbs; the rest of the meat was prepared for the evening meal and copiously sprinkled with *niamakoudji* and *dolo*. . . .

At the end of the meal, the griot asked, in the name of the king, for a divination reading. The hunter once again invoked the name of Kondolon Ni Sané, the twin gods of hunters, praying to them to allow his eyes to be more piercing than his tongue, and his tongue to be as exact as his arm. . . . Only then did he trace a geomantic figure in the soil and take out some cowrie shells. . . . After throwing the cowries down a few times, his voice became audible, soft and precise:

"Mystery fills the world, oh king, and I shall speak only of what I see. The tallest trees like the smallest ones grow from a tiny seed. Who can recognize a great king in a tiny drop of sperm? The strong are born from the weak, the handsome from the ugly. Where is truth?"

He turned around as if to look for it on the faces, stomachs, legs, anyplace where his inquisitive gaze would rest; the nobles, feeling ill at ease, straightened up in competition with each other, attempting to suck in their paunches, to close their legs and gaping mouths, wide open in a revelatory lack of self-awareness. . . . And the hunter kept on searching for the truth . . . he was throwing, gathering up, and re-throwing the cowries on traces of geomancy, which he would draw with an unsettling dexterity. . . .

"Ah, but . . . I see! I see two men arriving over there. . . ."

Everyone turned excitedly toward the door of surprises, which now stood wide open onto the night's blackness, and they remained alert as if they were expecting to be hit by an arrow! The hunter gathered up his cowries and brought them to his lips, murmuring a litany to them, and then threw them back on the ground.

"Destiny is marching toward the Mandinka with huge steps, followed by two hunters and a woman. . . . A new star has risen in the East and heaven is illuminated! All peoples are coming out of the night!"

One could sense his enormous exaltation as he faced his vision and spoke with a vibrant voice that gave people goosebumps. . . . The griot had to interrupt him briefly, fearing he might go into a trance.

"Easy now, Simbon, and please speak in the king's tongue, the clear words of this clear land! Speak, the king is listening to you. . . . "

But he arched up even more and shouted at the griot:

"Griot! Receive and relay the message of the Earth to your king. Receive it in the tongue of the Earth and translate it into the language of the king, that is your duty! A king of integrity, but without any ambition other than to transmit peace to his heirs! But the handsome king has not yet sired an HEIR! Destiny is marching to the Mandinka with huge steps, preceded by two men; two hunters followed by a woman. . . . An ugly woman, really ugly. . . . The kind of ugliness that gives birth to beauty and light! The Child will be born and will give immortality back to mankind, and fear shall be buried with his placenta. Destiny marches on, is marching with huge steps and might become lost. . . . In order to bring it here with all certainty, the king shall immolate a red bull to nourish the earth with this blood of power and to render it fragrant and appealing. . . . "

He gathered up his cowrie shells and put them away. He wiped his mouth with both his hands and erased the traces on the ground: he had spoken. . . .

Cease your roaming child of mankind
And I am calling you by your name
The name by which you shall respond to the Eternal

"Son-Courage
Lion heart tortoise heart
All warm all patient
All transparent all discreet-secret"
Nothing is stronger than a heart that looks at itself and reflects
Sees itself recognizes itself knows itself and is silent
And reacts and acts!
It will attract every light every shade of difference
Every energy of life
Magnet-Spiral radiating with courage and man's survival
It defies space and does not know time
Son-Courage seat your heart inside the belly
And I shall reveal the secret of the man of courage
Hilolombi as you know
Makes grace rain down once every year
During the season of hailstones
Like children the men go off to collect the gifts
Happy the child who has found a moonstone among the hailstones
And most happy the man who gathers up aspiration among the gifts
The hailstones melt away, the moonstone remains
As does aspiration taller than anyone's head
And bigger than the stomach
The man who picks that up finds courage with it
While others crawl he jumps high
When all heads are riveted to the ground
His gaze searches the clouds
His stomach becomes hollow to leave some space for the moonstone
When all other bellies stuff themselves with hailstones. . . .
Stop your weeping then
Heart of fire heart of moonstone
Raise your eyes to the heights. . . .

155

Love-across-a-Hundred-Lives

Yes, and Grandmother, too, had spoken. But had the wind carried her words away to points of strength that determine achievement or had it left them to flutter about wherever hesitation, doubt, and fear might carry them, those emotions that drain the active energy that brings success? These doubts, fears, this quavering that would always send Lem off into flight?

A flight like an arabesque, a dance, a flight that runs from itself to the point of telling lies in front of a mirror. . . . Since he tried to slip away from her again, she spoke to him one day:

"You flee and you walk the way others dance, but, you see, me, I want only warriors' steps and not dance steps. . . . Life is not complete without death, and freedom feeds on suffering. Look deeply into your pain and your failures and you'll see freedom spread itself into petals of giving, excelling, and providing service. Draw from it deeply! But draw from it with all your senses and your hands open wide! I want only warriors' steps. . . . Each step is a step toward life or toward death. Each step must be taken resolutely, as if it were to be the very last one, because, in fact, it could be the very last one. . . .

She hugged him close to her body, and he became intoxicated with her scent. She now had an astonishing face, on a long neck, and this put her gaze out of reach. And she murmured to him:

"So take my blood, son of an evil serpent, and let it prohibit your abdication. . . . "

Every one of his senses panicked, and Lem was afraid he would see himself grow other heads, other arms, other sex organs, and become a dragon of desire. Raucous cries escaped from him, and he heard them as sounds coming from outside, enemies. . . . Again he closed his eyes and tears sprang from them with the force of a long-delayed ejaculation. . . . He was trembling now and speaking without any concern for the coherence of his words. . . .

*
**

Madjo, I shall never be a soldier.

Shouted commands stupefy me and the noise of weapons drives me insane! Hate-filled eyes frighten me as much as eyes full of love. Fear, they say, makes men evil, and maybe I am not a man: fear freezes my hands and puts fire at my tail, and irresistibly I flee!

The next time, I will not scream again! I won't close my eyes, I won't hold myself back. I shall see the depth of life, I shall look death in the face. The next time. . . . And every time. . . . Oh Madjo, how does one become a warrior?

As soon as your smile grows dim and your voice grows silent, chaos takes over and wins every battle: time becomes confused, spaces superimpose themselves, noise of boots, slogans and curse words . . . dignity has lived its life! And your grandson once again becomes a trembling little child, and once again I take to my heels. . . .

Ah yes! I had fled again! And yet . . .

I was one of the most ardent among those who carried the banner of the strike and led the flood tide of the revolution (to think that we were calling it that . . .). But the radio journalist aired a commentary, vehement in its own way, that the "great party's" communiqué should be upheld: "This is a pathetic attempt at destabilization, hatched in a most cowardly fashion by the external enemy, who has corrupted . . . "

I took to my heels without listening to the rest! Could it be that I had participated in selling out the country? That there really had been a coalition against our institutions, organized by the Foreigner, and that we had been mere tools? But what had we received in exchange when swapping the country? We had nothing, we were as empty as always, empty heads, empty hands. . . . "And what if it were just the simple hope for an overdose of drops?" my navel whispered, and I fled, I fled. . . .

Truly, was it merely for that? I no longer knew anything at all! Still, come to think of it really, what had happened?

We had rebelled against too many failures. We had risen up against scornful insinuations regarding our abilities. That's only human, isn't it? And then, too, we were tired of hearing about the economic crisis while some people—and always the same ones—kept on moving nice and steady, and with them their most distant relatives! Then they spoke to us of our laziness, our lack of consciousness, our incompetence, how educational standards were becoming miserably low, without ever explaining in what way this was our fault! Making us doubt our abilities, was that not simply a way by which to condition us into accepting the fact there would be no employment guaranteed at the end of a course of study the direction of which had been imposed upon us?

Perhaps we should have demanded a more competent faculty, more logical programming, a more realistic educational approach, better adapted to our needs. . . . Undoubtedly, we should have denounced certain rotten situations by refusing to adhere to them ourselves. . . . But . . . they had insulted us! After all these centuries of insults. . . . Our blood had curdled only once! A voice said: "We'll break down their building and take revenge." It wasn't very convincing, but we left anyway. Our revenge against whom? In what way? And why should we tear everything apart? Could the country afford the luxury of being torn apart? Was that what revolution was? Or was it perhaps the form of revolution that suited us? How would the thousand-year-old Machine react, and then what would we do? We hadn't thought about that; we only knew that we could no longer, would no longer accept these things: they had to be brought to an end. . . .

⁂

And, as might have been expected, the Machine had indicated "Tilt"! And there they were with their arms dangling, as if surprised by some anesthesia running its course, hanging on to every word from radio and television stations, only to be subjected to news of marriages and burials. . . . Weeks of silence that just about denied their very existence, small corners of happiness and natural disasters that would laugh at their small-time metaphysical anguish, as if "a man who is hungry" could afford the luxury of reflection! Africa was hungry; all she had to do was be content to search for her sustenance! And Lem took flight, fled from this custom-made destiny, cut too small for his thirst for action. And he was fleeing, fleeing, and Madjo's voice had trouble bringing him back to precisely this point of the Story, where a higher will seemed to be trying desperately to impose an inescapable destiny toward certain turning points of life. . . .

*
**

Child of mankind stop running
Stop running your destiny is running after you
The day of your birth is like the end of the night
Even if there is an eclipse, light bursts forth and derides the clouds black with storms. . . .
Yes the day of your birth is like the birth of the night
The One-eyed Monarch peers out in vain
Earth turns its back to him and darkness sings in praise of its life
What can you do better than live your life and die of your death
For if you do not go toward your life it will go to you
And if you flee from your death it will ram into you!
So stop running and let your destiny catch up with you
And live and die with eyes wide open
Facing your life your death
Facing yourself
Do you see?
One morning, the Mandinka's destiny caught up with him.

Two hunters arrived at the door of surprises, followed by a woman; a woman so ugly that one couldn't tell whether she was young or old. Her eyes bulged from her head as if to look at everything the world did not dare look at. Her mouth would have devoured everything the world had wasted, and never would there be enough air for her enormous nostrils to breathe. And wasn't it every crime in the world that she was carrying there inside the hump on her back? She was walking with a stoop, looking pitiful, with a hint of supreme compassion that inspired respect and contemplation, so strong that people felt like looking up at heaven, sensing that beauty had fled from this earth! Yes, indeed, Sogolon was ugly. . . .

The two hunters offered her to the king, in homage to his very great hospitality. They recounted that they had won this woman for having killed a buffalo who was destroying the land of Do. The buffalo had already killed a hundred and seven hunters and injured another seventy-seven, looking for greatness-empty-of-compensation. . . . And the buffalo had found it in them. The king of Do had promised the most beautiful princess to the one who would kill this dreadful buffalo with the golden tail. They had chosen this princess on the very advice of the buffalo, who had made them promise they would ask for her before submitting to them. The two hunters thought that the great king Maghan deserved this amazing virgin. . . . Maghan accepted: had he not watered the ground with the warm and strong blood of a red bull in order to guide the steps of the ugly woman toward him?

It was decided that the marriage would take place when the moon was full. The new princess visited the kingdom, and the people came running to see this woman who was so ugly that she again caused them to raise their eyes to the skies above. . . .

Truly, she was a king's wife: an ordinary mortal would never have had the strength or the courage to offer himself such a sight, for truly she was a sight! Even Maghan himself couldn't bring himself to enter Sogolon's bed for several days after the wedding. . . . As soon as he would come near, he had the impression he was being pricked by the hair and the horns of a buffalo! And he would slink away. . . .

This went on for forty nights! Maghan had gone through every stage: he had lost his appetite and his imposing bearing; he lost his serenity and became irascible, then fell silent, and then became solitary. Truly, surprise had returned to the Mandinka kingdom! The nobles had to leave their comfortable waiting place underneath the tree of words. The village would grow empty at the first light of dawn, as the people followed in the silent wake of their king, who would attack trees and big game. The women were growing crops here and there as they whispered together; at night, people were going to bed with the chickens because the king was in a hurry once again to go to battle with the invincible Sogolon. Sweet nothings and flattery passed over her as dew over a rose petal of porcelain: it left no traces! Threats caused her to rise to her full height, and her gaze then became untenable. Any discussion was nipped in the bud: she wanted nothing to do with a worm on his knees begging for her attention; she wanted nothing to do with a brute whose only claim was the power of his muscles! She needed neither gold nor silver nor power, and as far as love was concerned, she swore there was none of it left on earth! And Maghan twisted and turned, desperately seeking some way to convince her. He was waging the first real battle of his life. He lost sleep over it!

This had been going on for forty nights. . . .

That evening, as he was watching the One-eyed Monarch give up his place for the moon, the last red ray blazing in gold as if to bring greater strength to the queen of the night, he felt as if a veil was being torn inside his head, there near his forehead, at his temples, at the crown of his skull. He was so overwhelmed that he lost all notion of time. When he came to, darkness had long ago taken over from the daylight, for there was no daytime without night and no night without daytime to complete the full cycle of the day. He understood that she was night and he was day. He felt serene, and for the first time the day rose within him. He went to take a bath, changed, and perfumed his body as would a bridegroom. When he returned to the room of Sogolon Kédjou, he thought he was seeing the young woman for the first time and found her to be as profound as life itself, her eyes like an all-knowing mirror; her skin was warm and soft like a motherly breast and a scent of beehive and honey. . . . A deep desire began to ascend from the very base of his vital core and rise like a tide. . . . He entered her bed, and without a word they gave themselves to each other.

Oh Madjo this desire deep desire for you
Tidal wave to be contained at any price
And the scent of beehive honey drug-scent
And your gaze transposed onto other faces
And one of my other faces hovering over you like that scent
Like a fog
And your hand that guides me and holds me back
My love of many faces
Grandmother in the night. . . .

That very night, Sogolon conceived the child foretold
The child that was going to be the alliance between the buffalo's secret represented by his mother
And the lion's secret long and deeply buried inside his father. . . .
The day that you must die, Child, you shall be drowned in a spring!
The day that you must be born it is hot too hot inside your mother's womb

Even if you grow wings son your destiny will catch you
Have I told you that before?
And so he was born as if despite himself
Twelve moons later, the child foretold like a water well
Limbs as long as times of trouble
And a belly as round as the moon.

They came from across the whole world to see this long-awaited child, who was eating enough to devour a kingdom and growing like a weed and who, seven years later, was still not walking!

Eyes as wide as windows and a mouth

Sundjata as they called him
Was born with a head as big as his father's kingdom
He crawled like a boa, dragging a swarm of filth behind him, among which there were the passersby, flies and spies, beggars and parasites of all kinds. . . .

Sogolon gave birth to two other children, daughters who with their mother were subjected to the mockery: had anyone ever seen a crawling buffalo, a crippled lion. . . .

Sassouma Bérété, the rival, laughed her malicious laughter like a waterfall, saying to anyone who was willing to listen that she preferred having a simple human son than a crippled buffalo-lion that crawled around eating shit! For Sundjata even ate cow dung! He was really a half-starved land looking desperately for fertilizer.

And his mother would weep with despair and shame. Her husband absolutely insisted on having another son, convinced that this one was not the predicted child. And each time, a daughter would be born. . . . And Sogolon knew it would always be like that. Sundjata was indeed the one she had been waiting for. But why was he not walking?

Every sign had indicated it was he: the sudden eclipse of the sun at his birth, preceded by a storm. . . . That horde of hunters who had all come together in front of the door of surprises, some pursuing a buffalo, others a lion, which they had killed there, at the very moment he gave his first cry! The blacksmiths who had come to bring him gifts of golden rings and that sword. . . . And then the king's griot who had given him his son to watch over the child! All the occult forces had recognized him; but why was he not walking?

Maghan Kon Fata, feeling the approach of his death, called in a marabou and a simbon. . . . To whom should he leave his kingdom? One doesn't entrust a kingdom to a cripple. And his oldest son was already seventeen years old, had passed through the hunters' initiation and was circumcised. . . .

"Great trees first root deeply into the soil before they rise majestically to the sky. . . . " said the master of the hunt.

"Birds must bring their feathers in close before they take flight," added the marabou. "The man who is to bring the

Mandinka dignity must first bring in all his slumbering energies to himself. . . . "

"A new star has risen in the East, but in the West there were too many clouds," the simbon said again. "One must remain belly to the ground so as to let the storm-chasers pass through, and the light shall shine."

"Destiny is marching with huge steps toward the Mandinka, who will not be able to hide from it," the marabou insisted. "Oh king, do not entrust the kingdom to your oldest son. He will make a point of taking it himself, but he shall not be able to occupy a place he is not capable of filling. . . . Entrust the secret of the succession to your griot, who will reveal it to the nobles when the right time comes. . . . "

So they spoke and went away, and the king kept their counsel in mind. . . . During this time, Sassouma Bérété was scheming as much as she could, inciting the nobles to have the king designate her son as heir to the throne. Was that not normal, in fact? Was her son not the oldest, the natural choice to succeed his father? Sure, he was neither lion nor buffalo, but he could walk, and he was a formidable hunter. . . . In case of war, one could at least count on his skill; while a cripple . . .

And Sundjata just went on dragging along the ground stuffing himself with cow dung and sheep turds. . . . And his mother continued her lamenting and scolded him: what was he waiting for to start walking? Had she not suffered enough yet, had she not paid her debts? Had she not been humiliated enough? Sundjata threw his mother an angry look, whereupon she averted her eyes, then he went crawling off in another direction. . . .

Seven years Child! A complete cycle of uninterrupted contact with the earth, the dust, the bottom of the ladder! For seven years Sundjata was crawling on the ground!

Then came the day that he was to walk
Inescapable as the day of birth and the day of death
That day, son, rocks dissolve underneath your feet
If the sky does not fall on your skull!

Maghan Kon Fata had gone to join his ancestors, and Sassouma was acting as regent, as she had always dreamed! Her son would lose the throne forever if she did not impose her will. Besides, it was for herself that she wanted the power, not for that ton of flesh of a son, whose sole ambition it was to go after small game! How could a man so big and so strong in appearance be so weak and so small on the inside? For truly, Sassouma's son was small and weak. He was barely competent in executing orders. But would he manage to conceive ideas and take initiative? Sassouma wore herself out encouraging him to acts of bravery, hoping he would develop a taste for greatness. . . .

Then came the day that Sundjata was to walk
Inescapable as the night as the day
Everything is a pretext for the deed that must be accomplished
That day, there was some jesting as usual
Sassouma's son had brought his mother leaves from the baobab tree
And she was rejoicing in all this attention
What a pleasure to have a son who stands on his two legs
In truth even if he is not a lion
He can climb a baobab tree
Pick the most tender of leaves for his mother
Those sweet and aroma-filled condiments
Never to be tasted by sterile women. . . .
Nor by the mother of a cripple!
That day Child
Sogolon could no longer control herself. . . .

She burst into loud sobs, went off to grab her son and shook him as one shakes a plum tree; she accused him of being an unworthy son, whose mother would never know the taste of baobab leaves. She pummeled him, scolded him, insulted him, beat him black and blue and screamed in his stead, enough to cut off her breath forever. Her cries resounded inside Sundjata's huge head and made his entire body vibrate as the storm shakes a reed. An interminable cry. An eternal cry. A cry that might give life or take it away. Sundjata received life for a second time. He stared at his mother intently and said to her:

"Fine, I shall walk
Bring me a stick
Today I shall walk."

Sundjata's griot did not wait to hear this repeated. He ran to the blacksmiths to ask for a stick. Think of it, to the blacksmiths! In the royal forge there was a steel bar that had been there for so long that the name of the blacksmith who had made it had been long since forgotten. . . .

It took seven people to transport the bar into Sundjata's court: blacksmiths, hunters, and the court's griots. . . . Had they not thrown the bait into the water together? Together they must pull up the fish. . . . And that day, they were once again with a woman: Sogolon Kédjou. . . .

Sundjata grabbed the steel bar with one hand as if it were a simple stick. He clutched it, and such strength poured forth from him that he might have seemed to be changing the world's axis! Raucous sounds came from his abdomen and his chest; the cracking of his joints made one think of the fall of a baobab tree! And all around there was nothing but silence. All the people were holding their breath and stopped moving as if to lend him their energy. . . .

Our Lion finally tore himself away from the ground. He took a first staggering step, then a second one, a third, and with the fifth step he let go of the steel bar. A real gasp came from everyone's heart, and in one second the news spread to the four corners of Niani-Ba: Sundjata was walking!

With her knees, hands, and forehead on the ground, Sogolon gave thanks to the ancestors: her mission was on the right path. . . . At the same moment that she wanted to get up, she heard Sundjata's voice:

"You wanted baobab leaves, Mother? Well, here they are!"

She raised her eyes and saw an entire baobab tree lying before her, with roots and all! The first deed of Sundjata standing upright had been to uproot a baobab!

All in its own time Child
Stop running your destiny is running after you. . . .

*
**

In the village, the convulsions of Lem's navel had stopped. The radio was forced to admit that some were being headstrong. Among these was his professor, Ziworé. And he said to me

"As long as he remains standing
Dirt will never enter my mouth
The nape of my neck will never touch the dust
My head will not accept emptiness anymore
My feet will grow roots deep into the heart of the earth
And my eyes will sweep the stars
As long as Ziworé remains standing
My heart will walk with my man's head held high
And whether it displeases my navel or not
Never again will they see me tremble
Never again will they see me take to my heels
Oh Nyambè, make him stand for nine moons
The nine moons that a newly circumcised boy needs to become a complete man
I ask you this with all of my being. . . . "

And so he was praying as the hour of the newscast approached, with such anguish that I couldn't help but join him in his prayer as I added:

"May it be so, oh Nyambè, and you shall be praised forever, for the rest of my lives. . . . "

*
**

Time is long Child
And man is in a rush
Life is a full cube
And all man sees is a flat surface
And when the images are three-dimensional
There still remain the contents people do not see
How poor are the five senses, Son!

And surely, they saw Sundjata walk, hunt, they heard him roar, Son. . . . His voice was authority itself. His eyes, his huge eyes of fire, his arms, powerful arms of steel, that's what people believed, that's what they heard. But, Child, what did they know of his knowledge, of what went on inside him? What could they possibly know? Which eyes were capable of seeing the rainbow in the depth of night?

Yet

While he was nailed to the ground

He learned the secret of the air: the pure air of words of truth, of the most sacred history of his people. . . .

When he rose up into the air

He learned the secret of the earth

The earth of the hunt and of healing herbs

And it was revealed to him why the buffalo was his mother's double

The only thing seen and heard was that he was given the title Simbon hereafter: Master of the hunt

Life unfolds and is unveiled under our eyes under our nose

The greatest of mysteries resound in our ears

The most powerful magic flows in our veins underneath our skin

The eternal word melts on our tongue

And we see only smoke

How poor are the five senses, Son!

Sundjata would get to know water, he had to know fire, inexorably one could assume, but how was he to attain that knowledge? Who was going to initiate him? When? Where? Those were questions nobody gave any thought to. Really, people like what awes them and are only rarely interested in the reasons why. It is enough that power appears to give of itself. . . .

And Sundjata seemed truly to be giving of himself. He proved himself to be the most hardworking, more rigorous with himself than with others. His bearing said: "Ever further." His gaze replied: "Ever higher." His hands confirmed: "Ever more beautiful." His mouth went one step further: "Ever more true." And the mediocre were being driven up the wall with indignation! And Sassouma Bérété saw her dreams of power collapse: her son was becoming more and more unobtrusive and was willingly serving Sundjata. He felt comfortable when close to that tower of strength, as it directed him, showed him the best way in which to exploit and express himself, that strength that channeled him and helped him to avoid the aggravations of choice and responsibility. . . .

Sassouma conceived the plan of killing Sundjata. She wanted nothing to do with this giant who seemed able to overshadow everything, to the great joy of his people. She wanted to be tall and stretch her head to the clouds. She wanted power for its own sake and for herself. Never would she give up her place. If her son wanted no part of power, then she would take it herself! And it was necessary to get rid of Sundjata.

She called upon the assembly of witches. . . .

The nine most fearsome witches of the Mandinka.

She made them believe that Sundjata was becoming a public danger.

Thirsting for power. . . .

She complained about his selfishness.

And, as you know, Child, nothing is more contemptible than a selfish sovereign, true?

The witches decided to rid the Mandinka of the scourge, of shame. . . .

When the time for the first harvest arrived, they went to Sundjata's field to pick the first fruits: corn, okra, eggplant, and the first ripe tomatoes. They arranged it so that they would be surprised by Sundjata, hoping in this way to unleash his rage, which would have given them the right to retaliate. For you know, don't you, child, that sorcery is also an art of harmony? One retaliates only with the echo of the attacking force. . . .

Sundjata moved toward the witches, his left knee on the ground, his head lowered, signs of humility and deep respect, and said to them: "How absent-minded I am, mothers of mine! I hadn't yet noticed that the first fruit had already ripened, and thus I have been lax in my duty to bring the first picking to your home, as a son owes it to his mothers. You are teaching me the lesson I need to learn. I beg you to accept my most sincere apologies and to allow me to make up for my error. . . . " As he said this, he filled the basket of each one of the nine old women and ordered his servants to escort his mothers home. . . .

Surprised by this irreproachable behavior, the witches were completely nonplused and understood that they were dealing with something much stronger than they. . . . They knew that this clearly was the man who had to be the king the Mandinka needed, and they grew frightened: Sassouma's hatred and the ruse she had displayed were real dangers for Sundjata. Sundjata was still only a child and had to be protected, for the well-being of the Mandinka. . . .

In unanimous agreement, they took Sundjata under their wing and entrusted him with a secret: the Water of emotions and of clairvoyance. . . . The troubled Water of badly revealed, unformulated emotions. The warm Water of strong feelings that grow nobler. The cold Water of generosity that stirs on and instigates action. The clear Water of compassion that provokes Vision. The secret of all the waters of life and of death. . . .

Do you see, Child, why the stepmother or the wicked father of folktales, who upset and torment the child, are the finest initiators?

And so Sundjata became familiar with the Waters. He understood he was not yet strong enough to hold his own and had to go into exile. . . . He needed to learn patience, the fire of will, and he needed to learn how to die, and perhaps also how to kill. . . .

> Time is long and man is in a rush, Child. . . .
> Time dies only to live forever
> And man does not know how to die
> Stop running son
> Your time will catch up with you!

*
**

To remain there waiting to be caught. . . . Perhaps it was the voice of wisdom. But is it wise to be wise at the age when ardent passion is the greatest reserve of energy, the most readily available sap of life, and when waiting is almost fatal?

Had he been a warrior in Madjo's sense, Lem would have offered the kinds of actions that kill or give life as the only alternative. But he wasn't, not yet, and his only action was flight, a half-measure. . . . But, in the end, is flight not the action of a warrior to the extent that it saves life and gains time to rethink strategy?

He had fled the city for the village, in order not to stupidly obey the injunctions of his navel and the movements of the starving-sheeplike-crowds who had pushed him to crawl in front of the Machine, to ask for droplets and to sanction the debasement that kills the awareness of shame and of mockery forever.

And now, these convulsions shaking his navel were rather promising for an opening up, for an evolution. . . . But let us listen to him. . . .

*
**

"The convulsions would catch me right in my navel again, every time the radio gave the list of those deserters-turned-white, and I'd hold my breath. The list seemed interminable, and every name sounded like that of my professor. My support. My state of mind. My model. My pillar. He wasn't going to succumb! He wasn't going to be infected!

At the end of the broadcasts I could breathe again! He was standing tall, an incorruptible rock. Eternity opened up before me. . . .

Three moons. Five moons. I no longer felt my navel. I was almost completely saved, no longer addicted to the droplets, the shock was covered by scar tissue.

I began to paint. . . . I wanted to create an 'oeuvre,' bring it to fruition, the birth of something divine.

It seemed to me that if I were to succeed in molding a thought, a specific dream, and if I were to find the strength to remain on my feet long enough to complete a painting of power and beauty, then some part of me would always remain upright, even if the guardian-oeuvre were to be torn away from me. . . .

But you must be rich to create a great work, rich in something that brings exaltation, that invigorates and empties you out suddenly, or perhaps very slowly and gently. Something you smell, see, taste, hear, or touch, and that is so enormous and so strong that it hurts too much if you cannot share it. . . . It seemed to me that wealth of that sort and generosity were the secret of creation. . . .

If I had a few impulses of generosity, some incomprehensible desires and instincts of which I was ashamed, I was rather poor in that particular kind of wealth. Perhaps I hadn't looked at death enough, or seen enough of life. Surely I hadn't suffered enough, shouted enough, nor felt enough joy. I was impoverished where great feelings and madly assumed sensations were concerned, and so I had nothing to share. I needed to enrich myself. . . . And quickly, too! Discover something astonishing to tell, to give. Something that would be born inside me like a divinity: with a snap of my fingers, the bursting of a dewdrop on a taro leaf, the blossoming of a gaze that discovers and recognizes. . . . Just like that, miraculously. . . . And why not?

For five moons I was watching every face, every seashell, every leaf, every sound and rhythm, all the fluctuations of the continent: stillborn empires, greedy colonels with big hearts, salvation of the peoples' councils, vampire-generals, and the fall of eagles. . . . For five moons I worked ceaselessly on my sketch. One evening, our aunt, who wouldn't take her eyes off me, cried out: 'My word! This really is one of those pieces that will never get done! So, have you decided to leave us yet?'

It was the following day that I left you. . . .

I took a train. . . .

The train that belongs to those others who come from a square piece of land. A parcel of land of which the edges are eaten away, lacking the *okoumé* forests of Gabon and the cedars of Lebanon, a bit of land at the other end of the sea, with plenty of Overseas Territories that have no sea as their frontier. A kernel of land that spurts forth a mass of 'volunteers for progress,' who go off to the four corners of the world with science and God in their pockets, weapons in hand, to bring the civilization of History and the prestige of Culture to the world's clans. Like soap balls of steel, they land in Bangui, in N'Djamena. . . . And the train goes on. . . .

The 'giants of the forests,' the 'powerful of the villages,' and the 'wise men of the people' collapse in its path: two thousand hectares a year! Two thousand hectares without any monuments, any dates, without a History, without Culture, without Civilization. . . . Two thousand hectares a year where seasons counted only in terms of sowing and harvesting. And you wouldn't speculate on monuments but on life, knowing that life, which is a monument, is eternal and manages without any dates. . . .

I took a train dated from the birth of Christ. I wanted to start counting my age, my time, and to date my new life: 'The year one of the loans. . . . ' But they declared that my age was the age at which Christ had died! Two thousand years of dreams of heaven and a seat to the right of the throne. A hundred thousand periods of Judas and of inquisitions. *One more time* of the secrets of confession delivered to Polichinelle. . . .

I took their train. I wanted to see other faces, other seashells, other sounds of bells. . . . I went far away, as far as the bumpy train would go. And I tried to stay as close as possible to everything my eyes were able to see. And one night I saw them. . . . Caught red-handed in the act of plunder. In their bumpy train, they fertilized and aborted the Overseas Territories, just as the interests of their parcel of homeland dictated. They would seat and invest emperors, then drive them away from the right side of the throne. They would carve authentic-imitation-thrones for themselves, which they'd deliver to the plundering mercenaries. They would transmute men into straw and would burn them up in a bonfire. And the train would go on. . . . I was late by two thousand years, and I had gotten off to a bad start! The train went on. . . .

And still I was looking for my stunning piece: the birth of a divinity, 'the impossible' for my sketch. My eyes popping, my lips tight, my ears cocked, my heart pulsating, my head on fire, my body tossed around by the jostling roll of their hellish train, my self-portrait! My first painting. . . .

And then one morning, the miracle: I saw! I saw its birth. . . . Just like that . . . from a whisper in the hollow of a shoulder, I saw a divinity being born.

Their train had decimated all the giants, the powerful and the wise, swept them off the surface of the continent, it had castrated all the males and taken possession of all the women, and now it was raining soot on the decaying world. And all the fires had been put out, we were sure of that! I named Bipol!

But persistent embers were smoldering in the ashes of the men of straw. There was a wondrous integrity in his man's warmth and his faith in his countrymen, Bipol-Lynx-Eye, who had decided to conquer pollution, corruption, by not offering men a grimace any more and a revolting caricature, but rather a fine smile, a lovely image, a word of truth. The men from here were all too accustomed to ugliness, and not a single horror would have made them tremble. . . .

Bipol, survivor of the fire of straw, ghost of the shipwreck engendered by the longest straw man's reign: a quarter of a century of double dealing!

Bipol, the diamond that no filth corrodes, the light that no contamination can tarnish. . . .

He was burning and shining with that strength and that lucidity that only integrity secures. His warmth was radiant, gave hope back to the ashes, gave life to the earth. His light emerged irresistibly, and the darkness moved aside to make room.

Yes, I saw him being born just like that, one morning, without any apparent effort, he was born from the wink of an eye. And I exclaimed: 'Just in time. Before nature dies and all beings fade away, before corruption smothers all dignity forever, just in time!' And it seemed I heard a chorus pick it up: 'Just in time. . . . '

Then he, Bipol, spoke. And he said: 'I am the son of Truth and of Love. The blood of your yearnings flows through my veins. It can neither fail nor tell lies. You can count on me, I have faith in you.'

But a nameless voice murmured: 'We shall kill you. . . . ' I must obstruct his path!

So that, if I rise and paint my story without notes, my failures of a hundred different dates and my hopes of a single morning, you who are listening to me will not start to say again that everything is always too old or too young where the black people live, on the oldest land of the oldest monkey skeletons. . . .

Because now that I have already been working desperately for five moons on my sketch and keeping my senses opened wide. . . .

Now that I have seen a divinity be born, I think there is nothing left to add to my drawing. I'll just emphasize the curve of the leaf, right there underneath the right foot of the divinity, to allow the eye to see both the inside and the outside of the leaf at the same time. . . . "

Lem, oh my brother! When you soar, you make me understand the sadness of my petty destiny all the more, surrendered as it is to the contingencies of laws as unavoidable for the average person as gravity, as karma. . . . How can I follow you in your flights when I am already obstructing my imagination from fear of hearsay? For, indeed, how would I manage if they treated me like a crazy person, as they did with you? You, you come out of it already grown, crowned with the title of artist! Me, I'd probably croak in a padded cell! That's why I always have to make an effort to understand your words in a language my logic can fit into. . . .

I think I understand this period corresponded for you to the "peaceful change that had taken place at the head of the neighboring State," when there appeared a man believed to be nothing more than a straw heir, meant to perpetuate the system of their Machine, without anything new, without any opening on the horizon. . . .

But he, Bipol, had spoken. And he stirred a hope believed to have been forever entombed, and once again men began to dream of "liberalization," of "democracy," of "participation," "moralization," "responsibility," and of "rigor"—watchwords proclaiming that which they were quick to call "renewal." . . .

And you, you had grown so excited that you were building the large outlines of this renewal by the mere power of your thinking. You were reconstructing a door of surprises in every town as in your kingdoms of dreams to favor discovery, invention, creativity, and to allow human beings to better liberate their energies in the service of something greater than their own personality. . . . Something that would elevate them to serve a nation, a continent, a planet, and that would break through the self-centered dams installed by the straw men who served the oppressor, served the enemy of man. . . . If only you had political power, my brother! But perhaps your only power and your only duty were those of creating dreams for us, inviting us to make thinking the first act of creation, in the same solitude and deprivation as on that first day's dawn, in the before-thought, before-God era?

*
**

Son
There is Only One
And men believe themselves to be multiple
The Only One is always alone
And man flees his own nature
What can he do, the man who has never known loneliness
He who has never seen his own face
That face which is discovered only when alone in loneliness
Alone facing Oneself, the Only One. . . .
Bonds smother you
Guardians suck you dry
Friends let you get lost
Loves cheat you
As long as you have not discovered yourself
Unique in loneliness
Oneself facing one's only self
Alone facing the Only One. . . .

Sassouma snatched Sundjata's griot away from him. The Griot of Words of pure Air. The memory of time. His Eye, his Mouth, his Guardian. She snatched him and kept him out of his reach. . . .

In exile, alone, Sundjata had to look through his own eyes, speak through his own sound, his own gestures. He had to taste and judge by his own tongue and learned to moisten his own skin, while he also had to take care of his mother's skin, as well as of his younger half brother and friend, Manding-Bori. He learned to champ the bit and see himself ruminate. He learned to die and then was able to kill. . . . The king who had welcomed him in exile taught him how to handle weapons and revealed the secret of Fire to him: the Fire of the Will, the will to live and to die, to be reborn, to take away and to give life. The will to know and to know himself. . . .

Thus, everything one can receive from nature was given him. The rest was merely a matter of conquest. . . .

Do you see why the stepmother who torments the frail orphan is the best of all initiators?

And, alone in his torment, Sundjata received that which nature gives to that being alone who has seen the Only One, who has seen himself. . . .

He became a man. . . .

The rest was merely a matter of conquest.

And conquest is the business of man. . . .

And Lem, standing before the Voice that created men and divulged History at will, became a man, for he achieved his first conquest. And as conquests go, it certainly was one: while he was fighting to emerge from the torpor in which he was stuck because of his refusal to have feelings he deemed improper, a kind of veil tore open before his eyes, and he saw himself feeble on the ground, grandmother Sogolon's gaze setting him on fire and telling him he was an unworthy son! He simply said: "It's all right, Mother. I tell you that today I shall walk. Let them bring me a stick. Today I shall walk." And as the veil closed over his vision again, he saw Madjo with her eyes of every day, Madjo who seemed to be waiting for him to rise at last, as in the olden days. He leaped up and grasped his rope of umbilical danglings as if to renew his first step taken one day way back then, at the dawn of time. . . .

And he tells me that at that exact moment he felt an energy that could have made him jump as high as the top of the maternity-tree, but other impulses came back to cloud his view! Despite everything, he wanted to fight for success, since conquest is the business of man and he was feeling his birth as a man. . . . So he persisted. . . .

"I must manage, just for once, my god! I must make it! I must at least succeed in casting one bridge in this life of mine that's been nothing but a casting of failed bridges. I must reach the top of this *karité* tree and tie my rope way up high. My rope-cross of umbilical strands, my stranded-rope of crosses, my cross of strands. . . . Damn! Anyway! I have to go further, try harder, climb higher, I have to manage that. . . .

I cannot have lived an entire life without one single action, without one single thing brought to fruition. . . . I cannot have failed to cast a single bridge between myself and one act, between one act and the next. I have to succeed. . . .

My rubbing against the trunk of the *karité* has torn my clothes, and I feel bits of bark on my skin, between my legs, on my belly, and surely I am bleeding, but no matter! I have to succeed.

The rope tied around my hips pulls me down, things never change! There's always an umbilical cord pulling us down! A stake of support that makes us crawl instead of raising us up to the sky! I must have been a breech birth and I would not be surprised if my mother fornicated with a pig or a duck! It would explain why the direction of my tendencies leads downward to stagnant ponds. But today I shall go upward, I want to go up, I have to manage that much. . . .

Today I'm aiming at the heights, and it is I who shall elevate abysses to crests. I am pulverizing my dirt in the wind and filling the ground with fresh air. When I balance on my rope, when I fall, I won't touch dirt anymore, I'll fly away. Flush with the ground, sure, at my own level, but it will be a flight all the same! I have to manage that. . . .

There! Now I'm tying my rope to this branch, this beautiful and solid branch.

Hurrah!

Didn't I say I would boost my frailty up to the clouds. Perhaps it will embellish me and become strength. . . . Now I have to go down, to find the air again, Grandmother's voice, which I no longer hear this high up, Grandmother's voice, which doesn't reach the top of the *karité* but which I want to extend, send forth toward the sun through my own last cry. She must be heard by every ear in the world. . . .

Descend but not fall! I must behave and guide myself, alone and straight toward the goal! My hands are torn to shreds, but what of it! I must hold up. I shall hold up down to my very bones! I have to manage that.

There.

I'm on the ground, one action completed!

Sure, my hands are ossified and don't want to open. Sure, my legs don't want to carry me anymore, are buckling under me. But I have time. . . .

And Grandmother? And her voice? Where did they go? I only hear the echo now, all I see is the reflection of my dirty face. I feel bits of my cord-cross slither down my back, and on my tongue there is the bitter taste of a slow death-struggle. . . . I take my time, the time my legs need to recover from their numbness and do my bidding once again. And the final act shall be accomplished. I'll climb back up to the first branch of the *karité,* where my rope of cords stops. I'll make a noose, put it around my neck, and I'll jump into my ultimate flight. . . .

Where are you, Grandmother, you who know miracle-medicine? You could have soothed my fingers, my feet, and hurried to help me realize my plan. . . . I'm impatient now that I've had a taste of action. I'm in a rush to get started again. Where are you? I beg you, speak to me, speak to me some more. . . ."

*
**

Then Lem felt hands on his feet, and he understood why God had to lend a hand to create mankind. Is not the hand the symbol of creation? There is such power that comes through hands, and through hands alone. . . . Someone who has never been touched by a hand cannot be aware of his own life. The hand is necessary to reveal volume, weight, space, and difference. The hand is necessary to reveal the flesh replete with life. . . .

Grandmother touched his hand, and he knew he was still alive, and for the first time ever he wondered about the feeling of lifeless flesh, and he was afraid he wouldn't appreciate it when there would no longer be any hands to touch him. . . .

Big tears streamed down his cheeks. . . . This time he was weeping over the hands he had just discovered and would be losing. . . .

His legs were now completely relaxed, and he no longer felt any pain in his hands. Yet he stayed there, prone on the ground. . . .

There was still too much dirt in him, and he told himself he was not yet light enough to balance elegantly on the end of a rope. He still needed to weep more, to be drained of yet more liquid, to be emptied out. . . .

His sob filled his head and the entire universe, he thought. He could see the moment when the roaring of wild beasts, of thunder or the song of birds would be heard no longer! He wanted to see the effect of a sob.

But all he heard was Grandmother's voice, and he said to himself that the original sound probably couldn't have been a sob: creation would have miscarried for sure. . . . The original sound was a voice. A voice of deep vibrations, with multiple and continuous intonations like the music of the spheres. The sound had begun very softly, growing louder little by little, until nothing else existed beyond the sound itself. Everything emanated from it, just as at this moment he himself emanated from the sound. For a second time, he saw a very clear picture of himself. "I am a particle of sound and not a sob," he told himself, and he flowed more deeply into Madjo's sound-voice. . . .

*
**

Child of mankind stop your weeping
Stop your weeping I am covering you with my hands
I am touching you there where life enters into you
I am rubbing your fontanel through which you divide yourself
Stay here in your frozen flesh
Stay here and let me warm you

Love-across-a-Hundred-Lives

Stay with me and I shall sing to you with my hands
I shall sing you your penultimate life. . . .
You are born and you live
You contract debts
You pay a few of them
You die and you are passing through to the land of balance sheets
You do your accounts
And on your account you enter your own well-understood truth
You collect the dividends and you are reborn
But Son watch out for debts forgotten
You shall pay them upon distraint
Interest and principal
How carelessly you did them, little father, those accounts of yours
How little time you took
You threw yourself precipitously ahead
Yesterday like today
You haven't stopped running
And life ran along with you
One never does escape from it
You are always reborn where you stopped living
If you die hanging from a tree
You shall be reborn underneath that tree and pay your forgotten debts. . . .
Stop your weeping little father
Every dead thing goes off to live again
That's the way it always is with the advent of the child foretold
That's how it was before the birth of Roumben. . . .
Before
In secret
Not so very long ago. . . .

Before . . . in Secret . . .
Not So Very Long Ago . . .

It was a long time ago that Nyobè-Nyum had gained possession of the Axe-that-slices and the Curved-cane, and that he had influenced the affairs of the Seizers with all his wisdom. But he couldn't find the inner peace that was his right. And yet . . .

He was the husband of a golden woman, Gol, as her name implied. . . . Sweet and firm, brilliant and modest, simple and profound, beautiful and intelligent, all at the same time!

She had given the nine sons indispensable for a guardian of the "Axe-that-slices" and the "Curved-cane." Nine sons to represent the nine clans of the Seizers. Nine sons who handled everything that shone and caused envy in those days. . . .

People spoke of exact sciences, public office, political science, institutes of higher learning, medicine, diplomacy, armed forces, and the priesthood. . . . It was a race to acquire the greatest number of degrees. . . .

But not one of Nyobè-Nyum's sons concerned himself with what he called "the Energy that makes the world go round." . . .

"They're driven by Energy like animals and plants. They're manipulated like marionettes, and they believe themselves to be real personalities," their father thought. "The man whose forehead bears the star is not born twice in a row to a same family, and real men leave no heirs behind," the Seizers said. These were words that collided with each other inside Nyobè-Nyum's head, and he did not find the peace that was his right. He was in despair night and day: he found no one to whom he could entrust the secret of the thousand-time secular Energy that he was burdened with having to pass on at any price, he who was its last trustee. Somewhere the chain had been broken, the world was in the process of evacuating its people and refilling itself with scarecrows operated by remote control. Wisdom is not the attribute of machines, after all!

The man had to be found. . . . And fast!
It is true.
The world is never as ugly as in those times of the world's end
When men resemble robots
And women look like magpies!
The physician of official medicine who arrives first does not stop this putrefaction.
There are world endings like fields slashed and burned
They enrich the soil with their ashes
And restore what they have consumed
But . . .
The first blacksmith to arrive
Does not transmute the robots' steel and plastic into humus. . . .
That Oeuvre is reserved for the Masters of Energy
And there was not one among the sons of Nyobè-Nyum. . . .

Seated with his back against his *mbènda,* Nyobè-Nyum was talking with a crowd of children in his interior courtyard. On certain days, he was expected to play teacher, which he did with rare enthusiasm. He was always hoping that in the group he would find the promised child, who would relieve him of the secret and let him live at last. . . . "Pépère, like everyone else." At the age of forty he had to start giving serious thought to such things, with the shortened life expectancy in underdeveloped countries!

He could not really live lightheartedly, burdened as he was with the knowledge that he himself was the only one responsible for the secret.

Often he would gaze intensely into the eyes of a child, as if to recognize his soul. Sometimes his muscles froze, and such great anguish would issue forth from him that the children became immobilized, the birds grew silent, and flies fell to the ground dead. . . .

At such moments, Gol would always come running. She alone seemed capable of bringing life back to him. Her voice was the music of the spheres, and her gaze two drops of light.

"My one true friend," she'd say to Nyobè-Nyum, "you knew that the promised child would be a 'son from the heart of the land,' and you chose to get married. You also knew that it is you, yourself, who must sire him, and yet you keep looking for him elsewhere. . . . Why do you delude yourself? Why do you recoil?"

Nyobè-Nyum's eyelashes were flickering painfully, and a weak smile unclenched his cheeks. It was true that he knew all this. This time, the promised child was not to be born within a family. But his love for Gol was too great not to have married her. . . . And since then he had refused to go off and look elsewhere, if only to sire the promised child! He had begun to pray that someone else would beget the Rainbow. Alas! There were only robots, and the "Rainbow Pillar of the Seizers" was to be a child of man or was not to be at all!

And somewhere a young virgin was awaiting . . . the seed. . . .

As soon as the smile returned to Nyobè-Nyum's face, the birds began to sing again, flies began to take off, and the children began to play once more: they would utter proverbs, mimic stories, imagine different worlds, laugh, and time would quietly vanish. . . .

When evening fell, Nyobè-Nyum had the feeling that he had only had time to blink. . . . Another day without any action. . . .

Yet, he knew this very well: in order to copulate with action as to copulate with life one had to begin by accepting. Accepting himself and carrying his own weight, doing violence to himself, desecrating himself. . . . True gymnastics, an ascesis. . . . And action is born from the fertilization of oneself with the self. And luck lifts every ambiguity and unburdens the frail shoulders that have carried it this way to full term, throughout the difficult days.

Luck is energy's eldest daughter. . . .

*
**

And Lem, too, had his luck, he was deeply convinced of this. His idol continued to hold out firmly, not to go begging on his belly for his daily dose of droplets from the Machine.

Six months already! And he was exultant.

"I no longer remembered fear. I was walking vertically, with something close to 360-degree vision."

Three more moons and he would be a man: he would know where we had slipped, why we had fallen. He would know how to rid us of the Drop-by-Drop-Machine. He would know what else might be put in its stead. He'd know the shrewd vocabulary of the green berets and the red helmets. He'd know the weight of stripes and medals, the value of titles and diplomas. . . .

"As a result, I began to write. I wanted to do a cesarean on words and pull a living child from them, capable of relaying a secret, the meaning of words. I wanted to listen more closely to these guiding-words to which I clung: revolution, initiation, evolution, development. . . . I was imagining a great change that would turn everything upside down and inside out, even enrich perceptions, a new beginning that would cause the dewdrop to burst open as for the birth of a divinity. A road that would open itself before everyone, requiring only that one start to walk! And since we would put one foot in front of the other, on our own, and start anew, we would no longer be the same after every step. It would be a new being who added a new step to the one that had come before. . . . A Master! What I needed was a Master. Someone who would already know because he had tried it out. . . . "

And Lem had walked and walked and walked. . . . As long as his feet could carry him, and they had carried him to the threshold. . . . He'd been told: "He knows, he'll know what to tell you. The meaning of the word, the cause of the word, and you, you will be the one who won't know how to write."

So Lem had met the little old man. . . .

"He smelled good, the little old man, and he took away your anxiety about growing old. His look was lively and profound, his voice soft and precise: 'Hee, hee, hee!' he was laughing maliciously. 'Revolution? But. . . . That's leaving, making the rounds and coming back to the starting point. . . . Hee, hee, hee! Initiation? That's looking, listening, doing. . . . Hee, hee, hee! Evolution? That's beginning again, leaving again, with a new thrust. . . . Well then, go for it! But. . . . You must begin. . . . '"

And he was watching a bewildered Lem and laughing with tears in his eyes. . . . Begin What? To speak? To write? Was it really he who would give birth to the Meaning of the Word?

On this the oldest of lands with the oldest of monkey skeletons and with nations less than a year old.

On this land where they talk about the rendezvous of giving and receiving and where they put down their signature in the name of *métissage.*

You who are reading me, I bet you'd say with all the others:

"Down with racism! Let the oppressed be liberated! Let all injustice be suppressed! Oh, how courageous they are those blacks! Just put yourself in their place! All they've suffered! With that limited capacity of theirs, you know. . . . It's quite something! Give them a very high mark."

I bet you'd no longer tell a black person: "You're a jerk, my friend, go to hell!"

I bet that you'd smile at him, your lips tight, full of consent, then mumble behind his back: "Damn! He can go eat his own shit!" And while covering him with praises, prizes, titles, and medals, you'd quietly cheat him out of grey matter and raw materials, even if you had to swim with him in his shit. Money has no smell, neither does power. But conscience has one, and, for it to be good, you'd tell yourself that it is for handling that blasted touchiness of the blacks. . . .

So if Lem were writing our life without History, the History of our life with its thousands of stories, performing a cesarean on every word . . . wouldn't you also be saying that History is never old enough for these vindictive blacks who never stop lamenting a History that's gone, and who do nothing but sing and paint the same old story, twenty years after the independences?

At a time when all of humanity is turning toward our people and telling it: "It's your turn to suckle us, your turn to open our eyes for us, your turn to show us the Way. . . . "

Do you think Lem would have a painless delivery?

Cesarean!

And to find strength, Lem cried out

"Help, Ziworé with tiger's feet tracking and scratching words without disabling them
Help, refuge of the days jumbled by words!"

And he had only two moons left to go. . . . No more than two moons!

I really believe it had made his beard grow, from virility, and that he'd grown his last few inches toward manhood, greatness, and a towering vision. During that period, just think of it!

He was finally going to understand "communism," "socialism," "capitalism," "protectionism," "conscientism," "spiritism," all those fascinating words that Ziworé scattered around to dance in his classes and that completely escaped Lem. At last he was going to understand them, in practice. Ziworé's resistance would better disclose their mechanics to him. He was going to understand through the pedagogical power of example. . . . He would understand, choose, adapt, re-create.

He already understood that the drop was quite simply the virus of fear. He who deprived himself of it would no longer feel the convulsive shivers on his neck and in his guts. . . . His large navel was going to re-enter the secret dungeons of his calmed entrails, for with Ziworé's victory fear would die.

How lucky he was! Isn't the person who sees the living example a hundred times more privileged than he who hears the myth? And he, he would see Ziworé with his own eyes.

He would see him walk strong
Straight toward abdication
Without bending without breaking
Walk strong under the blows

Straight toward intimidation. . . .

"You'll fast and forgo the drops without losing an ounce of your pride
You'll write 'No' on the forehead of your disciples
You'll paint proud steps onto their feet
Head high gaze clear gestures precise without any ambiguity
I shall see you with my own eyes Ziworé
Stronger than myth
Ziworé the incorruptible. . . ."

And he was reliving that exaltation lost since then, like one of the innumerable paths of flight. . . . But Grandmother's voice was imposing itself more and more like a vise, withdrawing him from his gentle inertia and subjecting him to a rhythm in which inattentiveness might become murderous, simply because important clues might pass him by unnoticed and leave him once again at the door of his own meanderings. . . . He decided to pull himself together and follow the thread, without fail. . . .

*
**

Was it not time then for everyone to play his role
Should gold not shine
The ring not embellish
And the finger not point. . . .
The ring is a question of environment
Tell me which is yours and I shall tell you who you are. . . .
So she was there, our Londè
Ring of pure gold which Gol had molded at the time of her infancy.

It was her very last sister, who had survived only by the miracle of her love. The mother had died in childbirth, and the desperate father had decided that, if the child survived, she would not marry: she would stay here to birth the boys destined to perpetuate the name of the Um, those boys her mother had not had the time to make. . . . You know how this happened among the Seizers, don't you? The girl so designated was free to choose her companion or companions. The children would bear her father's name and belong to his clan, even if everyone knew who had sired them. . . . Sons and nephews of the same clan, these children were called "children of the heart of the land." They were considered to be different personalities who came to resuscitate a dying branch. Among them, the greatest men who caused their world to evolve could be recognized. Remember Sénd Biok, Chaka. . . . Did they not create the very idea of a great nation?

And so Gol had finished her part of the work: she had raised the pure gold ring virgin–Light of *Mawu,* the receptacle carved to be the setting for the child of mankind.

Great men are spirit-ideas that take shape inside the bodies of great women.

The child is worth what its mother is worth
Have I told you that before, Child?
Thus she was there the one they were awaiting
Londè-Um, Aïda-moonflower
Ring of pure rainbow light
She was there
And Da-Energy would be able to call back Njoo-Mbongo-Legba. . . .
She was there, she who awaited the spirit's egg.

And Nyobè-Nyum was praying before the altar-of-the-departed.

"Yes, I know. I have chosen a wife. You had destined me for something more powerful and perhaps more beautiful. . . . But it was too abstract for me. I have chosen Love, and love has flourished. The harvest has been beyond expectation. I have enjoyed all man's joys and I bring you my gratitude. But I still have the Secret, and it is burning me, it hums inside my blood. Why can I not have the joy of passing it on? Is not that joy a part of the joys of man?"

"Man who chose Love
Why do you need to be inspired by anything other than love?
Should not love be the source of all inspiration, of all strength, and of all action?" replied the voices of the dead. . . .

And Nyobè-Nyum looked at himself head on, naked, for the first time. He saw again Gol's gestures, he heard her voice, reviewed her acts, and he understood that he had never invested enough in his love. So he could not ask everything of it. He had lived the Secret, he had only fed the obsession of the Secret, and the Secret had obstructed his sight and his path. He had not even seen that Gol had shared his love and his Secret from the first day onward. He had not understood that love really had wrought the miracle and that the harvest had gone well beyond the most marvelous of dreams. Gol had given him every joy of man and brought him every joy in existence. He could fulfill himself and realize his destiny.

A light poured from his heart, and he felt Gol's hand seeking his. He took it and there they met, before the departed dead. . . . Nyobè-Nyum accepted himself for the first time, both action and luck were going to be part of his being from now on.

Nevertheless, he waited five days before setting out. . . . Five man days he took upon himself to be silent and to be light itself inside the light of consciousness. Five days of fasting and purification, his heart and his belly wide open, pecked at by the rays of awareness.

And he was ready, the awaited one. . . .
He who steals fire
He who crosses through time
One step in space
One step in the spirit
He who had to hand it over. . . .

"Those-who-call-the-Spirit" were standing before the "Great Judgment"
"*Um Ram Am*!" the flowers intoned

"*Ziri é dum Zri*!" the birds took over
"*Ki fou ki ra*!" answered the stones

The clouds were superimposed over each other in a skillful ballet of emotions, illuminated by a thousand lightning bolts.

Two rainbows crossed each other in the sky and linked the four cardinal points.

Everything was only color and song.

Um Ram Am, Ziri é dum Zri, Ki fou ki ra, Ommm. . . .
Sounds and songs
Thus it was for his conception
And thus for his birth
Until the moment of his first cry which retrieved all singing
They named him "ROUMBEN"
"THE RAINBOW PILLAR"

Who would be the cornerstone of the Great Architect's building in this wild forest.

The Child promised to the Seizers, who was to bring knowledge, consciousness, and freedom to the four corners of the black lands. . . .

*
**

What was that moistness there underneath Lem's feet? A placenta that had come loose from his rope of umbilical cords. . . .

A placenta like the one in which he was born at the zenith of the night.

Like a chick inside an egg!

His mother had literally laid him with a hen's alacrity. . . .

And Gol the midwife—his aunt, my sister—had to open the placenta with a kitchen knife under the light of an oil lamp, a feeble light of hope at midnight. . . . This sensation of wetness on his feet. . . . The same feeling that had made him give his first incantation-cry then, and the same disgust that his nth cry of fear always calls forth in him and still does to this day; the cry of fear that forces Madjo to raise her voice, speed up the rhythm, and tirelessly pursue the story, their History. . . .

Naturally, after he'd been weaned the child was entrusted to his father-grandfather to learn to speak as a Seizer should. . . . However, since Roumben's first chant-cry, his voice had never been heard again! Every specialist had examined him and they unanimously agreed: the child was not mute. . . . If he was not speaking, if he was not crying, it was because he did not want to! He watched, he listened, but said nothing. Undoubtedly, he already knew that the kola shell doesn't crack before it's ripe and ready to deliver its treasure. . . . In a culture where the word is the only art and the intrinsic demonstration of any creativity, could the future Pillar allow himself any chatter?

His gaze made people uncomfortable: red like glowing embers, protuberant, piercing things and beings.

His ears stood out and were taut like radars. . . . He heard everything and understood. He was called and he came. He was asked to do some work and he accomplished it. But when he was asked a question, he countered it with his gaze, and too bad for those who could not interpret this. Doubtlessly, he had spoken too much in his earlier lives: his mouth was large, the lips still swollen from the effort. . . . His lips remembered! They remembered every venomous word, every mealy-mouthed word, all the flattering words overblown with illusions and pretentions. They remembered wheedling words used to mollify and put to sleep, all those that slam, beg, run away, flow by, and have never created a single thing!

Never again would these lips open for anything! They wouldn't make any pointless efforts again; they were healing now and thinking in stillness. And the more the child grew, the less swollen they became, curling delicately now like fertilized flower petals, ready to bear fruit.

And because he did not speak, Roumben was forgotten in the end. To such a point that nobody remembers his childhood, nobody saw him grow up. The sorcerers, on the lookout for "the growing man," "the man to be brought down," thus to equalize all by the lowest standard, even they no longer remembered the promised Child, symbol of the end of sordid regimes! Do you see why they say he was born old, his mouth filled with teeth, with white hair and skin as tough as a crocodile's. . . .

Yet, he followed old Um everywhere, carrying his "bag of knowledge," but he was so self-effacing that everything was said and done in his presence as if he did not exist. Of course, he was circumcised when he was twelve, as he had to be; of course, he hurled the "spears of Ngué" with just the "correct" movement, enough not to fail and yet not enough to be noticed. Of course, he went to school and obtained a "diploma," but a literate mute does not create much of a stir!

During the holidays, when he was not in the fields or at the assemblies with old Um, he would spend long hours with his mother, Londè-Um, and his aunt Gol Nyobè. She would tell him the genealogy, the epics, and the mythology of his tribe, as well as the songs and proverbs. He would listen with closed eyes as if to absorb the sound and rhythm better. . . .

During the "exploits of youth" at puberty, he shone by his absence and did not awaken any lustful desires in girls, who forgot him completely.

The day he turned twenty-one, his father-grandfather called him in to show him his piece of land, where he was to build the house of his manhood and envision the future. What was he going to do? What was he planning on doing? Would he work in the city with the government? Would he settle in the village to enlarge the plantation, now that the exportation of cash crops was growing by leaps and bounds? Although it was pointless to suggest new professions to him that would require the use of speech: buyer of products, carrier of products, interpreter or delegate of the people. . . .

"Delegate of the people, that is to say a deputy. . . . Why not? Delegate of the Seizers. . . . Speak for them, speak on their behalf, speak about them. . . . Yes, why not?"

Those were his first words, spoken in a firm voice, deep, clear, as if he had always spoken! Old Um's legs buckled! Roumben had to push a bench toward him so that he wouldn't fall. He sat down and looked the young man full in the face as if he were seeing him for the first time.

It really was the first time that he saw him as he truly was and not as he had wanted to show himself. Until that day, he had been seen as a total mute: mute in body, mute in feeling and language, mute in spirit. One of those disabled people you don't want to look at, the way you don't want to look at the great void for fear of growing dizzy, afraid of that impetuous call that pushes you toward the unknown. . . . The unknown territory of feelings impossible to take on: pity, love. . . . Or simply the unknown of embarrassing feelings: attraction, desire for the invalid! How many people are able to assume that comfortably? So you lower your eyes, you speak awkwardly, you act tactlessly, you see in a blur. And so it was that he had shown himself or had kept himself hidden. But here, suddenly, old Um found himself facing another man: tall, impressive in his calm and his imposing presence. He had an open look, firm and sure gestures, and a will as strong as iron that seemed to spring from his entire being, his breath, his aura. . . .

And for the first time, too, old Um thought of Roumben's sire. As you well know, the sire does not count for much among the Seizers. The father is he who accepts and raises a child. The problem of the sire arises only when the child is not accepted and someone is needed to insure an inheritance for him: a piece of land, a name, a clan. . . . But that was not the reason old Um was thinking of Roumben's natural father. He was the last one of those who knew the name of the trustee of the Secret. He also knew that Nyobè-Nyum was his grandson's sire. In the beginning, he had kept an eye on him to find out whether he would transmit the Secret. It might have been to his own advantage and earned him a bit more respect in the "Assembly of wise men."

But no one ever saw father and son together. Of course, it had been noticed that Nyobè-Nyum was happier, more lighthearted, after Roumben had turned nine. But since there was no change whatsoever in the life of the boy, old Um no longer tried to approach him and came to the conclusion that Nyobè-

Nyum would never transmit the Secret to a natural son who did not bear his name and would therefore not carry that name on. You know very well, of course, that among these people survival is closely linked to name.

In the wink of an eye, it seemed to him that he was looking at the last guardian of the Secret right there before him, and the image of Nyobè-Nyum seemed to hover over the young man! That tension around the temples, that almost cadaverous motionlessness, that electric gaze. . . . Now that he was speaking, it was completely the voice of Nyobè-Nyum! Suddenly, old Um assumed the malady of muteness, but just thinking about that alone made him get up from the bench with a start and begin to pour out words in torrents like a river.

"Roumben! You're speaking! You know! You saw Nyobè! My God, how you've grown! You're a man! Deputy? But of course, since you speak now! Eh, but. . . . You're not married yet! And the lineage? And the name of the Um? Right. . . . I was going to suggest the youngest daughter of the Samick to you! That's the perfect one for a mute! Sweet, attentive, a hard worker, and pure. . . . "

"No!" Roumben said simply and went away.

Old Um stayed behind, delirious.

"The perfect one for a mute. . . . But he speaks! He has seen it, I could swear! Son of Nyobè! Evil serpent! And what about the name of Um?"

He was delirious for two days and one night. . . .

Curious, the impact of words on life, on humans. One word often is the key to a world, to a whole universe. It bounces off one cell in our memory, which contacts other cells that remember other facts, other pictures, and other words related to the first one. And here we are, inside a series of impressions, feelings, motions, and words, still others, and the journey could be continued indefinitely. And many of us live this way inside a chaotic bubbling of cellular infusion, imagining ourselves to be thinking. . . .

Is thinking not something different? Is that not a voluntary act, a formulation that precedes creation before it materializes, before it forms? Undoubtedly, this infusion, this jumble of feelings, was the before-God. . . . Then, one day, a name took shape, and a word was uttered. That was the birth of thought, and God was its name. And he began to formulate all these feelings, and he saw that it was good. That was the birth of the Word, and the Word became God.

At the very evocation of the word delirium, when Grandmother spoke of old Um, Lem tells me that he literally plunged into another, similar situation in which he wondered whether he was living in reality or in one of those overlapping spheres that made him delirious. . . .

Was it yesterday? Was it before or after? He only remembered there was just one more moon missing to complete the time he had bet on, the time he had given himself for restructuring, a time during which he still needed to lean on his idol, his support, his crutch.

Having nearly lost the habit of watching for the news hour with that obsession of the first months, he almost jumped at the solemnity of the announcer's voice and especially at the crowd amassing around the set, which had become unusual since then. He had missed the first part completely, and it was the second monster, rumor, that attracted his attention.

"You lost, my friend! You owe me a bottle of *koutoukou*! I don't know who is crazy to think that the man is ready to starve to death while the drops fall with the regularity of clockwork into the mouths of the biggest fools!"

And the radio had more to say. . . .

"Considering that the Drop-by-Drop-Machine has always been honest toward its faithful. . . . "

"Whoa! Me, Zézé, if I was in that there fancy university professor's place, I sure would find the same way of earning rations, *Walaï*!"

"Considering that every Drop-by-Drop-Machine in the area has dried up and that our neighbors are dying of hunger and thirst. . . . "

"Me, Moussa, I ain't gonna be put near that Sahel-Machine there to have my throat scratching under the sun, don't even think about it! Me just die!"

"Considering that the efforts put out by our Drop-by-Drop-Machine in order to insure the daily droplet-rations have been particularly effective: we have moved from a single million to ten times that many people receiving aid from our Machine in only thirty years since independence (which makes for a growth rate of a thousand percent), while even the most developed countries attain that record with difficulty in these times of economic crisis. . . . "

"Didn't I tell you that Radio Moscow announced this morning that imperialism had enlisted the chief-comrades into the counterrevolution!"

"Why don't you be quiet, we can't hear a thing!"

" . . . That such efforts can be rewarded only with fervent gratitude and that the least sign of recrimination is flagrant proof of lack of gratitude and a . . . "

"Me, Zézé, I tell ya, this is some fancy university French, not a mistake in there."

" . . . Will be stoned in public like evil adulterers. . . . "

"*Walaï,* they're crazy these intellectuals! Are they kidding, first they go on strike and then they come trembling like a chicken that's caught malaria?"

"Let us make amends for the greed we showed, the greed of mediocre, embittered malcontents. . . . "

"Wanna bet that there imperialism gave plenty plenty dollars to make a deal with that old Machine, cause otherwise that old thing is going to cut off the oil supply! Really and truly, that there Machine got power! Even White folks be beggin' it for them drops. . . . "

"Let us appeal to the legendary clemency of the Machine to forgive the prodigal sons one more time."

"Whadd' I tell ya! Cousin, I knowed it. I always do know! There, isn't that him, him too ask for droplets right there in that university?"

"You crazy, cousin?"

"Let us ask that it be turned on again. . . . the Droppp Drop-by-Drop-Machine. . . . For the good of everyone. . . . Signed: Ziboté, Zamara, Ziworé. . . . "

"NOOOOOOO!" Lem screamed while the announcer's voice, a woman's voice, concluded: "Ladies and gentlemen, this is the end of our evening broadcast, we wish you a very good night."

I do believe that Lem must have fainted somewhere during his trek. Oh yes, he couldn't resist the flight. . . . When he woke up, he noticed that he was lying in a ditch filled with squalid garbage. It was obvious that something was rotting away not far from him. He rose and tried to walk. But his legs no longer wanted to carry him, because he had crumpled again and knocked over a kind of garbage can. But rather than garbage, it was more something like meats, he noticed! As he looked around, he realized that he was in the backyard of the maternity clinic. And the meats in question were nothing other than placentas! An abundance of placentas dragging their long tails. . . . No, umbilical cords! What a weird destiny! To die in a pile of umbilical cords, for a man who had never managed to cut his own, this was justice for once!

Ah yes! He had just decided to die. Ziworé had fallen, and he couldn't live on his belly, and he couldn't stand up by himself, not yet. . . .

It was true. Lem had always needed a stake of support, as a heavily burdened banana tree needs support, as does a creeping plant. . . . Even as a child, when he was learning to walk, they had to tell him stories about strength so that he could feel them in his legs before he was able to walk! And when the story would leave his feet, he would fall. . . . Fortunately, Madjo was there. . . .

We had always heard it said around us that the pupil could not overtake the master, that the child had to follow his father, the wife her husband, the employee his boss. We receive an imposed assistance from the moment of conception on: to each his umbilical cord, to each his stake of support. We receive an education that aids us: to each his idol, his model. I didn't understand how some people succeeded in cutting the cord, in bypassing the model, in freeing themselves from any desire for assistance. Lem himself was still dragging his umbilical cord along. He had accepted the separation from his mother badly, he had not accepted a father who refused to be a model; he hadn't tolerated teachers who had nothing to teach us, smothering girls with dried-up chests. He hadn't accepted heroes who died before the victory because the storm that rips away the stake of support also knocks the banana tree down, whether it is ripe or not. . . . Heroes who die before the victory die as many times as their supporters do!

"Ziworé, you shall die twice. You shall know the dreadful second death of hell, you who denied me the ninth moon. Through my death your name shall be forever forgotten and your soul will never again have any rest. Ziworé! Damned among damned heroes! You who tore off my umbilical cord before my navel could form a scar, you will drink shame for the rest of your life from my decayed navel, hung from all the other cords that I wasn't able to cut . . . ," Lem was grumbling. Fortunately, Madjo's voice managed to cover his rancor and his bitterness and to open worlds to him in which beauty had existed because people had refused to become mired in the chaotic jumble of unformulated things. . . .

*
**

The day that Roumben spoke for the first time
Son of my son
I who now speak to you I was there
The coconut trees became simple palm trees
Palm trees were transformed into coconut trees
It did not rain on that day
There was barely any sunshine
The Whites who were ploughing our pathways scorched all their cigarettes. . . . And they began to smoke bamboo twigs
The day he spoke
I who now speak to you I was there, Cha cha!

The day that Roumben laughed for the first time
Female elephants surpassed each other in giving birth
Antelope were urged to do the swaddling
The Whites who were ploughing our pathways emptied their cartridges in baobab trees while monkeys were pissing on their flat hair
The day that he laughed, I who smile at you now, I was there, Cha cha!
His first words were for the Seizers
His first words were for the tribe
He who does not know how to organize a tribe
Would he have more knowledge of building a nation?
His first resounding thoughts were for the nation
Oceans would not exist if the sources had not existed

When old Um had come back to his senses and called for Roumben to ask him to confirm his plans, the latter simply said:

"When I spoke and the wind took my words away
I Roumben
Should I have to run after the wind through the forest to catch them again?"

Son of my son
I speak to you of the ram crashing through the brush
And the sheep following him close on his heels
I speak to you of the hummingbird waking the panther
And the panther erupts without seeing the culprit. . . .
Listen to the story of the dwarf ant
Who penetrates the elephant's trunk
And the elephant struggles in vain
And the elephant hangs his spoon. . . .
The day that he spoke for the first time
I who speak to you now I was there, Cha cha!
And since he spoke and the wind took his words away
He stuck by them
Since he spoke it was thus

The tribe walked behind him
The women and children walked in front
Holding high the torch
You know that the elephant does not walk with the young behind him
The peoples sang Roumben
Din-of-Nyobè-Nyum
Gorilla-marked-with-a-white-spot
Stinging-nettle-bean-no-bare-hand-will-touch
Thorny-liana-no-serpent-will-crawl-up
Foaming-waterfall
Humming-bell
Sonorous-drum-of-great-days
When he spoke son of my son
A fight of serpents would take place between action and word
Since he spoke and kept his word
I who speak to you can draw you his word-actions
Since I was there, Cha cha!"

"And I, Lem Liang Mianga. . . .
If only I were there to help with the metamorphosis
With all the lucidity and all the distance
Needed to observe analyze synthesize re-create. . . .
If only I were there to see the coarse trunk of the palm tree
Launch forth and become the svelte beam of a coconut tree
If only I were there to surprise the secret of a veritable mutation
To know it and to understand it at last
To teach it and to transmit it
See Madjo how I am being transformed. . . .
My body is becoming lighter my heart more firm my head more open. . . .
I am going through a metamorphosis without quite understanding why. . . .
I am on the inside of the metamorphosis
And the nape of the neck refuses to see itself

And the heel refuses to walk in front
If I live again what shall I teach the children
And if I die what shall I say in the great beyond?
I am in the fullness of metamorphosis
I no longer feel my navel
And my skin no longer crawls in convulsive shudders

I have dissociated myself from the trembling little boy inside me who used to clasp his hands together between his legs to repress his fear, the fear of being discovered when a simple look would come in his direction. . . . I remember him: how I used to hate him! How I used to detest him there inside me! His instability, his unfaithfulness, his indescribable shortcomings, my ignorance about any lived and true feeling that stabilizes. . . . So. . . . So I invented a beautiful life for myself passionately tied to a dreamworld being, you, Madjo. . . .

I hated all those incomplete beings who had participated in the sharing of bread crumbs: they had received a crumb here, a crumb there, this one a bit of goodness, a bit of loyalty, that one a crumb of wealth, of generosity, yet another a crumb of intelligence, a crumb of power. . . . But nobody had received enough crumbs to make a whole bread!

So I would construct miraculous beings who had everything and were true lords, filled with compassion and love, wealth and power. Hearts and heads would open up as they passed. People would smile at them, admire them, respect them, love them. And inside the head of the trembling little boy I would sketch the story of these lords whom he would have loved with a divided love.

It is true. . . .
I have always wanted to be tall and handsome
I have always dreamed of being faithful and overflowing with love
Passionately and everlastingly in love
I have always wanted to be immensely rich
And royally generous

Love-across-a-Hundred-Lives

I have always wished for the authority and power
To render justice, to protect, to give and to serve
And it seemed to me I had once before been all of those at once.

But what then was I doing here inside the skin of a trembling little child? A trembling little boy born poor in the midst of poverty, with cursed parents barely earning a living wage who weren't even sure they were his true progenitors. . . . You know perfectly well, Madjo, that if you hadn't been there. . . . And I hated that little trembling child inside me, headstrong, obtuse, who was determined in his desire to appear handsome, rich, great, and beloved, even if it meant pilfering everything, running after each new face, shadows of love or power, giving himself with his heart and body wide open. . . . He had no knowledge of either good or evil, he only knew the pretty picture I would tirelessly paint and repaint for him. And sometimes the picture would be so beautiful that it truly raised me higher, and I'd become someone they said was admirable. . . .

And in my euphoria I became a defender of the people, a parliamentarian, and it seemed to represent something of note on that plane. I would speak on behalf of black peoples, on behalf of humans and their dignity whatever their color might be. . . . And you were always by my side, Madjo: I lived within your womb and I'd emerge from it like a life-giving sap in which everyone would hasten to delight. . . .

I would feel the sap rising in me. . . . You were beautiful. I would inhale you. I would be nourished by you and I'd take up my struggle ever more convincingly, ever more convinced.

Ouch! A gash! The clanging of weapons! A bullet in my neck. . . . And the picture would be destroyed. . . .

Oh, Madjo. . . .

As soon as the image was cracked, as soon as the painting flaked off, the void lay in wait at our door: poverty persisted in surrounding the trembling little child, in sharing his bed, in sleeping inside his heart, which was still incapable of loving. . . . And I once again became incapable of reflection, of constructing one single coherent thought, of taking one single initiative. . . . The little boy would begin to steal again, to tell lies again, to prostitute himself and to tremble more with dissatisfaction, helplessness, but never with shame! He didn't know any shame, that little boy! How could I have known shame, since I had lost all awareness of my own existence, at the same time that I was losing my beautiful image? When I'd flee, when I'd take to my heels, it was always out of fear, that mute fear of the void that would tie my navel into knots, the fear of ugliness. . . . In my nightmares the stumps of lepers would grab at me, maggots would eat me, slugs and reptiles would crawl all over me dribbling spittle! I'd scream and lose consciousness so as to escape from my disgust, and I'd wake up in a lovely image of beauty: I had no more self-hatred within me, and you were my queen. . . . Everything that was ugly in my gestures and my actions would not be etched in my conscience; how would I have known shame, I who was abnormal, amoral, I who desired you so much that it would set my skull on fire and make me ready to transgress any law. . . .

The trembling little boy and I were a monster
A monster created by nature and society
Both having always refused to set the example for us
The total being complete in itself
Both having always suggested crumbs, bits, disparities to us
When what we desired was something complete
Something noble and generous.

And all we had was that image, which we owed to our imagination alone. What would happen if we were to lose track of that? We'd lose our life, without a doubt. . . . And didn't we have the right to live despite everything? Our survival instinct was the perfect response to that of nature and society: we had to live, survive at any price. . . .

And we survived, and I grew up, a monster of fear and imagination. It is true: the only emotion I have ever lived was fear. It would liquefy my extremities, would make me dyslexic; it would make me run, steal, lie, it would render me monstrous in amorality. It would make me sing, create, be happy. . . . It would render me monstrous in abnormality. Every other feeling that underlay our lovely image was nothing other than projections: we would create them but wouldn't submit them to the test of living; they supported us like crutches, but we knew nothing of their essence, their true flavor. . . .

Yes, I was a little boy, a trembling little monster, me, Lem Lian!

And I put on a mask and I fled my whole life long.

From fear and the fear of death.

And here I am now calm in the face of death.

My skin is monstrously relaxed and motionless.

The image has disappeared as have the convulsive shivers from fear of epilepsy.

The little trembling boy has died in me, and I am still alive full of the same unsated desires.

Ah, if only I had been there the day that Roumben spoke for the first time, to know and understand the secret of a true mutation!

Everything has died in me, and I am multiplying in everything. . . .

Who am I?"

*
**

Child of mankind stop your weeping
Stop your weeping over yesterday History inhabits you
Writings have been burned photographs torn up
The names of places have been changed and the names of men reversed
Facts are truncated maps are scrambled
They think they've erased History
But look at what's under the moonlight
And see the Akasha's gaze glimmer
From ear to ear
Memories in dreams

Come back to sing yesterday's thoughts
Come back to bloom the actions of the dead
Stop your weeping Child and let History inhabit you. . . .
You are twenty years old son
And I am a hundred times older
Metamorphoses and moultings
Transformations and evolutions, I have seen a few. . . .
But the one Roumben went through Son
I can draw it for you
For I who carry you
I was there Cha cha chaaa. . . .
The body has its laws son
The body has its laws that the law does not foresee
When a fruit ripens and must fall
When it becomes impossible to forbid
What does the law prescribe?
The flesh has its laws that the law does not understand
When you are in the East why should you turn to the East again?
Since Roumben was spirit
He had to turn toward flesh
He had to find himself in a body
The body has its laws Son. . . .

*
**

And so Madjo spoke to Lem of Roumben and of Ngo Kal Djob, the woman whose name was inseparably linked to the myth of Roumben. . . . Of course, she did tell the essential points; but her manner of speaking about that woman was so sober, so terse, that I prefer to bring you, here, the version of Gol, my older midwife sister.

She was a fervent admirer, what am I saying! a fanatic disciple of Roumben, and she was the only one who spoke freely about him to me; I would even go so far as to say that she quite literally indoctrinated me, to such a point that I do not know how to distinguish the historical fact from the pure recreation of my sister Gol! She ingenuously mixed her own ideals, her dreams, her hopes with those of the national hero whose life she considered to be an ideal of love, and if one had a chance to live it if only for one day, a whole lifetime would not be high enough a price to pay, that is how much it could open one's soul, raise it higher, make it greater. . . .

Yes, without a doubt, the body had its laws that the law did not know. Why did I always get gooseflesh when they spoke about Roumben, who had died well before my birth and whom I'd met only in myth and its rumblings? A myth that surely had been embellished by souls desirous of grasping on to a model and to patriotic ideals, a desire that seemed to characterize the people in this family. . . . What secret bonded me to this man to the point that just the very mention of his name would fill my head with questions and my heart with a mixture of respectful exaltation and bitterness? And why did Lem's image insist on becoming confused with his? Was it because he was one of his favorite idols? Or was it perhaps only Madjo's famous invocation of his name as soon as Lem uttered the cry, before she fainted and the fire burnt her face, which had made a very strong impression on me? An impression that was strengthened by the mystery surrounding his name at the least allusion to it in my presence. . . .

Here then, loosely, is how my sister Gol described Ngo Kal Djob to me and how she sketched the portrait of her love with Roumben and the impact of that love upon their life. . . .

*
**

"So, Roumben's eyes fell upon a body.

I have mentioned the body of 'Ngo Kal Djob.'

'The daughter of God's words,' only that. . . .

A body with intelligent feet that knew where to place themselves, and delicately so. . . .

Feet cast in the mold of a great artist and chiseled by a goldsmith of genius. He had refined her ankles nicely to set them more beautifully in her jewel-like feet. Her legs and thighs had been modeled on a day without cold, without sudden surprises. . . . The artist had availed himself of all tranquillity to put the finishing touches on his work and to envelop her in a skin as silky as a young banana tree. . . .

Her waist fit exactly between Roumben's two spread hands.

Her chest was as round and succulent as a pink grapefruit. . . .

The curve of her back had done its best to greet the moon in a very pronounced thanksgiving, and with every step her buttocks said: 'So be it. . . . '

Her shoulders had sworn to hold high the heavy inheritance of her warrior fathers, allies of the Warrior Ants. These shoulders had sworn it and they kept their word without ever bending the spine. Her arms, conscientious witnesses, sang of the elegance of promises kept and of work well done. . . .

And her hands. . . .

Oh, those hands!

Firm and generous palms, yellow partridge.

Solidly implanted fingers.

These fingers would never let go of what had been conquered.

Her fingers with their ivory claws, their mother-of-pearl nails.

It was the finery of these fascinating hands that would foreshadow caresses . . . and the act. . . .

I'm drawing you a picture of the body of Ngo Kal Djob.

I have named the daughter of God's words, only that. . . .

Can we escape the inescapable?

The neck had taken on a swanlike allure meant to bear an astonishing face quite high.

Enormous and wide jet-black eyes in cloud-white.

Her eyes devoured more than a third of her face.

Her eyes had undoubtedly seen too much and had been too much surprised, as if astonishment were ceasing to be the fate of mankind's children to become that of the trees. . . .

The mouth, too, had taken up a third of her face.

Her mouth compelled recognition through the heavy thickness of her flower-lips, heavy petals of a mysterious black iris, which would open out over the brilliant teeth of a famished feline when Ngo Kal Djob would smile. . . .

Her forehead must have drawn back very far, hunted down by her hair in order to obtain the place it deserved: the place for a full moon; a high, rounded forehead, saturated with hundreds of lives. . . . But the war against the hair must have been a hard one, for her hair, my sister, was really tough: growing like rye grass, it came falling down in twists and coils in which one's hand got lost. . . . Sure, it had made some place for her enormous forehead, but it had gained space in the neck, and heavy braids lay coiled there before coming back down on her proud shoulders. . . .

Between her giant neck, her enormous hair, her giant forehead, her enormous eyes, her huge mouth encircled by small bouquets of tattoos that came up from her hands, two dwarfs: a tiny little tight nose that made an effort to form a bridge, and small, pointed ears which Ngo Kal Djob would constantly keep free. . . .

I have drawn Ngo Kal Djob, only that
Beyond beauty
Beyond ugliness
The strength-daughter joy-daughter ripe-daughter
I have sung the law-daughter, daughter of God's words
The body has its laws. . . .
Can he who has lain down still fall?
But perched on the peaks
He looks at the abyss into which he'll fall
That is the law
The body has its laws."

And while she was speaking of Ngo Kal Djob, masses of descriptive elements seemed to coincide with Grandmother, and my discomfort would only increase. . . . Despite it all, this time I was very careful not to interrupt her, at the risk of once again not knowing the rest. . . .

"And Roumben, perched high on one of the peaks of the spirit, had to glance down on a body, and his eyes fell upon the body of Ngo Kal Djob."

"My sister,
I am drawing you the story of a metamorphosis.

Here then is Roumben with his lips like a cupping-glass and his eyes of fire
His eyes of fire fell upon her body of carved stone
I am telling you about the body of Ngo Kal Djob only that
A body sculpted in pride and nobility.

It wasn't one of those remnants of volcanic fire, lava grown cold, that roll noisily down the mountainside, crash against hand hoes, dull the pick axes, nick the shovels, taking pride in being stones and melting under the first heat of the flames. . . .
She wasn't one of those 'precious' women who wrap themselves in pagne after pagne and jewelry, walking with their head high, their back straight, with the false bearing of a queen, who confuse gold with nobility: surely, both are pure and precious, but the one is bought at the first vendor's and flies off with the first thief; the other cannot be acquired, not even with religiously imposed lessons. One must be born with it and develop it in a continuous asceticism. . . . And whether at work in the fields, milking sows, or at posh evening parties, it embellishes us better than the most precious of jewels.

His eyes of fire settled on a body of nobility that did not take fire. . . .
And Roumben filled with fire circled around and around the body of nobility
I have named the daughter of God's words
With the man of fire dancing around a body like a flame
A whirlwind of flames around a woman's body
Ngo Kal Djob was watching the man with her eyes of stone
And she said to him:
'All I want are warriors' steps, not those of the dance. . . .
No more dances that blaze and wiggle about
Then snore next to dying fires
Dead to all joy
Dead to enthusiasm and reflection
All I want are warriors' steps that strike the earth with determination and advance upon the enemy who retreats

Fear that retreats
Strike the earth with knowledge that advances upon the enemy in retreat
Wretchedness in retreat mediocrity in retreat
Greatness advancing greatness awakening me
And you, son of Nyobè-Nyum, you know very well
That you never look at the one who awakens you from up high
You observe him in all of his prominence. . . .
Go then son of the Rainbow-Serpent
Go and become a great warrior
Come back to awaken me
For I say unto you, to you
Rainbow-Pillar
I can't bear to sleep anymore. . . . '

She was the first one and the only one to call him Son of Nyobè-Nyum. She spoke as others sing. . . .

And Roumben began to dance as others walk
Striking the earth with his whole foot
Pounding the earth with his full weight
His heel penetrating the soil as if for mating
For me warrior dances of the Zulu of the Bantu nations
To walk as others dance
To dance as others walk
To drink the sap of the earth
To rise up again as a giant
Okumé-bridge between heaven and earth
Another act of love
She spoke as others sing
And Roumben rose up into heaven
And I say this to you my sister
You would have shattered him standing upright rather than force him to lay the nape of his neck in the dust. . . .
He went off to war my sister
For the love of Ngo Kal Djob

Ah what a pity that women today no longer demand of men to be great
And no longer expect of love to construct worlds. . . .
When Roumben was suffocating
He breathed her in
In her he would find his storehouse of air
When he dissipated his efforts
In her he pulled himself together again
When he became despairing and weakened
It was she who renewed his strength
All she asked of him was to be great
All she asked of him was to be that ceaseless call toward progress. . . . The act beyond oneself
When he fell, he knew he must get up again, and fast!
Get up with dignity, without a whimper
For she would say to him:
'All I want is blood, no tears
They are too limp, too heavy
They would transform our tasks into burdens
And our path into the way of the cross
For what do we have to repent?
For the blood of our skins, our hands?
For the blood of our inflexible and inescapable steps?
For the blood blue with pride over actions that bloom?
All I want is blood, no tears
They are too bitter and too viscous
They would transform our war cries into sobs
And our thirst for peace into the willingness to be martyrs

I want the warm blood of that embrace you gave us at the dawn of time, which caused explosions in mineral rock, in hymens, and in water pockets! Do you remember that a thousand worlds were born from that kiss and are still waiting to suckle the blood of your actions that flower at the brink of each new day?'

Oh my sister, what a pity you never knew him, before his death, and before the burns. . . . It was I who used to bring them their food to the 'love nest.' Knowing such a couple does not make you want to live the tepid feelings of an ordinary couple. . . . I believe that's why I didn't marry and will probably never marry, unless I have the luck our mother had to meet a man like that. . . . "

At this point, I couldn't stop myself, I interrupted her. . . .

"But. . . . Do you mean to tell me that Madjo's famous lover was Roumben? But. . . . Then what about the no less famous Ngo Kal Djob? Did he have two mistresses then?"

"Look here, you, . . . " she said dumbfounded. "You're not going to tell me that you don't know that mother's name, her 'mother's own name,' is Ngo Kal Djob?"

I thought my head was going to explode. . . .

But then. . . . If my mother was Ngo Kal Djob, if Roumben was the famous lover, he was my natural father, my sire! That's why his name had always fascinated me so. . . . Here was the why to all these mysteries, all these silences, all these hushed tones. . . . Ah, the body really had its laws. . . . I was seized by an agitation hard to control; I had to concentrate on something outside my own head in which a farandole of ideas was dancing around. . . . I begged my sister to go on and, above all, to tell me more about Roumben. . . .

"Roumben had come at the time that the Blacks had allowed themselves to be convinced they were the descendants of Ham-the-accursed-son-of-Noah and concluded they would be slaves for all eternity with God's blessing. This vindictive and rancorous Old Man, immanent with goodness and love, would punish the least mistake through the fourth generation. It had been revealed to Blacks that to this Bearded One a thousand years counted for barely one day; so try to figure out what four generations might come to. . . . Since men were even more wicked than this god, the malediction would be perpetuated over the lineage for at least a hundred thousand generations, were it to be converted into God's time! All of which was to say that Blacks would be cursed-slaves forever!

This prospect had so revolted some people that they wanted to refuse to assume this curse. They struggled, they battled in single and multiple wars, and they were vanquished: to confirm the assertion. . . . Others expressed doubt about their belonging to the lineage of Ham-the-accursed, but the sky fell in on their heads: to confirm the assertion. . . .

And since centuries passed without any change, Blacks accepted their fate. . . . And you know, with their 'optimistic tendencies' and their 'happy temperament,' they were on their way up again! Singing and dancing, they multiplied like flies and died the same way. Singing and dancing, they confirmed the established order with all the respect due to the ancestors. . . . Singing the dance of their life, dancing the song of their death, they rose up against anyone who would attempt to violate the least prohibition. And there were plenty of those prohibitions! Added to the 'ten commandments' was an entire 'catechism,' an entire 'civil and military code,' all the 'interior and sanitary rules' of the commander, the boss, the missionary-explorers annoyed by mosquitoes and amoebas, and every program for tourists exasperated by the reversal of the seasons!

Dancing and singing in the face of insults, of blows, forsaking the bearing of man, Blacks, in conciliation, confirmed the established order in nonhuman postures: back hunched, head lowered, language reduced to some sounds unable to defend any ideas, to question, to accuse, to refuse. . . . 'Yes, Sah! Yes, Chief! Pardon, Boss!' Singing life, dancing death, Blacks. . . .

And it was at this period that Roumben-the-Mute spoke for the first time and said that he would speak for the Seizers, that he would speak about them in their own words. . . .

He said that the word of the Seizers was going to set the universe straight. That man would be Man in every place that he spoke his mind with the sincere heart of mankind. And he spoke sincerely, believe me!

He said that Blacks did not descend from Ham, but from the Word which created the world, and that the Seizers came from a free and noble land, from the Stone-in-the Hole, descendants of Ancients and Times Gone By united one day upon the Stone of the Universe, in a divine mating. An act of light in Mapubi, a fertile act in Ngog Mbock!

He said that everything was possible: cities of earth and stone would be built. Light would spring forth from water and men would move on at the speed of light. He spoke of brotherhood: it was not color but aspiration that would justify brotherhood. All men who aspired to justice and freedom were brothers. All those who thought Mankind in the fullness of their heart's center were brothers. He spoke of equality: it was not the same degree of wealth and power that made men equal, but thought and the form it took. Art, in short. . . . All those who saw themselves included in the word Mankind as they thought mankind in the fullness of their heart's center were equals. All those who drew aside from the greater group, seeing themselves as supermen or sub-men, were each other's equal and were creating the division-insult to humanity. In their thoughts and in their actions they had an inhuman shape that confused difference with value. And they had a repulsive way of reducing everything that did not fit into their code. Their art denied mankind. . . .

Then he spoke of the future. . . .

The future had to stop being a fatal unknown in order to become a child that is created here and now, by questioning yesterday and by acting upon today. He said that the future belonged to mankind since the future belonged to God and mankind is the son of God. . . . He said that Ham, too, was the son of God and that there was no curse whatsoever that could change the essence of any thing or any being.

So, my sister, believe me if you will. . . . Blacks were seen becoming warriors again. They rose up like archangels against Roumben, who dared to advocate equality between a man and a son of Ham-the-Accursed. They remembered Lot's wife transformed into a 'pillar of salt.' They invoked God's fulgurations against this madman who wanted to aggravate Black people's misery. . . . They decided to lynch him and offer his head to the men of God, to testify to their loyalty and fidelity.

The moon was full that night.

Roumben had gone to meet Ngo Kal Djob in their love nest. He confided his fears to her, spoke to her of errors he thought he had made, concessions he was promising himself to make in order to 'restrict the damage,' and the failures he was planning to accept. . . .

She, Ngo Kal Djob, let out a cry! The daughter of God's words, a cry.

I am telling you of a bipolarized cry, a pulverizing and reorganizing cry, a cry. . . . She spoke to him:

'Shout, son of Nyobè-Nyum
Tell me one word that I shall hear and not forget.'

He spoke to her:

'I name you daughter of mankind, you who know what suffering is.'

She spoke to him:

'Suffer then from my mankind suffering.'

Then she spoke again:

'Take my blood, son of Nyobè-Nyum,
And let it forbid you to abdicate
My blood crazy with inescapable progress
I forbid you to renounce
Son of Evil Serpent, wicked mouth. . . . '

At that moment, a loud noise against the door was heard. The whole hut was shaking. A voice cried out: 'Open up, Ngo Kal Djob, and deliver him to us!'

She opened herself to him and he penetrated her. She absorbed all of him. He inhabited her, and she clothed his spirit with her flesh. . . .

When the bolts gave way and the Blacks surged into the little room, Ngo Kal Djob seemed to be fast asleep. The leader of the group found her, and they all stood bedazzled by that inhabited body breathing spirit. They searched for Roumben everywhere. They opened the chests, the covered plates, the pots, the books, anything that could be opened. They lifted up the bed, the blankets, even the mats on the floor. . . .

Ngo Kal Djob was sleeping her deep sleep. . . .

The leader of the group ordered them to cover her up again, and they went away, confused, but still firm in their decision to deliver Roumben, out of respect for the established order.

And every time they were on his tracks, mankind's daughter would speak to him:

'Take my blood Son of Nyobè-Nyum
And let it forbid you to abdicate
Cry of my cries
Suffer my suffering
And be free to set us free
My blood proud of progress, Son of the Rainbow-Serpent. . . .'

He became body inside her body and clothed himself in her body of flesh and spirit. And it was a man who raised himself up, quickly and with dignity, singing as others speak, speaking as others act, and dancing as others walk, steps that move forward. . . .

Drums. . . . To sleep as others watch.

Words. . . . To walk forward as the earth is fertilized with steps that bear the fruit of action.

Gestures. . . . To speak as one speaks the Word that caused the world to spurt forth and began to command it, the Mbock!

And the mute one was speaking words that no one would ever forget:

'Man will be noble when he will be Man amongst men, Being amongst beings, Life in Love, and Gift in life.'

And the gaze of fire became a luminous window: the blind approached and saw fabulous worlds in a thousand colors of the rainbow. Black and loving stars threw themselves into sweet and powerful embraces that radiated the black, red, yellow, white lands, and a diamond-blue race sprang up from the black and loving stars in a sound of re-creation. A sound descended from the new race in a chanting-breath.

'We are the Sum of sums Ommmm.'

My sister, I am telling you of a metamorphosis registered in the Akasha of History. . . .

The mute began to speak, and the word obtained administrative Independence. Those who were believed to be with sight discovered they were blind. The blind could see and decided to walk toward the Vision; passions that had been swallowed up under the yoke awakened like old volcanoes. Warriors discovered their true and only adversary: the animal inside themselves. . . .

They were walking tall, the Seizers, brandishing the banner red with the blood of the dead, black Crab of the Black skins and lands. . . .

They were walking tall, the Seizers, underneath the White leaden metal, the 'Bon Ba Long,' underneath the White lead.

Upright and proud.

Dying upright underneath the White lead, the 'Ngwélés.'

Man became noble and great again. Woman sublime and immortal.

I am telling you of a metamorphosis that saw the White lead become pulverized like an old snake skin. . . .

They will speak forever of the laws of metamorphosis, my sister. . . . "

And Madjo had concluded, as my sister:

"The body has its laws, Son. . . .

For a third time, Roumben had to take on another form: he was married according to custom, made children, spoke at the UN, Pan-African dream. . . . He returned to the maquis, and had to die with the secret, for the sake of the survival of the Seizers. But you know that, don't you? Since it was no longer anything but a question of conquest and conquest is the business of man. . . . A game of warriors. . . . "

As I relive the emotion that was mine the day that Gol told me the story of Roumben, I can easily imagine Lem's emotion when Madjo revealed to him that she was Ngo Kal Djob and that Lem's idol had been her only lover. . . . I can imagine every deduction, every bit of fervor, every re-creation, for which only he possessed the secret. . . .

What Lem was feeling at that moment was so alarming that he preferred to think of someone else, and he thought of Ziworé. . . .

"Speak to me Ziworé
Speak to me of yourself, of your life. . . .
Speak to me of your anguish, your fears, your doubts
Speak to me of your grudges, your reproaches, the hues of your suspicions
Do you still have dreams, desires
Speak to me of the colors of your sleepless nights
Speak to me of the temptations of your body
Of the fervor of your resolutions
Speak to me of the whims of destiny the lines in your hands
Tell me, what is the weather like down there?
Here the drums no longer connect
The pigeons no longer come close to the doves
Audacity flees from me and failure is watching me
Noises frighten me and silence barely tolerates me. . . .
But I am clinging on. . . .
I cling on to memories, the fugitive happiness of dreams
Love in every life and from life to life
Love-across-a-hundred-lives
Sun-drenched mysteries concentrated in a single minute
The time of a thought-year
Finding each other in the reign of the past. . . .
But tell me, what is the weather like down there?

Down there in the shade of infamy where idols disintegrate
Hair becomes anemic like the silk on dried corn
Fawns flee from death like cats
Friends abandon the skiff and let go of the moorings. . . .
Tell me, what is the weather like down there?
Perhaps you are listening to the hibiscus
Perhaps you hear the cicada
Perhaps O Yém Mback!
Perhaps you are awaiting the end of the rains oh Mayi
My friend of yesterday and of tomorrow oh Ziworé
My cursed friend and a thousand times blessed
Tell me, what is the weather like down there?
Since you have stayed down there
The aerial roots of the Sèm no longer sting the soil
The long and deeply hidden tubers are emerging from the earth
And cause the splatter of many saps to surge out. . . .
But the wish to live descends from heaven and everything becomes sound
Which whispers to my heart that my life is not a Life
Your disciples and the orphans are whispering to my heart
That my life is not Life
Misery and tortures are whispering to my heart
That my life is not Life
And I cling on. . . .
I cling on to every thread of light to every being of the dream

And the wish to live again descends from heaven, down the full length of my rope of umbilical cords, and I think us anew, I remodel us, touch us up, and re-create us as sons of light. . . . Well now! Hold on, my brother, let's hold on, my friend, we shall have other times, other loves, other lives. . . .

Yes, Madjo, the body truly has its laws. . . . It is you who taught me that once again, and one more time, it is I who am feeling like a conqueror there where you have opened every door! When shall I do my part in the action? When shall it be my turn to lighten your path, my love, my twin sister?"

Love-across-a-Hundred-Lives

Yes, henceforth he knew that conquest was the business of man, his business, a game of warriors like that warrior he had been condemned to become so that this life might not be useless, so that he wouldn't yet again fail his other side, his yesterday's double, his love-across-a-hundred lives. . . .

It seemed to him it was within hand's reach. . . . But he didn't dare believe it. . . .

It is not for nothing that he had been named "the art of casting bridges," of that he was now convinced. One never bears a name by accident. . . . He felt that he still had to launch another bridge, between this "before . . . in secret . . . not so very long ago" and today, that is to say to understand yesterday, Roumben's tragic end, and why the transmission of the Secret had been interrupted. . . .

Assuredly, it was the end of a world, the end of a stage. . . . Something else would have to be started, and he would certainly have a role to play, a new Secret to transmit. . . . But he felt the need to rethink yesterday, and he didn't even realize that Madjo had gotten up, frozen by the night cold, and was busy fighting death, in trying to make it home by herself although her legs were hardly able to carry her any longer. . . .

And he remembered what my sister, Gol, used to tell us, she who had been in the maquis close to Roumben. . . .

She would follow him everywhere and so had witnessed his end. But once again, his eagerness still seemed very "unscientific" to me, and I said to myself there were bits and pieces to choose from in what she was saying. . . . But in these times of intense emotion for Lem, I don't think he was overly concerned with historical truth. . . . He was on a plane where he needed only thrusts and motivation, and the more fantastic the story, the better it would mark him. . . .

Here then is Gol's version, as it came back to the feverish mind of Lem Liang Mianga. . . .

Yesterday . . .

The end began yesterday. . . .
They declared Roumben to be an outlaw
And "the trashcan man" was proclaimed "Wisest of the wise"
For knowing how to glorify predilection for personal power, charisma. . . .
High above people
Much stronger than Mother-Earth. . . .

By unanimous decision of the Assembly, Tafar said yes. Sédar said yes. Caado said yes, a thousand times yes! And down the line to Raïs, who said yes, as if Solomon's blood seemed to have grown dangerously tepid inside its veins or so it seemed to him. . . .

Under the gaze of "the trashcan man." . . .

Then the excitement was broken up into fifty Africas. The Union of the Peoples was reduced to tribal subsections. Man was reduced to a bag of straw, the revolutionary to revolutionist, the warrior to rebel, the Catholic to indecency, woman to a display window of a sepulchre, the Protestant to cynic, the child to soccer-shooter, rightful claims to advocations of revenge. . . . Hope was reduced to crumbs, ideals to sustenance, life to emptiness. . . .

And watch out for the besotted Bété, a beast panic-stricken by the fire leveling its villages, who would have confused a Bassa with a Bamiléké had he been questioned by the police about the bulging leather of the party's purses! The Bassa would have jumped at his throat with rage, thinking of all those Swiss accounts grown fatter through his faith and taken over behind his back by the rickshaws . . . in turn protected by the Bambara infantrymen. . . .

Christ's sword now separated sons from their fathers, daughters from their mothers, dividing in order to conquer more effectively. . . . The great fire of small ambitions, napalm of the jealousy of the embittered when confronted with the unfairly privileged, the grafting strategies of geopoliticians, the militia of information-documentation . . . with terror in their gut, hatred in their hands, a phony smile on their face, with impudence in their genitals, lasciviousness in their heads, and the void in their hearts. . . . Children-nations of the fathers of nations, little men and petty women-great-helmsmen!

And they said yes a thousand times yes while people sang to them:

Bamtsé,
Azikiwé bamtsé éé bamtsé
Mba Léon bamtsé éé bamtsé
Tsiranana Philibert bamtsé éé bamtsé
Bamtsé bamtsé bamtsé bamtsé na wo é chéris bamtsé éé bamtsé. . . .

"*Boum i tché*" among the Seizers, with that yes that made the Pillar into an outlaw came the end of the world!

The people, outlaw, solidarity, outlaw!

Intelligence, outlaw.

Art, outlaw.

The law of the nouveaux riches, fathers of nations, a law that chased men away from their homes in order to hunt them down and shoot at them as at hares in the bush! Bodies. Dead bodies. Suffering. Hunger and wretchedness. Fire. Raids. Silence!

Days of woe. . . .

Then the men fled and dove into the "elephant-forest," having decided to fight, to defend their cause at the cost of their lives. . . . They were walking on all fours, stooped over, contorted, trampling on decaying carcasses. They caught elephantiasis, sleeping sickness, and they were croaking like dogs. But they carried their hearts with pride, their great hearts, as long as he, their Pillar, was living. . . .

They died and were resuscitated. They fell and stood back up. They were surviving, they were proliferating, these men, as long as he, their Pillar, was living. . . .

And the smell of man became unbearable to the men of straw. Camped out to block the road against charisma alone, they knew they would find man ahead of them always and everywhere, as long as he, the Pillar, were alive. . . .

Foaming at the mouth with rage, exploding, the great Marim made grand resolutions, and he proclaimed these words: "I shall burn down the land of the Seizers in twenty-four hours," he said. "I shall expunge Man from the surface of the Earth." He spoke and had freighters come filled with napalm. . . .

It was then the Pillar was afraid for the first time: he had been born to raise man high, and the forest was full of men. There would always be men as long as the forest was there, he thought. The forest must not burn; the elephants must continue to trumpet so that men would continue to hold their hearts close to their bellies. There would be nothing left to raise up high if there were no more men. He chose man and decreed him to have priority. His own life came last.

"Let's talk," he said and gave himself up.

They told him: "Your life for Mankind, mankind or your life."

Knowing that his last hour had come, he waged his last battle for man. He demanded that he have the right to choose, for that alone makes a man of him, a responsible being. . . . He attempted to sow a liking for responsibility among the straw men. He threw the seeds by the handful, he threw them to the wind: "The courage to speak, to liberalize, the freedom to undo, the daring to start anew, to start from scratch . . . ," these are the things that make a Man, and the straw men were not able to understand. . . . They had been manipulated by the "hard Hand of Gaul," which was taking things in hand once again, wanting to clear the slate in order to redress its shrinking Gaul. . . .

They told him: "Become straw with us, and you will fatten yourself. Become straw with us, and your burden will be lightened." But he persisted in singing his song of Man, and they shot him down like a hare with his smell of Man, the thirteenth of a bad month. . . . And the people were singing of "Caado the new hope," he who had taken power some time earlier as he returned the napalm to the Népalm, which is accustomed to burning. . . .

He died as he was singing: "Take my life, Stone-in-the-Hole, drink my blood, cradle of free Man, my life for your liberty, my life for your survival, forest of men. . . . "

And they shot him in the back while he sang of Man in the mists of a too early morning, and while the people were singing of Caado the new hope who was perfidiously shooting at the Pillar! Caado who had to be thanked for having spared the elephant-forest of the Men of the Seizers, and they gave the Mbock to him, saying:

"Caado, guard the land well
The great Marim was ashamed
Guard our men well
The great Marim was ashamed
Guard our hearts well, Caado. . . . "

People registered for his party in enormous numbers; they pleaded for him. For him they violated the elephant-forest in search of the great Secret. They invoked the great liberation, as Roumben had taught; he could not lie to our faith. He had said: "We shall construct our temple around the dignity of free Man, and all sorrow, all misery shall be erased. And on that day, I shall be with you, whatever happens. . . . "

So no one wept when his decapitated body was exhibited, and no one was shocked by the smell of decay. . . . They looked at him and they said to each other that he could not have lied to our faith: he would be there with us on the day of the great liberation and he would smell fresh again of Man.

The smells of decay were nothing other than the smells of our lack of passion, solidarity, and courage. . . . We had to regroup around the new hope and tighten our ranks. The struggle had to go on until the day of victory. . . . When we have forgotten our dead sons and we imagine them marching by our side, Man's weapons in their hands. . . . When we forget our burned-down homes, our devastated fields, and when we see before our eyes only the untamable elephant-forest bought back with his blood. . . . When animosity is abolished and chased away from our hearts of Men. . . . When we fight like brothers, hand in hand for the same cause, and when we are victorious. . . . Then we shall see the day of the great liberation, and on that day, whatever happens, he shall be with us. . . .

"Remain
Remain awake, vigilant sons of the people
Young
Youth of the Black Crab
Roum
Roumben is ready to live again
All he is waiting for is the reconciliation,"

thus we sang every day of struggle and of hope, until the great Day of the New Year.

Then they placed the great flag on the main square of every village. The men gathered around, reserving a space for the Pillar. . . . The women and children had to climb into trees or onto the rooftops to see the reserved place, determined to see his solar face cast the beam of liberation into their eyes. . . . And they would sing a while, and they would wait a while, and they would sing more loudly still:

"All he is waiting for is passion
All he is waiting for is sincerity
All he is waiting for is friendship."

And they were radiating passion, sincerely, and with friendliness, and they would wait another while, their eyes open wide, good god!

"He shall spurt forth from the ground like a geyser, a python-dragon from the lake, a *poteau-mitan.* And we, we shall set ourselves around him. I, I shall be a brick, and I, I shall be beam, I a rock, and I a bolt on the door. . . . "

"Silence, vigilance! There. . . . The earth is moving! I tell you, the earth did move! He'll spout up from the soil like a geyser. . . . "

"Oh, no! He'll come down from heaven like a tank of fire, a beaming ray, a core of light, a young sun. I, I shall be a molecule, I a vapor, a spark, and together with him we shall radiate the Light-that-is-Man. . . . Be vigilant, he is coming! I tell you, a lightning bolt has torn the sun apart!"

And in the smallest village, all across the land, people were staring at the sky, the earth, and the waterways. They invoked him, they beseeched him. . . . He would revive, he would be with us no matter what happened, he had promised, he could not lie to our faith! As long as midnight had not come. . . .

The bells of the mother-church rang twelve times for the second time that day, and a smell of carrion arose from the bell as if it had stirred every latrine and every new grave in the land. Nothing remained anymore of the people but a swarming slithering mass catching everyone's spittle right in the face. . . . And in the sky, will-o'-the-wisp, the bodiless head of the Pillar, eyes rolled upward, completely ludicrous in his bodiless faith! But why then had he spoken and struggled, why had he died? So that men would slither forever or flutter about like straw?

He had lied to our faith, and that was the beginning of the end. . . .

The persistent smell of carrion rose to the people's head, and the competition of the most decayed was begun: Punks, Picks. . . . And it was for the one who would steal, the one who was the best swindler, the one who would trample the most frail, the oldest, the one who would sully the most pure and the most honest. It was for him who would crawl most through the shit, the one who would best lick the filled scrota. . . . And they began to drug themselves, and they were getting drunk in this plague. They were becoming more and more stuck together by the slime. They were flies whose feet had gotten stuck in the nets of Gaul, vampiring us day and night for its own survival. . . .

Oh, how tenacious these Blacks are! As tenacious as time in its seeming indolence. . . . They can't be made to croak, they are indomitable, these Blacks! They're the true allies of matter and inertia: you can shake them up all you want, rip off their skin, their flesh, their blood, they never die, they never evaporate. They proliferate, these devils! They certainly possess the true secret of Evolution!

And inside the scourge, the slime, the traps, unruffled, slowly and inexorably, they became closer, they bonded, they were clutching each other by their umbilicals one more tightly than the next, until they were nothing but a cohesive block that was surviving, sometimes equalizing at its lowest point, but it would revive, persist, multiply and evolve toward eternity. . . .

From the death to the rebirth of Man, passing through every stage, inexorably: straw-man, passive beast-of-burden-man, wild-beast-man, hunter-man, warrior-man, inexorably. . . .

Slowly, the noxious drug, a slow metamorphosis into a dream perfume. . . .

Slowly, the persistent carrion tempts the fertilization of mother-humus. . . .

Imperceptible, the slime cracks under the pressure of flies' feet
The paws of Blacks pushing down like the roots of Sèm
And anchoring themselves deeply in immortality
There where earth has drunk the blood of Man
The blood of Man's responsibility
The blood of his liberty
Where oppression has crushed dignity
The dignity of love and of the gift of life

Where every memory of the divine lies buried
Slowly
Gently
The day bursts forth and the image is reflected in the sacred pool.
Ngambi told that a universe-son of the promise would be born
From fire and water
From charcoal and kaolin. . . .

He had predicted Roumben's birth, when all hope would be dead, when the mere idea of purity would be ridiculed, when virginity would be something to be ashamed of. He said that peace would be established amidst the full blare of wars and that flowers would grow on soil soaked with blood and ashes. . . .

When every man would once again have learned to fight for the whole and the whole for each one, when they would move the center of the world from their own navels and place it high above their skulls, when they would no longer be afraid of death and would understand that life is eternal. . . .

Then Ngo Kal Djob's song will rise high into the night and every man will see Roumben lighting his own path. . . .

And Lem is exultant: "My God, I do believe I can hear it already. . . . Shh!"

"Suffer then, suffer my pain
And make yourself free for our liberty
Accept then, accept this my blood
And let it forbid you to abdicate
My blood, crazed from the tight and inescapable steps
I forbid you any renunciation. . . . "

*
**

And this story, which Gol began over and over a thousand times, and which was new every time, welled up again right there inside Lem's head like the eye of a cyclone, turning memories over, tearing at the last knots of unnamed and nameless emotions, as if he wanted to explain the inexplicable at all cost. . . .

Yes, he was remembering. . . . He had to remember: it was a matter of life and death. . . .

He was remembering every last little feeling: that sense of being completely absorbed, of living inside her as if inside a sloughing cocoon. . . . That beehive smell that would rupture all his reserves and deliver him to her. . . . That feeling of having found completeness and integrity once again, that would increase his faith, his fervor, his capacity to resist and to fight tenfold. . . . That pride in Being. . . . That vision of Man's greatness, that opening out onto boundlessness, onto eternity. . . . That intimate understanding of Pleasure as the Secret of the Divine. . . .

The mask of burns had leaped off Madjo's face, stripping it down to that of the Lover Daughter of God's words. . . . He now understood every urge and every mad desire for that woman so much beloved yesterday, which everything now prevented him from feeling: age, the nature of family connection, the taboos of society. . . .

He was also remembering that foul and foggy morning. . . . Very early they had come to get him from the cell in which they had thrown him like a bandit. . . . For the last time they suggested that he come around, that he renounce. . . . They might as well have told him to deny himself, to deny her! Yet, was it not better to live, to survive at all cost in order to preserve her? To make a few concessions. . . . To infiltrate. . . . To enter into the system like Ngok Ikwèn Manyim into the belly of the monster, after carefully preparing himself? But in any event, not to die like this, not to lose her, not to leave without a single farewell, without having inhabited her one last time. . . .

The evening before he was supposed to give himself up, she had said to him: "Be careful, I'm expecting a child by you. . . . Perhaps a guardian of the Secret?" With a bit of luck. . . . He had to live. . . . He would accept. . . .

It was at exactly that moment that he felt a burning in his

neck and an explosion inside his skull! He had begun to take enormous leaps: he had to go back to her, nobody could stop him!

In the love nest, Ngo Kal Djob was holding her head with both her hands, twisting in silent pain, as if overcome by an atrocious migraine. . . . He moved toward her and placed his hands on her. . . . She raised eyes filled with tears and despair and went out without seeing him. . . . It was then that he understood he had died. He took another leap and returned to the site of the crime; his body lay soaking in a pool of blood, in the backyard of the motor squad, and he had been decapitated! His skull had burst at its top, and his eyes had popped out. . . . His navel was swollen like a balloon, a final and abortive attempt at splitting himself. . . . He was leaping from one place to another, desperately seeking to communicate with someone, and especially to console Ngo Kal Djob, who had enclosed herself inside a silence of ill boding. . . . She was moving around mechanically, accomplishing her tasks without showing any interest in them, until the day when, in her anxiety over her grandson, who was suffocating inside a placenta in the middle of the night, she succeeded miraculously in creating light. . . . So then Roumben slipped into the body of the newborn infant and couldn't stop himself from giving her a signal. . . . Was it fear then or her own volition to cover up that made her fall into the flame that masked her face? Having become her grandson, would Roumben have known how to live in this new relationship that made them taboo to each other, had she kept the same face?

Thus, imprisoned inside a child's body that prevented him from joining with his beloved in the yogic sense of the term, without killing his spirit however, the small and trembling child was no longer able to stop the flight begun one day by a dead man who did not want to die. . . .

And now that Lem was remembering, his navel turned fully back into his belly, leaving nothing but a hole like a chalice from which his wife would perhaps drink some nectar. . . . No longer was there any impulse toward flight in him. . . . He had cast a bridge between his lives and now he felt ready to assume this one with all its depravity: his abandoned studies, the Machine . . . Ziworé, his professor and his friend, whom he was sure he had known elsewhere as well. . . . He had a moving thought for him:

> "My mother often sang it for us, Ziworé, do you remember?
> Her always mysterious songs speaking of love
> Yet never forgetting death
> 'No love exists without death no happiness without a past. . . .'
> My mother often sang it for us, Z. . . .
> Do you remember?
> Do you remember the sun in her words
> The hope in her eyes
> The fire in our hearts
> The love in our heads
> And the strength in our hands?
> We were reborn every morning as we awoke to start again . . . to start the world anew!
> We were reborn at every stage to renew the effort once again
> A hundred times, a thousand times the very same road
> To go faster and farther with every turn
> We were reborn with every encounter to render things perfect. . . .
> What then is the secret of the wind that carries off so many things
> Without ever crumbling under the weight and leaving oblivion everywhere?
> That madness that would intrigue us and fascinate us so, Ziworé. . . .
> Do you remember?
> My mother often sang it for us:
> 'Two madmen on the roads of life
> Fused together at the hands and the heart
> Would brave the countercurrent winds
> Singing of life in the realm of death

Singing of love in the realm of hate
They would walk a thousand miles without boots on their flat feet
Toward the cardboard castles and the cities of sand
And the contaminated kings would desert their kingdoms built of cards
And would follow them on the roads of life
Do you know why?
Two madmen on the roads of life spoke to them of life'
That madness that intrigued us so, Z. . . .
My mother always sang us that song. . . . But. . . .
Tell me, what is the weather like down there?"

Over there where he made the decision to return in order to take part in the action; there where he might help to disconnect the old Machine, perhaps, to rethink Man, to discover other vital secrets, other methods with which to uphold the divine in man. . . .

He turned around expecting to see Grandmother; he had decided that this time he would look deep into her eyes and tell her: "Here I am again, *come back love. . . .* "

He opened his eyes. . . . But I prefer to let him tell you this himself. . . .

My Name Is . . . Lem Liang Mianga. . . .

Nobody around. . . .

One would have thought the region had been abandoned. Not a sound, not even a child playing in a corner!

There I was, lying on the ground, flat on my belly; a bit of rope licking at my cheek like an evil serpent. Finally I was able to turn around, and I saw him coming down the *karité* tree like a dragon! I leapt with all my strength to dodge the monster. . . .

I believe that at that moment I truly woke up. What was I doing here? Where was I? Was the bridge between my conscience in its waking state and my dream life beyond going to crack once again? For, very obviously, I had been sleeping. . . . But where? Come on. . . .

I was in a cocoa plantation. The ground was carpeted with dead leaves. I was underneath a huge tree. A kola tree? No, a *karité*. A hundred-year-old *karité,* at least, judging by its height. . . .

I was dressed in a faded pair of blue jeans and a red shirt, which must have come off on me, because I had blood-like blotches on my hands. My sticky hands. . . .

My hair was strewn with twigs and dead leaves; it, too, was sticky!

Nobody around!

But where? Where had the village gone, where had the world gone? That silence. . . . As far as one could see, cocoa trees with yellow, red, green pods shimmering strangely in the semidark. . . . The shade of the trees, the silence. . . . Silence?

Pierced by the whistling of the cicadas, the song of birds, and the buzzing of bees and flies. . . .

Above all of flies. . . . There had to be a whole swarm of them somewhere. . . . But where?

And where, then, was I? I sensed some pestilence. . . . I was as if imprisoned in a slow-motion movie. I was moving and reasoning at snail's pace. And there was the swarm of flies humming away; I had disturbed it as I stumbled against something that seemed to be a liana in the elephant-forest and that made me want to clutch on to it and to take enormous swings like Tarzan and to leave this forest of coçoa trees that was growing bigger under my very eyes. . . .

The Tarzan-like cry that was already rising to my lips was silenced by the swarm of flies deserting its rotted liana!

My rope of dangling umbilical cords!

My first bridge cast between heaven and earth. My bridge of umbilical cords as if to compromise the least link between my heaven and my earth forever. . . . Heaven would be closed to me forever. I had to cast another bridge and fast! A solid bridge of oak and steel, a bridge of gold between my heaven and my earth. . . .

But where?

Where then was my earth? And my heaven?

Where cocoa and coffee, kola and *karité* were growing was where my earth was, watered by the sweat of a generous people that asked nothing other than to be offered on the altar of love and to give away its free will and pleasure in working so that everything might be, because life is everything. . . .

But the lion-sun had frightened the rain and the gazelles: the earth had been baked and cracked. The grass had died. The fauna had fled. Desert had settled in, but Man was holding out! They were watering it with their blood and their sweat, and beautiful fruit was scoffing at the lion-sun.

Yes, my earth was these people, these "masses" who were judged to be uneducated simply because they didn't know how to read. And yet, they were more cultured than most of the intellectuals: at least they knew where they came from, who they were and why they were there. . . . But it was decided they should be educated: soccer games, soccer balls, official languages and commercials in national languages, deadly seminars, broadcasts pulled out of the storage sheds of other people's forgotten materials, trunks of secondhand clothes filled with the AIDS virus, disjointed conversations. . . . But the people were holding out and threw their Moussa French, full of their men's humor, back in their faces. . . . My masses were being drowned in demagogy; and, outdistanced, they were laughing their men's laughter. . . . And time didn't count for them, because they, they knew full well that life is eternal and makes a mockery of dates. . . .

They were made to wear garish colors, though they liked only red, white, and black, though they were all lines, curves, circles and sinusoids, rising spirals. . . .

This was my earth, my land of rhythms and symbols, of lives moving inside a limping statuette yet miraculously balanced, on an uneven surface, in an asymmetrical figure, my land of symmetry of inversions. . . . No, my masses were not the ones that needed lessons and sermons. . . . My land, my masses needed only an elite, and beacons. . . . the greatest deficiency lay there, the lack of a wise and responsible elite, a star in the night, a shimmer of hope, a heaven. . . .

My heaven . . . ? My heaven would be the place where men would have conquered their navel, their big mouth, and their loins. . . . They would have suffered bruises in this war against the beast and fear inside them, and they would have been left with testimonial scars to be fingered by the doubting Thomases. . . . And in the name of these victorious scars, they would have conquered power, might, love, and privileges: the power of conquering man inside the beast, the might to gather nations of builders, the love of leading mankind in their lives, and the privilege of serving them. . . .

My hand, my Thomas hand, skimmed your scars, oh Sogolon Jata. And yours as well, Chaka-Zulu, with your hands of blood! I have touched your scars, Rainbow Pillar of the

Seizers! And yours, Yém Mback! I have touched the scars of so very many sons of light in my dreams. . . . In heaven, my dream. . . .

But where? Where have these men gone?

My heaven would be the place where men will have conquered their slavish desire for the drop and where they will stand up for themselves at all times, so that mankind may continue to walk with its head held high. And even if one were to be crushed by the Drop-by-Drop-Machine, the image would remain forever there on the side of the Machine, witness to Man's survival, the indelible imprint there for every hand of every Thomas to touch. . . .

And your imprint has remained stuck to my hand, Ziworé, I who abandoned you when you might perhaps have been able to cling to me, and keep high the heads of all your followers! Yet, your imprint will shine on the Machine, and myth will open the doors of eternity to you where your followers will see you among the sons of light. . . .

And you, too, Sékou-of-the-red-hands, pulling the horde of hopes behind you, you will be among the sons of light. . . .

And you, the Artist who caused black woman and the Mask to sing, and who crossbred the Académie Française, so as to consecrate the definitive end of a period, of a race. . . .

You, too, Bipol-the-upright-one, who gave us back faith in the birth of a divinity. . . . My dream, my heaven. . . .

But where?

But where then had my love gone?

The one that follows me from land to land, from life to life, from heaven to heaven. . . . My love. . . . My dream. . . .

She told me:

"I want blood, hot blood of that embrace you gave us at the dawn of time, which caused all the straitjackets, hymens, and pockets of water to explode. A thousand worlds were born from that kiss and are still waiting to suckle at the sound of your actions which will bloom again, here at the dawn of every new day. . . . "

My dream, my love. . . .

And in front of me, my rope of dangling umbilical cords, my decomposed bridge between heaven and earth. . . .

No!

What I needed was an indestructible bridge, a bridge of awareness, a bridge of love. . . .

My dream, my love. . . .

I decided to give what was decayed back to mother-earth, who was alone in knowing how to transmute everything to life. . . . I was going to bury my fears, my flights, my pretexts, and my thirst for droplets with these umbilical cords braided into a rope for the bridge of rot, in order never again to take to my heels, never again to abandon friends as one abandons a sinking ship, never again to clutch on to stakes of support. . . .

Then I will walk with my Man's head held high, hand and heart fused to the sons of light like that couple of madmen who brave the winds on the roads of life and speak to kings of their life. . . .

My dream, my love. . . .

She told me: "I forbid you to abdicate."

And so I dig. . . .

With my hands I dig my soil, here where my cousins were born. . . . With my hands I dig my soil, here where I must plant the foundations of my bridge of light to be cast toward the heavens with the speed of light. . . .

I was digging. . . .

With my hands I have dug the soil injected with material woes and poisonous imported riches
Dug my soil glutted with aid
With my hands I have dug and I have buried the protectorate
Buried the stakes of support
With the rope of umbilical danglings
Since I had to live, for this was my duty. . . .
For the steep and inescapable steps that move forward
And the enemy who retreats

My warrior's feet had to strike the ground with determination
So that fear will recoil
So that knowledge will advance
And that slavery will recoil, misery recoil
That inertia recoil and that the passion for love will move forward. . . .
My love, my dream. . . .
She told me:
"Live. Go and become a great warrior
And come back to awaken me
And never again will I look down upon you."

My dream, my love. . . . But where?
Where then has my love gone?

*
**

At the very moment that he finished burying his bridge of placentas emptied of life, the sound of the drum announcing a death struggle in the village reached him. He began to walk very fast, his heart beating with anguished premonition. And so that he would not fall back into prognostications that might perturb him, he began to sing:

"Bring me back, Mother, to where I am loved
So that eyes will look at me lovingly caress me
So that hands will touch me embrace me massage me where words become the clamor of healers:
Stinging piercing
Dynamic rhythms enclosed within the sounds of drums
But calming the nerves and the aching hearts
Drums beating Voices heating Hands clapping
So that the voices fall silent and words flow
Let my heart sing
My love who then would banish me when you are living?
I'm running, jumping, and flying toward you. . . . "

But where?

But where then was life fleeing to?

In the village every house was closed. Everything seemed frozen. The birds were no longer singing. One would have thought that even the chickens had heard a fox roaming around. . . . And the sheep were no longer bleating!

Lem's heart was beating more and more loudly. He ran through the village. A silent crowd stood in front of Grandmother's courtyard. . . . He felt the blood freeze in his veins and he moved no more. . . .

"Quick, quick, you're the one she's waiting for!" a cousin cried out.

Several others ran toward him and grabbed him. He no longer felt as if he were walking. Surely they had lifted him up and placed him on a bench next to the bed where Grandmother was lying. . . .

She opened her eyes as if after a long waiting period. . . . The others moved several steps back. . . . Lem took a breath. . . .

"Why did you leave without me? Why didn't you call me?" he murmured to her with reproach in his voice.

"Because you weren't ready yet, of course!"

Her voice. . . . As clear and calm as always. Her hands. . . . He took her hands and they squeezed his, calling forth a melee of all his feelings, which now were clear to him, feelings he would now be able and would want to take on, because he placed them above any human law. . . . But Madjo didn't let him get carried away. . . . She brought him back to this new truth, the last test-of-separation they would have to suffer. . . .

"Now that everything is ready, say good-bye to me. . . ."

"Wait, Grandmother. . . . Let me tell you the dream you told me last night when I wanted to die and you called me back, do you remember, Grandmother? Before, in secret, it was very long ago. . . . "

"Yes, I remember. . . . "

"Before, in secret, not so very long ago. . . . "

"Yes, I remember. . . . "

"Yesterday. . . . "

"No, I didn't tell you about yesterday, since you knew that already. It was you who told me about yesterday in order to cast your first bridge of awareness. Now that it has been accomplished, tell me good-bye. . . . "

"No, wait, my love. . . . I am going to tell you about tomorrow and the day after tomorrow as well, if you want, but stay. . . . Wait. . . . I beg of you! I will give you a kiss like the one of the first dawn. I will create shimmering worlds where you will place your jewel-feet without soiling them. I will win every trophy of dignity to keep your neck in its natural grace. Stay . . . please stay. For you I will dance the war of the sons of heaven, the Zulu. I will strike the ground with light. Please, Grandmother, I beg of you, I will give you the kiss of love. I will awaken you and you will see me all grown. . . . "

"For you, now, the rest is nothing more than conquest, and you know from here on in that conquest is the business of men. Go then, my man . . . go and come back. I shall always be there for you, you who think Africa, you who think men in the deepest core of the heart. I shall keep the links of the lineage open, the chain knotted at the dawn of time, there, beyond where the eyes can see. . . . Go and come back. You who know how to keep that which is invisible at the depth of your gaze, can you now maintain that you come from nowhere and swear that it's the truth? A thousand times conqueror, a thousand times conquered, can you deny yesterday and eternity?

Didn't you know that death regenerates? Could you deny the death of every day of every birth and the birth of every death?

And yet, you begged me to teach you freedom and I swore to you that the time of the ancient prophecy would surely come: integrity in the service of freedom, freedom in the service of destiny of the design. For ever, for sure. . . . "

"Stay, Grandmother. . . . I will have myself submerged in the same source as Sogolon Jata, and I will have myself baptized son of light by the fire that killed Roumben, so that your eyes shall never see the larva and the beast inside mankind again, but stay, my love. . . . "

"All is and remains. Everything was there from the first day onward, from the first kiss onward. How could you have lived without seeing that? Really? Didn't you know that life is not complete if it is free of death? And that suffering is the very essence of freedom? And yet you begged me to teach you freedom. . . . And I say this to you again: don't look toward heaven and the infinite ether anymore as you flee from suffering. Look at failure, at sorrow. . . . Freedom lies there spread out and flows in petals of surpassing, of giving, and of service. Go then, my man, and remember. . . . "

"Stay in our flesh, in our body, the shared shelter of our twinned heart, and I shall inspire you with all that you believe in: the strength of our hands full of calluses, worn down with honest work, the hot breath of desire's forge, born from esteem and true encounter. The devouring act of lips that communicate experience. From your blood to my blood. Our shared body frozen in waiting. . . . stay, I beg you!"

"Why do you love me so if you do not believe in the Ancient, and if you think I am nothing but the bearer of defeat and resignation, incapable of recognizing our path and of following it freely, why do you still let a slip of yourself drag behind in my animism? You who bear on your forehead the star that is twin of mine, you who first created heat as you glued your chest against mine, do you know that a thousand failures have died from those hugs and kisses and that a thousand eyes have been opened to the light and are watching the infinite? A matrix of precious stone has burst open: we have just been reborn. . . . Our life will be free after all this suffering! If you don't believe that, if you think I am nothing but the bearer of the regret and rancor of centuries of defamation, humiliations, and the negation of who we are, why do you love me so?"

They said: "My God! She is going to die, she is slipping away."

But I could still hear her.

"Go and come back
Go, man who casts bridges.
Trace new paths. Open the road of tomorrow for us and remember. . . .
Go, my man, and come back, and remember."

Did tears cloud my eyes? I could still hear her.

"Tears spring forth from blood and violence from the life that is deaf from profit. . . . Our eternity.
I want only that life and no tears
Too heavy and limp
Which would transform our tasks into burdens
And our path into the way of the cross
Would you deny that Christ died for us as well?
Oh suffering!
Suffering yours mine, our suffering
Flower of knowledge which blooms because of love, of the freedom of life
Which unmistakably blooms
Go and come back, I forbid you to abdicate!"

They said: "She is gone. Close her eyes, which are still looking at Lem!"

I did not go to her funeral. I had already buried her old skin with my rope of umbilical cords and umbilical danglings underneath the *karité* where so many lives had been born. . . . But I could still hear her.

"I am speaking the language of non-innocence to you
No act, no struggle, no failure
No victory can be yours to encounter what you haven't already conquered, son of the great and only act
Remember, I forbid you to have a good conscience. . . . "

*
**

And so, Ziworé, I am coming back, I am coming back to pick up the challenge with you, my brother-friend.

The sky darkened at her dawning, Ziworé, so that her life given in hostage, the new harvest of these new times, will sprout in the humus. . . .

Here you are, and here we are, then. . . . See how all these hearts that have come running are vibrating and meditating and rustling. . . .

For my survival
In the space of her torment, I drag my innocent confusion
My sun has darkened at her dawning, Ziworé
My sun, tragically quartered at birth, my navel sprouted at the root of liquid manure
But her intense gaze remained fixed on the queen-cities of the new times, times of assault. . . .
I did not go to her funeral
It was yesterday it was the day before yesterday or this morning
I don't remember anymore but what does time matter. . . .
I hear her still:
"Go and come back, brother of my soul, and bring back that bow of opal music that left the garden of the ancestor
Take care that this world's madmen do not desecrate her
Do not sully her
And that she does not perish without this song of love that came from our twinned hearts having ever been heard
My caster of bridges
My music bow
My love
Go and come back and remember. . . . "

*
**

Good-bye then tender receiver of my childhood
Soon a new curve
A new departure
And tomorrow morning

I shall see the light with new eyes
And I shall lay the first stone of the structure for the return of my Love-across-a-hundred-lives. . . .

*
**

And he effectively negotiated a new turning point. . . .

First, he told me everything. . . .

Then he returned to the city to continue his studies without a scholarship. . . . After his master's in philosophy, he opened a sculptor's studio! With much research into new forms and plenty of students. . . .

He married a charming young woman, and I have told you the rest. . . .

Yes, my brother Lem is truly an exceptional being, next to whom you cannot live an ordinary life. . . .

I, for example, in the same life, I have managed to find a sire, a nephew, a brother, a friend, and an idol in the same person. . . . Surely you agree with me this is exceptional!

And yet, I am still wondering: me, who am I? Who was I for him at the time of those hundreds of lives of one eternal love?

Was I the father, Maghan Kon Fata, or Nyobé-Nyum?

Was I the half brother, in the background, but faithful friend, Manding Bori?

Was I the wicked stepmother Sassouma Bérété?

Or one of the sorceresses?

Or perhaps the son of Sassouma, Dankara Touman?

In any case, I don't believe I was a woman, for my father would not have attached a man's name to me in this life simply because a marabou had predicted the birth of a boy. . . .

So what am I doing here in these skirts that always bother me the way a straitjacket bothers a madman's feet?

Cocody. . . . Tour Sarah
27 April 1985, 7:05 P.M.

Afterword

Yes! the names of people and places reminiscent of people who exist or have existed are true and could not be "purely coincidental."

They exist in African history and mythology. . . .

Some of them are quite famous: Roumben, Sundjata, Sogolon, Ngo Kal Djob, Yém Mback, Bipol. . . .

There are those less famous: Ziworé, Lem, Gol. . . .

But . . . don't be rash! There is no historical truth here!

The conception, birth, life, and death of the characters have been completely reinvented, and the story of their life, their loves, and the passage from one life to another is entirely fictitious.

The phenomenon of reincarnation, which underlies most of the precolonial black African beliefs, has allowed me to follow the characters from the "dawn of time" throughout one love that survives and returns as the lives move on, from destiny to destiny, from ancestors to lineages, from link to link, in order to express a personal conviction that justifies the desire for a return to "the original," an untiring demand for an evolution, a better future for all. But this is not a defense of the theory of reincarnation, although I do not belong to those who confirm that they come from nowhere and swear that to be the Truth. . . . If I had to deliver my own theory of this phenomenon, I think I would do it differently, on the basis of other calculations. . . . Here, then, we are dealing with a purely literary ruse. . . .

What I would like, what I would love, is simply to give us back some hope and courage, to all of us, to the young in general and to Africans in particular, to all of us who despair of decay, corruption, injustice, and who await the apocalypse of salvation from heaven. I believe we evoke them so that we may have a good conscience in our resignation, in our irresponsibility. . . .

There have always been and there shall always be worlds that end. That is why there has been, and there always will be, rebirths. . . .

But rebirths have to be prepared!

Why not by us?

Let us be well aware that at this very moment people are active somewhere!

Let us look! Let us look, like the buffalo-woman, let us discover the Masters of Energy of the renewal, let us be part of it. . . .

For no failure, no joy, no victory can be ours if we have not "conquered" them with the sweat of our actions. . . .

Shhhhh!

Careful. . . . I think I hear. . . . The voice of Ngo Kal Djob!

"I am speaking the language of non-innocence to you
I forbid you to have a good conscience. . . . "

Shhhhh!

What else do I hear?

The rooster's crowing? Already? Well, look at that. . . . It is daytime!

OUR DAY
THIS VERY DAY!

THE END

Glossary

aloko: small slices of fried plantain

the Artist: a reference to Leopold Sedar Senghor, leader of the Negritude Movement, president of Senegal from 1960 to 1980

attieké: a kind of couscous made of manioc, the basis for most meals in the southern regions of the Ivory Coast

Bangui: palm wine

Bikoursi: a lyrical art, only for the Bassa women, much like the art of the *griottes,* but sung

boubou: a long, flowing garment

Boulot-Métro-Dodo: literally "Work-Subway-Shuteye," used primarily in Paris to indicate the monotony of everyday urban life

dolo: millet beer

Edouard Maunick: a Mauritian poet born in Flacq in 1931, preoccupied with *métissage* and the Creole language that was his mother tongue

foutou: a mash of porridge-like consistency, made of either yams, manioc, bananas, or any tuberous vegetables locally grown; *sauce-graine* is a sauce made of the oil of palm kernels

Hilolombi: the god of gods, the most ancient of the ancients for the Bassa; the literal meaning is "the most ancient"

Isba: the name of a nightclub

karité tree: a large tree better known in English as the shea tree—a source of vegetable oil; its fruit, a nut, holds a richly oily substance that is used to soften the skin, among other things, and known as *karité* butter

kom-imboye: a fruit that grows wild in the forest, all white flesh inside, somewhat similar to the kola nut

Kondolon and (Ni) Sané: for the Mandinka these are the two—twinned—gods of hunters

Koo: the most important of the woman's initiations, which allows her to consider herself a complete being (hermaphrodite); marriage is *her* choice, and, if she so chooses, it is considered to be her gift to society

koutoukou: a locally brewed palm wine

macabo: a variety of taro, a tuberous, edible plant

Maghan Kon Fata: the father of Sundjata

Mawu: among the Fon of Benin, God is seen as twin Mawu (female) and Lissa (male); generally, however, God is called Mawu

mbènda: a comfortable chair in which to relax

métissage: hybridization or cross-breeding

Mévoungou: an association of women, expressing itself through the lyrical art as well

misovire: a word invented by Liking as a counterpoint to "misogynist"

"mon mari est capable": means "my husband is able" and is, in fact, the name of a certain pagne's design; a motorbike may also be referred to by this name, as it indicates that the husband is able to provide well for his wife

Ngo Biyong Bi Kuban: the author's paternal grandmother, who taught her what she needed to know for her adult life

Ngok Ikwèn Manyim: from a folktale, the name of a headstrong boy who is asked by a multiheaded monster to "climb on my shoulder, climb on my lips" so he can swallow him; however, the child comes prepared with a pocketknife and a mash of hot pepper, ginger, and other fiery spices, which he rubs into the monster's intestines after first slashing these with his little knife. Ngok Ikwèn is symbolic of the person who enters, indeed infiltrates, a system in order to fight it from the inside. In the folktale, the monster howls and then is slain.

niamakoudji: a ginger-based, lemonade-like drink

pagne: woman's garment printed of batik fabric, sold usually in lengths of several yards, worn as skirts, wraps, sometimes with an additional piece to carry babies on the back

pépère: grandfather (or, father, used affectionately)

poteau-mitan: (in Haitian Creole *poto-mitan*) the center pillar in a Vodou sanctuary, where the supernatural and the natural worlds meet

radio-trottoir: literally, the "sidewalk-radio"; means hearsay—the local rumors being spread from mouth to mouth in the streets

sèm: a tree, the roots of which have a special configuration that lends itself well to the preservation of kola nuts, for example, which are hidden between these roots

si le grain ne meurt: a quote from the Bible, used by André Gide as the title of one of his novels (translated into English as *If It Die*)

simbon: a master of the hunt

soukoukalba: a parasitic plant that grows on other plants or trees and can eventually kill these off

Tima Bailly: an opponent to the regime; Diallo Telli was the first secretary of the OUA, killed in Guinea by Sékou

Touré; Ouandié was executed in public under the regime of Ahidjo (1960–82) in Cameroon

the tree of words: *l'arbre à palabres,* traditionally is the tree, often in the center of a village, underneath which the elders discuss the community's issues, resolve disputes, and hold meetings; it is also the tree where people gather to hear the tales of the storyteller

walaï: an interjection of surprise or shock

CARAF Books

Caribbean and African Literature

Translated from French

A number of writers from very different cultures in Africa and the Caribbean continue to write in French although their daily communication may be in another language. While this use of French brings their creative vision to a more diverse international public, it inevitably enriches and often deforms the conventions of classical French, producing new regional idioms worthy of notice in their own right. The works of these francophone writers offer valuable insights into a highly varied group of complex and evolving cultures. The CARAF Books series was founded in an effort to make these works available to a public of English-speaking readers.

For students, scholars, and general readers, CARAF offers selected novels, short stories, plays, poetry, and essays that have attracted attention across national boundaries. In most cases the works are published in English for the first time. The specialists presenting the works have often interviewed the author in preparing background materials, and each title includes an original essay situating the work within its own literary and social context and offering a guide to thoughtful reading.

CARAF Books

Guillaume Oyônô-Mbia and Seydou Badian
Faces of African Independence: Three Plays
Translated by Clive Wake

Olympe Bhêly-Quénum
Snares without End
Translated by Dorothy S. Blair

Bertène Juminer
The Bastards
Translated by Keith Q. Warner

Tchicaya U Tam'Si
The Madman and the Medusa
Translated by Sonja Haussmann Smith and William Jay Smith

Alioum Fantouré
Tropical Circle
Translated by Dorothy S. Blair

Edouard Glissant
Caribbean Discourse: Selected Essays
Translated by J. Michael Dash

Daniel Maximin
Lone Sun
Translated by Nidra Poller

Aimé Césaire
Lyric and Dramatic Poetry, 1946–82
Translated by Clayton Eshleman and Annette Smith

René Depestre
The Festival of the Greasy Pole
Translated by Carrol F. Coates

Kateb Yacine
Nedjma
Translated by Richard Howard

Léopold Sédar Senghor
The Collected Poetry
Translated by Melvin Dixon

Maryse Condé
I, Tituba, Black Witch of Salem
Translated by Richard Philcox

Assia Djebar
Women of Algiers in Their Apartment
Translated by Marjolijn de Jager

Dany Bébel-Gisler
Leonora: The Buried Story of Guadeloupe
Translated by Andrea Leskes

Lilas Desquiron
Reflections of Loko Miwa
Translated by Robin Orr Bodkin

Jacques Stephen Alexis
General Sun, My Brother
Translated by Carrol F. Coates

Malika Mokeddem
Of Dreams and Assassins
Translated by K. Melissa Marcus

Werewere Liking

It Shall Be of Jasper and Coral and

Love-across-a-Hundred-Lives

Translated by Marjolijn de Jager